I0740893

For The Love of D. H. Lawrence

B. R. ALMOND

ISBN: 978-0-9830147-3-7

Cover art by Thereas Liddle-Bernsen
Graphics by: Devanie

Editorial Consultant: KD Writer's Service
Woodville, Texas

Golden Triangle Writers Guild Books
PO BOX 541
Hillister Texas 77624

The Golden Triangle Writers Guild is a 501(C)(3) non-profit writers support and educational organization serving writers since 1983.

For the love of D. H. Lawrence, is a work of fiction. Any resemblance to actual persons or events is purely coincidental.

For Lily
Face your fears and never forget the strong women who came before you.

Thank you
To my mother, Betty Cross, and best of friends, Jeannie, Stacey, Tina, and Christy for reminding me life sometimes make a person lay their dreams to the side. The important thing is remembering where you left them.

I never saw a wild thing sorry for itself, a small bird will drop frozen from its bough never having felt sorry for itself. D.H. Lawrence

We spend our lives waiting for one monumental moment that defines our sense of purpose. For many years, I believed my moment came when Mom died leaving me with a three year old and a soul full of heartache headed toward the boxing ring. I was wrong.

Every step in my life was for preparation. My moment had arrived. My moment waited in a two-story farmhouse. Regardless if I triumphed or became the sacrificial lamb, I finally understood my purpose, save Katie no matter the consequences.

1

The Last Fight

*V*oices vibrated to a discordant hum overpowered by the rhythmic adrenaline pounding in my chest. Seconds ticked away. Our eyes locked in a standoff dance, waiting for the smallest indication of the other's next move. Respect ran short for the woman across the ring, but like Bill always said, never underestimate your opponent.

It was hard maintaining that type of outlook knowing the boxing ring held no place for Diana Strauss. She lacked the seasoned talent to call herself a contender. She had a few skills. I gave her that much credit. We both knew commercial appeal lured a promoter into the promise of riches and her getting a shot at the title. Maybe, just maybe, he hoped she might win by some fluke.

I never spoke to her outside the ring. The platinum

blonde mocked the sport with her very existence modeling the latest fashion of undergarments which she managed to incorporate into her boxing career. I had no issues with women modeling lingerie. But, one sporting a lacy bra, matching panties, boxing gloves, and uttering the phrase, 'Wearing Leather and Lace by Dago, you'll knock him out,' nauseated my very core.

The flickering commercial broke my concentration. That's when it happened. My brow twitched.

One quick jab sent the breath rushing out of me. "Umph." I twisted and tightened muscles absorbing the two that followed while sliding backwards a little off kilter. I almost regained my footing when her glove connected against my brow. My head forcefully pushed sideways parallel to my shoulder. Booming shouts surged throughout the arena.

"Move your feet, Jake."

Bill's rough Chicago accent cut through the roar shouting more demands. "Keep your hands up. Move, move, move!"

I ducked and skipped sideways avoiding the next padded fist zipping toward me. I saw my opening. She left her jaw exposed. I had all intentions of planting a fist against it.

When my arm extended, a sharp pain pierced my side. Gloves retreated to a protective mode along with a few words of profanity gushing forward. I bounced back a few steps regaining my composure and berating my own mistake.

It was ridiculous that the fight went on as long as it did. Diana should have gone down in the fourth round after my right hook rattled her teeth. Somehow, she stayed on her feet and gained a second wind in the fifth round. I worked too hard to let some Panty Princess take my title. Gloves slammed together warding off the pain in my side.

I charged forward.

Several punches to the midriff lifted her onto toes. A quick left struck her perfectly round chin. An upper cut followed reeling her backwards. The crowd exploded when Diana fell against the ropes using them to stay on her feet. I didn't give her a chance to recover but went after the wanna-be boxer with a vengeance. The bell rang closing the round. I ignored the sound until the referee's palm shoved me toward the corner. Just a few more seconds, and the fight would have been over.

I dropped my arms pacing quickly across the ring. The small trail of blood mixed with sweat trickled to the edge of my eye.

"Stupid! Plain stupid," I muttered with each step.

Bill climbed under the ropes and slid a stool into the corner. I chose to stand, showing the crowd Diana's punches meant nothing.

"Sit down, Jake," he demanded.

My rear plopped down onto the stool. "She cut me."

A cotton swab appeared from Bill's pocket. He pressed the small gash. "Get over it and get your head back in the fight." He removed the swab, assessed the damage, then applied more pressure.

"My head's in the fight," I snapped.

The acidy feel of cotton dug deeper. I winced. "Jesus, Bill, what'cha trying to do, push it through the other side?"

Bill wiped sweat from my forehead and continued to hold the swab in place. The lines of his mouth turned upward. "You keep bleeding and they'll stop the fight. Wanna end your career by getting an ass whooping from an underwear model?"

He was right. What I had done was just plain foolish. Only a rookie made the mistake of getting distracted. My top lip twitched. "I *ain't* losing. Just do what you have to do to get me back out there."

Bill grasped my chin turning for a better view. "Looks like it stopped. Don't let her hit you again. Use your head for something other than a punching bag."

A sharp burn fanned my side. I lowered seeking bravery to pull in oxygen. I hated admitting she did some damage with those three jabs but she did.

"You hear me, Jake? Don't let her hit you again!"

Deep breaths exploded torture. I gripped the ropes turning knuckles white. "Yeah, I hear ya."

A dip to the right seemed to ease the throbbing. Bill touched my favored side. I brushed his hand away. "Let's finish this."

His hands on his hips, Bill gave me a skeptical raise of the brow. I wrinkled my nose ignoring his concern. I glanced over my shoulder meeting my grandmother's frowning face. After all the years seated behind my corner, Gran still disliked the profession and worried each time I stepped into the ring. A quick nod let her know I was okay.

I caught a glimpse of my sister, Katie, seated next to Gran. No worries on her face just an amusing grin. She pushed out her bottom lip and rubbed an area around her temple. I shook my head inching a smile. No way would she ever let me forget the foolish mistake and probably made mental notes of the jokes to use after the fight.

A quick roll of the shoulders raised me from the stool. I clamped eyes shut taking small gulps of air. Ribs pulled apart when my muscles expanded much like the splitting of a turkey wishbone. God, it hurt. A deeper intake stretched blinding pain throughout my side flashing to another place and time as a reminder how physical pain held no equal to that which one never forgets. But, in my darkest hours, a light always shined dissolving the shadows of discomfort. It was then that I felt her presence and heard the caressing voice echo words of wisdom.

"I never saw a wild thing sorry for its self."

A deep swallow cleared away the anguish of knowing my mother should have been in the seat beside Gran and Katie but had long since passed, long before my career began. I submitted to the ghostly advice tracing the beams running the length of the ceiling. I shook arms and bounced on toes letting rage reside where lax emotions attempted to live.

The sound of the bell brought my head forward, eyes cold, unfeeling, staring at Diana Strauss with a hunger to destroy the surrogate cause of misery. I deafened ears to the surrounding noise and shifted feet checking the weight of my body before stalking the model with the skills of a wild animal hunting its prey.

She hadn't recovered from the last round. A minute into round six, her left hand dropped too far to the side. It was an opportunity to shut Diana down for good and I took it. One quick jab slid between her gloves and landed against the slim jaw line. The blonde head reeled right. She wasn't given the chance to counter or protect herself. During the recoil, my upper cut staggered her to a sway. I took advantage with several body punches doubling her over.

Each plant of the fist on her flesh was not without cost. Punching drew a pinching sensation sending a wave of agony throughout my side. At one point, my knees started to buckle from searing torture, but I quickly straightened and rebuked the pain pushing beyond the threshold of acceptance.

I continued attacking her midriff with alternating fists. She took a step back dropping both hands. A hard left finished the job. She was done. The beauty fell backwards onto the mat. I moved away listening to the spectators count, "...NINE, TEN!"

It was over. I threw my arms victoriously in the air turning to meet Bill rushing toward me.

"You did it, kid," he cheered.

I welcomed the open arms with the two of us celebrating the end of a great career.

Although there were multiple voices calling my name, it was Gran and Katie's that I heard above all others. I looked for them, but a reporter blocked my view.

"Jake, over here, Bob Williams, Sport's One. You are the undisputed women's world boxing champ. How does it feel going out on top with three consecutive title defenses under your belt?"

I didn't want to talk to him or any reporters until my arms were around my grandmother and sister. A stretched neck craned unable to find the familiar voices calling from beyond the sea of microphones awaiting my response.

"Great, good fight. Want to thank Diana for putting up a good challenge," I said trying to move forward.

Someone shoved another microphone in my face. "What's next, Jake? Can you walk away from the sport?"

They asked the question I pondered many times over the past months. Leaving the boxing world meant walking away from the one thing that saved me from my worst enemy, me. Who was Jake Conner without the gloves? Frankly, the thought of finding out unsettled me to say the least.

I spotted Bill escorting Gran and Katie through the crowd. My family, three people I loved the most. As long as I had them, I knew everything would be okay. I would be okay. I kept eyes on the trio and smiled. "Yeah, I can walk away."

2

$\mathcal{A}$ week in Vegas left me very homesick. Nothing compared to the tranquility found on our porch rocking the swing to the sound of crickets and frogs at dusk. The quiet countryside, the smell of fresh cut hay, the aroma from Gran's kitchen, I longed for Washington, Arkansas, that bit of heaven on earth where one basked in centuries of a simple, slow-paced life.

After several interviews, my family and I prepared to leave Las Vegas and a career that had been so good to me. I walked down the jet way checking over my shoulder assuring Gran was close behind me. Bringing attention forward, I bobbed a look over people searching for my sister.

"You see Katie?" I asked Bill.

He shook his head.

Somehow my sister managed to get ahead of us which was no surprise. Patience was never her strong suit.

Passing the welcoming flight attendant, the line came to a stop. Bill shifted weight from one leg to the other exposing his intolerance for delays.

After a couple of minutes, waiting wore on me. "What's the hold up?" I murmured.

"No idea," Bill said.

Several rows ahead, a woman's voice rang out with authority. "Miss, you have to check that bag."

The Miss who replied drew my head down. There

was no denying my fifteen-year-old sister's Southern belle voice,

"It'll fit. I just know it will."

Bill crossed his arms rocking to and fro. "Should've known."

I shifted around his shoulder. Katie braced a foot in one seat shoving an over packed bag into a compartment on the opposite side of the aisle. Her loose, waist length, blonde hair tussled about with each push.

"Miss, it won't fit. You have to check it," the attendant argued.

"I ain't checking it. Get in there," Katie huffed.

One good shove and the bag went in.

"Another win for the Sultress of Slam," she exclaimed, stepping off the seat.

Sultress of Slam, the name she bestowed on herself boasting a God given talent for softball. The only serious moments of her life showed on the softball field. She was good. Even I had to acknowledge her talent with pride.

The line advanced until Bill halted by his seat. He placed a bag in the compartment overhead. "See how easy that is, Katie? Not so hard when you leave the curling iron at home," he said.

Katie chuckled. "If I was as old as you, then I guess all I'd have to pack is Geritol and hemorrhoid cream, too."

Bill took a seat by the window and raised the shade. "Honey, if I had hemorrhoid cream in my bag, I'd smear it on you because you sure are a pain in my ass."

I stepped to the side letting Gran take her place beside Bill.

"I'd trade seats but not sure which one is the lesser of the evil," she said.

"Next time we book 'em in coach," I added.

I stowed my backpack under the seat and sat down next to my sister. Katie removed an Ipod from her purse and fluffed a pillow behind her head. *Let her go to sleep,* I prayed.

Katie squirmed in the seat until she found a fixed position. I dug for the buckle of my seat belt.

Suddenly, her fist came close to my mouth as if she were holding a microphone. "Jake Conner, you just won the title and retired. What are you gonna do next, go to Disneyland?"

I fastened the seatbelt. "Oh, I'm going to an amusement park all right. It's called Hope High School."

It was the beginning of May. If lucky, the rest of the month and the summer would pass with a turtle pace delaying what was sure to be inevitable boredom for the next thirty years of my life.

A chosen profession teaching high school history laid ahead contingent on graduating from college in the coming weeks and passing a license exam. The occupation replaced a boxing career and looked upon with less admiration. No matter how much convincing myself teaching might be an exciting challenge, the truth gnawed redundant days filled with teenagers and the loss of ever feeling the rush of raw power again.

Gum popped in the mouth of the teenager seated next to me. "Well, if it makes you feel better, I got over being mad and really looking forward to seeing you every day."

This from the girl who stormed out of our kitchen ranting, 'Can't you find a job somewhere else?' the day I told her I accepted the job at the same school she attends. I slowly turned in her direction. "Oh, really. Why the change of heart?"

She pumped her palms in the air. "Easy A in the house of J."

It was the proof needed declaring my sister delusional. "Do you actually think I'll let you slide by in my class?" I asked relaxing in the seat.

Katie produced a cunning grin. "Well, I'd hate to slip at school and call you Jacqueline."

If anyone knew how much I detested the use of my full name, it was Katie. I gave a big smile spouting in return. "Go for it. May the best sense of humor win. I'm calling roll every class. I can't wait to shout Katherine Glenn Connor."

A look of horror crossed the pretty face hearing the recital of the name given to her at birth. We agreed to Miss Conner and a promise of no shenanigans at school. None linked back to her. She pushed ear buds in and faded off to the music pouring from the IPOD.

Before long, the plane pushed back from the gate, glided toward the runway, and left the ground. The lullaby motion lured my tired body to a peaceful place of relaxation. Moderate pain radiated from the cut near my temple, a souvenir from Diana Strauss. After retaining my title, I still rebuked the mistake. The cut required only two stitches. My side, however, was quite tender.

Official retirement began but accepting it, well, that was another matter. The first time I stepped into the ring had been twelve years ago with more hurt and anger than any one person should have felt. Boxing saved my life. It gave me a future. The sadness of it ending measured the same emotions of two lovers separated after a lifelong relationship.

A sigh escaped from Katie who fell asleep most likely dreaming of ways to torture me, which happened to be her favorite pastime. No one passing our seats would ever think us related. Katie inherited our mother's features, blonde, light skinned with an angelic face masking a mischievous sense of humor. I didn't think of myself as unattractive with long brown hair and eyes to match, but projected a more hardened to the world type appearance on my dark complexioned face.

We were the same height, similar athletic build. Being a boxer, or a retired boxer, as the circumstance, I owned the more muscle tone. That tidbit remained open for debate with the Sultress of Slam.

Katie stirred against the pillow. I reached over and raised the fallen blanket above her shoulders. A moment of turbulence shook the plane. My injured side hit the armrest. A throbbing wave surged throughout my body. I held my breath grasping the epic center of pain. After a few seconds, it subsided.

Across the aisle I confirmed Gran missed the distressful moment. I wasn't a pain junky by any means. I just refused to let anyone see me in such a state of weakness. After all, a trained fighter programmed to conceal thoughts and feelings could not afford infirm emotions.

Gran raised her head lifting a smile. "You all right, sugar?"

"I'm fine. Just tired, and ready to get home."

"Me, too. I'm glad this business is over." She returned to reading the book she held.

I lowered my chin, veiling the smile, recalling the oath made to the sixty-nine year old woman.

After the first sanctioned boxing match the summer following high school graduation, Gran vocalized her expectations. "You go to college and stop that fighting," she had said.

I agreed to end my boxing days once a degree was in hand. The deliberate extension of college to eight years naturally lengthened my career. I often wondered if Gran thought I'd graduate with a degree in everything or maybe her granddaughter's IQ equaled that of dirt. That was until last winter.

During a Sunday church service, the pastor asked Gran to give the closing prayer. She started with, 'Lord, bless my granddaughter with a diploma even though she thinks she's smarter than me,' followed with, 'She's a good girl just needs reminding now and then of a promise made to an old woman.'

At twenty-seven with that much guilt hanging over my head, I decided to stop stringing Gran along and retired from the boxing world.

A loud snort buzzed from the other side of Gran. A shake of the head produced a broad grin on my lips. Bill Monroe, my trainer and best friend, was dashing and debonair in his own way. Lines mapped the edges of his sixty-year-old eyes from years of squinting trying to look tough. I always thought the tough guy eyes were the result of a stubborn man's reluctance to wear glasses. "I can see fine," he shouted, whenever I mentioned the word optometrist.

The locals nicknamed him Chicago Bill. He arrived in the neighboring town of Hope with his Swedish protégé, Sven, in tow claiming grief over the loss of his wife as the reason he left Illinois. A few years after Bill started my training, Sven returned to Chicago. From that point on, my sister, grandmother, and I became the widower's family. I inquired about his life before coming to Hope. He limited the information passed along. There was more to Bill than meets the eye, but he'd never tell it.

A light cough escaped stretching the muscle in my aching side. I held a death grip on the armrest waiting for the spasm to stop. When my eyes opened, they met a narrowed gaze from a man seated two rows ahead on the opposite side of the plane. He gave the once over with readable curiosity. I captured his stare tossing a harsh, "What are you looking at buddy?" forcing his eyes elsewhere.

I possessed a strong dislike for flying. It produced boredom for a person such as myself who stayed busy twenty-four seven. A Seventeen magazine lay in Katie's lap. The words, Is He into You, leaped off the cover. Boredom yes, desperation no, I surmised. I looked elsewhere for entertainment then remembered the book of poetry stashed in my backpack under the seat. A great debate occurred in regards to the agony ahead if I bent down and retrieved the worn out pages once belonging to my mother.

I wondered, at times, what the public might think if they were aware of the reigning champ's soft spot for poems. Truth was, my mother taught me to love poetry at an early age. Many times, she spouted verse after verse of her favorites choosing the appropriate lines to suit the situation. One ritual maintained over a boxing career was to hold the book drawing strength from mom's spirit, which I believed still lived in the pages.

Forget it. My body discovered a position relieving the nagging below the breast. I abandoned the book idea for quick nap before reaching Dallas-Fort Worth Airport and the connecting flight to Texarkana.

I managed to fall asleep rather quickly. Maybe the thought of the book of poetry, the pain my body refused to give into, or my life changing that led me to a place I preferred not to go. Although forever in my heart, it had been a long time since I dreamed of my mother, Bridgette Conner. Unfortunately, my subconscious chose her final struggle as the subject of the dream.

She was beautiful, smart, and witty but at the end of her life, she appeared tired and sad yet managed to hide the excruciating pain I knew she felt. That late summer afternoon, our hands held tightly wishing things turned out differently. There were no misgivings. Life for my mother was ending and mine, never to be the same.

I did not attempt to conceal a broken heart. Mom was strong enough for the both of us. At death's door, she held vigilant in her convictions.

"Don't cry, Jake. We never feel sorry for ourselves. Remember," she said, between shallow breaths.

With what were her final moments, she recited a favorite D. H. Lawrence poem used many times throughout my childhood.

"I never saw a wild thing sorry for itself, a small bird will drop frozen from its bough never having felt sorry for itself."

One last exhale, followed by silence, her eyes faded to a faraway place, no sign of pain or sorrow, just peace, drifting from my life forever.

I loved my mother but hated the memory of her death. It tugged at soft places best left concealed. I woke rather abruptly spying around the plane hoping no one saw the moisture threatening to spill down my cheeks.

I painfully straightened sore muscles and lingered a loving stare on the body asleep next to me. Katie was a few weeks shy of her third birthday when our mother died. I was fifteen, the same age as the sweet girl.

A quick sweep of the hand brushed away the few strands of hair that escaped her ponytail. I ached for her lack of memories but at the same time, relieved she had none. I never wanted her to carry the emotional baggage weighing down my back.

I was stiff and eased over in the seat toward Gran. She clutched a book tightly in her crossed arms drawing resting breaths. Overwhelming shame filled my heart. I admired the saintly woman above all others, but it wasn't always like that.

Chelsea Parker came into my life the morning after Momma died. I had known all my life of a grandmother living in Arkansas. That was all I knew. We never visited or called. Once, I asked Momma why. Her only answer had been, "Things happen. People go their separate ways."

I sat on my mother's bed still in shock over her death, listening to Gran's interpretation of how to get over the grief. "Be strong. In time you'll put this behind you and move on. It's what your mother would want."

I exploded in silent anger wondering how this total stranger had the gall to inject such an opinion. She didn't know me. She didn't know my sister, and it had been so long since she seen her daughter, I doubted she knew my mother.

I gave no thought of how Gran suffered nor cared. She drove all night from Washington, Arkansas to arrive in St. Louis, Missouri with no time to grieve over the loss of her only child who had disappeared years prior with no hint of her whereabouts. Instead, Gran focused her attention on packing our belongings, comforting a confused toddler asking repeatedly for her mother, not to mention, a mute teenager radiating hostility.

A month after Mom's funeral, my hatred deepened while living in the two story white farmhouse my sister and I called home. I loathed my grandmother for the uprooting and even Katie for reminding me of a mother so desperately needed.

School was another nightmare. The nearest was in Hope, which turned into a twenty-mile round trip on the yellow limousine every day. I found myself the butt of cruel remarks mostly geared toward my statured height. Depraved social skills and wearing headphones listening to an old Etta James cassette found in my mother's belongings made matters worse. I preferred to be alone so I kept my head down and ignored the nasty remarks from the other students.

For months, I tried everything to fill the empty space where my mother once resided. The pain of losing her grew until I no longer cared about anyone, including myself. I made friends with a pot-smoking clique nicknamed the Stoned Hengers and discovered alcohol and drugs seemed to dull the rage. Gran, God love her, tried to gain control over my behavior, but the harder she tried, the fiercer my rebellion became.

A few weeks before our first Christmas in Washington, a hazardous life caught up with me. At the end of an evening filled with alcohol and a variety of drugs, the idea of stealing a vehicle came to mind. Unfortunately for Tom Jackson, his pickup was my target.

He left the truck parked in front of his garage with keys in the ignition. It was a sign of good luck, or so I thought. I climbed behind the wheel, started the old Ford, and raced down the highway driving everywhere but on the pavement. The joy ride ended with a trip through Adell Williams' yard demolishing her nativity scene and landing the truck upside down in a nearby field. I walked away with a busted lip from hitting my mouth on the steering wheel.

Adell called Sheriff Harvey Jones who happened to be a close friend of my grandmother's. When he arrived he found me sitting beside the truck, a joint between my lips. He should have slapped the illegal cigarette from my mouth, thrown me across the trunk of his car, and placed handcuffs on my wrists. Instead, he ordered me to throw down the pot and get in the front seat.

At two o'clock in the morning, we pulled into the driveway. Gran opened the door. I was intoxicatingly drenched in blood.

The sheriff explained what happened and spoke in a sympathetic tone. "Chelsea, I won't take her in, but I gotta have your word you'll bring her to town in the morning. We have to see if Tom wants to press charges."

My grandmother looked tired and at her wits end. That night standing in the doorway, she made one of the hardest decisions of her life.

"Lock her up, Harvey," she said with a shaky voice. "She made her bed. Let her lie in it. Her mother would be so ashamed."

Gran's last words cut deep and made me livid. "Take my ass to jail. I don't need a damn thing from her!" I stormed to the sheriff's car.

I thought I was tough. Reality hit me after two days locked up in the Hempstead County Jail isolated from other prisoners. There were no visitors not even Gran. I spent the time wondering if the future held a juvenile center.

On the third day, I went before a judge and sentenced to two years' probation, working in Jackson's garage to pay for the damages to the truck, and two-hundred hours of community service cleaning a gym owned by Bill Monroe.

After many months of butting heads and strong determination on his part, Bill introduced me to an alternative to self-destruction in the form of boxing. I loved the nontraditional sport that gave me a sense of purpose and a way to release the pent up anger. But the purpose had ended in retirement and left me with one enormous question. What do I do now?

I lowered my head, drawing brows together, understanding life came full circle. My life changed never to be the same just as it had when Momma died, only this time the sense of loss existed in the form of self-uncertainty.

"Good afternoon, ladies and gentlemen, welcome to Dallas–Fort Worth International."

I patted my sister's leg. "Katie, wake up."

She raised her head. "What?"

"They want you to fly the plane." I smirked.

She stretched her arms fully awake, righting herself in the seat. "I can do it. If you remember, oh dear punching bag of Diana, I am the Pilot Master of the video world."

I cocked an eye in her direction. "Oh, yeah? Well Pilot Master, they don't have a pause and restart button in this version."

She met me with a glint of laughter twinkling in her eyes. She fingered the bandage covering my cut brow. "Who would have thought her small fist would do this much damage? Does it hurt?"

I tossed an irritated glare and knocked her hand away. "Bite my ass."

Gran called out from across the aisle. "What did you say, Jake?"

I avoided using profanity within Gran's hearing fearing a bar of soap might appear from the shopping-bag size purse she carried. I picked up the plastic cup sitting on the tray. "I told Katie not to knock over my glass."

Katie snorted. "Good cover, Jake."

Thankfully, maneuvering through the airport in Dallas posed no challenges. Two hours later, we were on the ground walking to the small terminal in Texarkana. The goal: Bring the car around, load luggage, pick up everyone, and see how fast Gran's Cadillac made the thirty-mile trip to Hope.

I retrieved the car from the lot pulling close to the curb next to Bill. Katie pounced into the front passenger seat.

"You could've at least offered to help him with the luggage," I scolded.

She gave me one of her famous whatever looks while thumbing through CDs in her backpack. I cradled a hand over my aching side walking to the back of the car. Bill waved me off.

Shortly into the ride, everyone in the back seat fell asleep. Katie loaded a CD into the player turning the volume to a low range. For the most part, Katie and I enjoyed the same music. A song from one of my favorite rock bands played. I tapped the steering wheel keeping time with the song while eyeing the traffic occasionally looking over to the teen who bounced her head to the beat of the music.

We reached the freeway merging from the ramp. Katie cut a look to the back seat monitoring the silver haired woman and trainer. She gave a broad grin mimicking a racetrack announcer. "It's a beautiful day at the Interstate 30 Speedway. The driver of the gray, corn fed girl, home grown tomato, sponsored Cadillac is taking the track."

I've had my moments of outrageous behavior, but the one problem I maintained was the need for speed. My grandmother, well aware of my heavy foot, rode my case about driving fast. The strong desire to get home over ruled any worry of Gran waking to discover her car flying down the freeway. My foot pressed harder on the accelerator moving the speedometer to a higher position.

"Be my spotter. Watch for cops and Grandma. We're going for a track record," I said.

Katie placed her favorite pair of large frame sunglasses over her eyes and gave the thumbs up. "Pass what you can, hit the others in the quarter panel if they won't get over."

We chatted for most of the drive to Hope. The conversations centered on the approaching summer softball season. Katie, always open with her feelings, expressed her concern over moving up into a different league. All she needed was a little reassurance from her older sister to boost her confidence.

"Well," I started with a little smile playing on my lips, "We both know how bad you suck. You can't hit and hey, let's be honest, you pitch like Carley Everett."

Katie scowled at the mention of her arch nemesis

name. The two's rivaled history with sports occasionally got out of hand. I chuckled. Pain surged from the movement. I clenched the menacing area. Katie caught the gesture.

"You okay, sis?"

I gripped the steering wheel tighter, nodded, and remained silent, fearing the pain might show in my voice. Once it eased, I returned to the softball conversation. "Good grief, Katie, you've got four coaches begging you to play. You'll be fine."

The words seemed exactly what my sister needed to hear. My approval and praise was all it took to turn her worry to calm. On some level, I found her dependence on me troublesome, depending on me to make everything right in her world. I understood better than anyone how life could change in a split second, with the person you depended on the most, gone forever.

I turned the car onto the street leading to Bill's small house located a few blocks from his gym. He hired local kids to care for the lawn. Doing his part to keep the youngsters out of trouble, he once explained. The man's heart was golden but one could never tell by the rough exterior he presented.

I discovered by accident that he used the house and gym as collateral to finance our summer vacations and weekend trips to Chicago and Boston to train and fight. With his connections, I fought my way to the top. After the first title win, I went straight to the bank and paid off the mortgage before he protested.

I tried unsuccessfully to talk him into selling the house and relocating to our farm.

"I like my privacy. No women, just testosterone and quiet," he explained every time the subject came up. No doubt, the weekly visits from his unofficial girlfriend, Shirley Dobbs, played a major factor with the privacy comment.

I brought the car to a stop and got out with the intentions of getting Bill's garment and duffle bags from the trunk. My sister scurried around taking the initiative. The fact Katie and Bill spent a good deal of time bantering cutting remarks to each other made Bill and I question her motives. She handed Bill the bags.

Bill spilled a sheepish grin. "Thank you, honey."

Trotting back toward the front of the car, Katie retorted, "Just doing my part to save the dinosaurs."

Never letting Katie get the best of him, Bill shot back, "Is that an insult against my age or the gas I've been passing for the past hour?"

Katie giggled. "It's all the same. Old men, old dinosaurs both turn into some form of gas."

I broke into a fit of laughter that led to a cough. I held my side inconspicuously. Surely after a few days rest, the injury would heal. I breathed, silently praying for an end to the pain. After a goodbye, with the promise of seeing Bill the next day, I pointed the car toward our home still some ten miles away north of Hope.

The sky held plenty of sunlight when we pulled into the driveway. The yard needed mowing. The flowers lining the house yearned for water. I made a mental note to take care of the chores the following morning. For a place I hated so much in the beginning, it was exactly where I always wanted to be. Home at last.

I rose from the driver's seat pacing around to the trunk unloading suitcases. After moving a small bag, I dipped deep inside the trunk for Katie's heavy suitcase. A firm tug didn't budge it. What had she packed? Probably everything in her room, I concluded.

I leaned further inside using both hands lifting and pulling. The suitcase slipped. My injured side smacked the edge of the trunk. Everything went dark when the sharp stab hit me. Fingers trembled and dug into the suitcase with a drip of sweat hitting the cloth.

It took some time to compose myself and free the bag. Once it touched the ground, my chest felt like a weight dropped on it and someone's hand squeezed my lung. I fell to my knees. An expulsion of, "Ahh," rushed from my mouth.

Gran rounded the car. "Jake? Honey, what is it?"

Sheer determination rebuked what my body felt. My fingers spread over the trunk. The tips imprinted a firm grip pulling myself to a half-standing, half-crouching position hanging onto the trunk for support desperately trying to suck air into my lungs. I accepted the fact. This was one time I couldn't meditate myself whole again.

"Gran," I forced out the word.

My grandmother wrapped an arm around the injured side.

"I can't." I stopped then gasped, "Breathe."

The pressure of her arm touched the injured side delivering a groan.

"Katie," Gran yelled and repeated louder, "Katie!"

The happy-go-lucky teenager alighted from the passenger side walking to the back with CDs in hand. She froze, witnessing the anguish written on my face. "Oh, my God, Jake, what is it?"

"Help me get her in the car. We're going to the hospital," Gran directed.

I've had plenty of injuries throughout my boxing career. Normally, the notion of seeking medical intervention was out of the question, but I didn't protest this time.

With one on each side, my grandmother and sister guided me to the back seat of the car. I shifted my aching body to a laying position. The sound of the luggage being scooted across the driveway preceded Katie jumping into the car and slamming the door. Excessive pressure on the accelerator caused the engine to roar back to life. We moved backward at a high speed. Gravel blasted the undercarriage of Gran's beloved Cadillac. I felt a bump when the car hit the pavement stopping long enough for Gran to change gears. The force of moving forward so quickly pressed my back against the seat delivering a low moan from my throat.

Katie's excited voice expelled, "Meet us at the hospital. I dunno her side is killin' her and she can't breathe." A few seconds later, she announced, "Bill said he'll get there ahead of us to let 'em know we're coming."

I never recalled my grandmother ever speeding but that evening, she drove with the accelerator flat on the floor. With a firm grip on the seat, I prayed, dear God if my side didn't kill me, Gran surely would.

3

The ride to Hempstead County Hospital was the longest ten miles of my life. The slightest turn of the road, or the simple task of inhaling oxygen, brought sweltering ache. I silently questioned Gran's ability to find the town of Hope, after living in the area her entire life.

"Jake, how're you doing back there?" Gran asked.

I took a shallow breath prepared to supply an answer but stopped short upon seeing a body wedged on the armrest between the seats.

"It takes a lot of strength and courage for a butterfly to burst out of a cocoon."

I was confused hearing the phrase my mother spouted the first time I painfully transitioned from a child to a woman.

Tired eyes strained tracing the face, which never spoke. A dimple creased the chin. Blue eyes filled with worry. Wisps of honey blonde hair hung loosely on her cheeks. Her voice, her presence, all hallucinations except for the truth. Katie looked just like Momma.

I lowered my lashes shutting out the image. It was hard enough concentrating on every breath, slowing to a smooth rhythm, making the discomfort tolerable. Thoughts of my mother were the last thing I needed.

The car took a sharp turn to the right. My lips compressed delivering a low, moaning curse while gripping the edge of the seat. A tickling sensation produced a cough. Tears sprung to my eyes and I felt certain my body would split in half. The thought of passing out crossed my mind yet I chose to focus on airflow.

I saw Katie's pouty lips quiver. Her body advanced further between the seats. "Jake, hang on. We're almost there."

Teeth sunk into the lower lip aiding my lie of, "I'm fine."

We stopped rather unexpectedly. I palmed the front seat feeling a moment of nausea creeping up. Bill climbed inside the car chastising what I covered up during the fight.

"I ought to take you over my knee. I knew something was wrong," he said, keeping a low tone.

I lay against his hard shoulder grasping a handful of headrest easing the effort from the car. Gran extended a hand on my elbow swinging her over sized purse behind her.

"What do you think's wrong, Bill?" she asked.

I interceded. "It's just a bad bruise."

Beyond the door, a nurse with wheelchair in tow kept a good distance away. She was a very slender redhead with an up turned nose. The same look worn if constantly smelling something bad. "Miss, can you get out on your own, or do you need assistance?"

Narrowed eyes shot daggers in her direction. She must have been blind if unable to see the struggle exiting the car. With Bill's support, I maneuvered out preventing any sound from escaping.

I waited for the nurse to push the chair closer. It didn't happen. To me, she was either lazy or just uncaring. Sucking in the deepest breath possible, I crossed the distance planting my rear in the seat.

One common flaw Bill and I shared was a razor sharp

tongue. "Think you can manage to wheel her in?" Bill snapped.

The nurse gave a sour look while pushing toward the emergency entrance not bothering to be gentle but hitting every crack in the concreted ambulance bay. What little sunlight remained faded with the advancement into the dimly lit entrance. Glass doors slid apart with a burst of light and the smell of disinfectant invaded my senses. I suppressed a cough.

We passed the desk surrounded by medical personnel busy pouring over charts. Moving on beyond several doors, the nurse turned into a room. I looked around for my family who had disappeared. She informed me of their detention at the desk filling out paper work.

The nurse parked several feet from the gurney. "All right dear," she said in an condescending voice. "Have a seat on the bed. Someone will be with you shortly."

She lounged against the entrance and took note of my fist-gripping steps, savoring each one with some sort of personal satisfaction. I shot pure hatred toward her. She read my facial expression and curled her rather thin lips uttering words dripping with disdain.

"We know who you are, but there are other critical patients ahead of you." She crossed her arms against her chest as if she were waiting for a reply.

I closed my eyes dealing with the task of easing onto the bed, hoping she went away before I lost my temper.

She turned to leave and said just loud enough for me to hear, "She doesn't impress me."

I never desired nor expected special treatment from anyone. I refused seating ahead of others in restaurants when the managers recognized me. People sent gifts, which I declined and asked the monetary value donated to charities. I let people check out ahead of me at the Food Mart. Be respectful. What goes around comes around was the philosophy Gran taught. I expected treatment like everyone else coming through the ER, none the better, none the worse.

The cutting remark mixed with the increased pain fueled the flames. I sat on the crisp white sheet covering the hard mattress and glared at the nurse. A strong desire to punch the over-tanned bone-protruding face ran through my mind. I gave it serious thought and wondered if the accommodations at the county jail had improved over the past twelve years.

"You know sweet pea, since we're in a hospital," I took a shallow breath. "You might want to see about having that stick removed from your ass."

Her eyes grew large, obviously wanting to say something, but chose wisely to leave the room.

I surveyed the sterile white surroundings. An assortment of bins and shelves bearing the name of their contents lined a portion of the walls. Across the room, a chart of some sort hung with different facial expressions and a value below, PAIN LEVEL. My body screamed a ten but I focused on staying toward the zero side. A shift in positions gave some relief. Lying down was an option but once my head hit the wafer-thin pillow, surely someone would be in to rouse me to a sitting position.

Before the thought finished, a heavyset dark skinned woman with a wide, toothy grin entered clutching a clipboard. "Hi, I'm Mary, and I'll be your RN for the evening," she said enthusiastically lifting a free hand in a gesture of Ta'dah! Surprise, it is me.

She was rather short. I'm sure, if I stood, Mary fell well below the chin line of my five foot ten. I shook my head. Great, first it's the nurse from hell and now, well, Little Mary Sunshine.

She smiled with genuine concern. "What's going on Miss Conner?"

I drew a ragged breath prepared to speak only pre-empted by the nurse. "Oops, I can hear what's going on. You got some wheezing, can you lie back for me honey?"

I clutched the right side easing down onto the bed. Nurse Mary helped with the struggle. "Honey, did you fall on your side?"

I explained the punching details of my recent occupation. "Ooh," she said with excitement. "You're Jake Conner, the fighter. You beat that woman on the pay-per-view."

She delivered a play by play of the short sixth round while sticking a thermometer in my mouth. I always wondered why doctors or nurses chose temperature first. Come to the emergency room with an eye hanging out of the socket, the first thing they do, check for a fever.

Her lips never stopped while she moved about connecting devices, checking pulse, and blood pressure. She unbuttoned my shirt and listened to my chest. How she managed to hear anything babbling on the way she did was beyond me. The shirt came together but remained unbuttoned. The stethoscope went around her thick neck. "I'll be right back."

Mary returned with a very young man in a white lab coat whom I assumed to be a doctor although he looked younger than I did. For most small towns, seasoned MD's clamoring to join hospitals paying significantly less than larger cities were hard to come by.

He introduced himself as Doctor Jensen. He re-opened the shirt listening to the left side, then center chest, moving across to the right side, and stroking the very visible reddish blue bruise. The baby-faced doctor navigated the area touching ribs and sternum. Each time he pressed an area toward the right side, a stabbing sensation paralyzed the muscles.

He applied stronger pressure to the area. I pulled

away from his intrusive touch.

"Tender?" he questioned.

I twisted my mouth in aggravation for what I thought was a stupid question. "Ah? Yeah," I replied rather sharply.

Standing erect, he wrote on the clipboard. "You got into a fight and took a couple of shots to the ribs? Why did you wait so long to come in?"

I explained the best way possible with difficulty pushing air in and out of my lungs about my career. "I didn't start having trouble breathing until I picked up the suitcase after we got home."

He raised a brow. "No pain before that?"

"Some, not too bad."

Gran appeared in the room supplying her version of the fight leading up to the present.

"How many punches did you take to the side?" he asked, pointing to the bruises.

I sucked in more air. "Three. Nothing very hard."

Without looking up and still writing, he addressed smiling Nurse Mary. "Let's get a few pictures, complete blood panel, and give her something to take the edge off the pain."

I've lived the life of a control freak willing my body to endure things most could not. The thought of medication stirred the memory of the last toll morphine took on my body after a procedure to fix a broken nose received during a fight in Boston. I did not like the feeling of weakness and confusion the drug inflicted. No way was I going through that again.

"I'm fine. I don't need anything for pain," I said.

Pursing his thick lips, the young doctor shrugged. "Suit yourself." He handed the chart to Nurse Mary who immediately disappeared following the doctor's instructions. He clicked his pen repeatedly and walked to a phone mounted on the wall near the door. "Hi, Greta, Dr. Jensen. Is Dr. Lawrence still in surgery? Great, ask him to stop by the ER for a consult." Returning his attention, he gave his thoughts. "I am sure there's a broken rib."

I blamed his youth and inexperience for such a misdiagnosis.

After a once over of the area above my eye, he commented on the well-sutured slit. When an x-ray tech entered the room with a huge machine in tow, Dr. Jensen took his cue and left.

A barrage of people came and went, each completing their appointed task. Katie sashayed her way inside somewhat calmer. "How you feeling," she said in a rather high-pitched voice.

I looked away, avoiding her. "Right as rain."

Katie's never met a person who remained a stranger for very long. She told me about someone in the emergency waiting room. A steel beam, swollen toe, I never quite understood the whole story and didn't feel like asking for a repeat.

Bill walked in. "How you doing Jake?"

I gave my chest a rub in an attempt to fight another cough. "I've had worse."

Bill came closer leaning down. "Liar, how bad is it?"

I shifted worried eyes in Gran and Katie's direction. Bill got the message and changed the subject.

Katie started to explain another person's ailments from her ER investigations when the door opened. What now? They poked, x-rayed, stuck patches all over me, and hooked me to machines making all kinds of noises. What else could they possibly want to do? Moving the least bit made me ill tempered.

I rolled my head to the side. A tall, wide shouldered male wearing black, half-framed glasses dressed in green surgical scrubs with a matching cap strolled across the room studying the chart in hand while making introductions. "Hi, Jacqueline, I'm Dr. Lawrence," came the deep voice.

A snicker slipped from Katie.

"Boxer," he questioned and went on reading the chart while shaking his head. "Injured during a fight." He huffed then raised his head noticing his audience.

A snarl built on my already frowning face. The disapproving tone in his voice rubbed me the wrong way. Of course, Katie, being Katie answered for me. "The champ, baby."

A broad smile parted the doctor's lips while reading the growing thick stack of papers. He laid the clipboard on a nearby table and unwound the stethoscope from his neck with the end held between rather long, thick fingers. The cold instrument pressed against my chest.

"Take a breath, deep as you can," he instructed.

I tried with useless effort.

A large hand braced the doctor's weight on the pillow to the side of my head. "Again," he ordered.

His height became more evident while looming over me listening to the air moving in and out of my lungs. For a brief moment, he locked sight on my face. I caught a glimpse of the dark irises hidden behind the glasses. His skin appeared tanned and smooth covering high cheekbones. One corner of his mouth turned upward. I looked away staring blankly at the wall avoiding further eye contact.

The pillow gave way letting me know he stood upright. I drifted downward observing cool fingers tracing the area of my side radiating prominent pain when pressed harder. I squinted against his touch. The doctor stepped back training his attention on my side studying the area. A knock at the door brought the same x-ray tech handing over a large envelope.

Dr. Lawrence moved to the end of the bed stopping in front of a lighted box on the wall. "Let's see what we have."

He held each x-ray against the screen, away from the screen, flipping to the next then back to the first, finally surmising. "It appears there may be a puncture in the pleural cavity. If you look closer," he pointed to a spot on the picture. Everyone but the incapacitated patient stepped forward getting a better view. "You'll see the culprit is a rib pushing against the lung which is why she's having trouble breathing." Looking down to Katie standing beside him, he grinned. "I would say caused by the champ taking a couple of well-laid punches."

I glared at the back of the surgical cap fitted snug against his head. What a jerk. He turned around about the time the thought entered my head. Judging by the one brow lift, there was no doubt he read my expression.

After educating my family on the anatomy of the human chest, he announced, "I want to admit you for observation and keep you still for the next twenty four hours with some IV pain medication. The lung's not completely collapsed so hopefully we won't have to insert a chest tube to re-inflate it."

I expected to hear you have some bruised ribs which will heal in a few days. I did not expect anything of this magnitude. How many punches had I taken to the ribs from better fighters than Diana? I mean, come on, for crying out loud. At sixteen, I took body punches from Bill's former protégé, the big Swedish monster, Sven.

Dragging air into my painful chest, I exclaimed, "What? The punches didn't move me an inch."

In my outrage of thinking there was the remote possibility the underwear queen broke my ribs, I struggled to raise my voice even louder. "Are you sure?"

Looking over the half glasses, the doctor presented a

surprised glower. A muscle twitched his cheek showing clear signs I had slapped his ego. "You either got hit harder than you remember or the stress on the ribs from the years of abuse has finally caught up to you," he said in a condescending manner.

Abuse. Did he actually say that word? My cheeks flamed with the rise of a hot temper wanting to say a few things to the doctor's lack of boxing knowledge. From my peripheral, I saw Katie working her hands against one another.

"She fell a couple of weeks ago in the barn when she was trying to get Sluggo's saddle," she blurted.

I shot a look in her direction, infuriated. It was true but it angered me that she revealed the incident after I told her to keep her mouth shut.

Dr. Lawrence ignored me and addressed Katie. "How far did she fall?"

Katie looked down. She nibbled on her thumbnail hesitantly replying, "From the loft, and she hit the work bench."

Bill and Gran's mouths gaped hearing of the incident for the first time. I closed my eyes wanting to thrash my sister for giving up the secret.

Shaking his head and jutting his chin, Dr. Lawrence wrote on the clipboard. "You probably broke the rib when you fell and further damaged it during the fight."

Writing more notes and never missing a beat, he added with sarcasm, "I'm surprised someone didn't catch this. I'm assuming there was a doctor who examined you before and after the fight."

I narrowed my eyes and thought, *What a judgmental egomaniac and probably a quack to boot.* I answered with strong bite, "Yeah I was examined before and after the fight, passed with flying colors."

He stopped writing on the clipboard and slowly raised

his head locking dark eyes on mine. A silent battle of wills ensued. He gave a little nod.

"I'm sure you hid it well, and to answer your question, yes, you need to stay at least overnight especially seeing how much you're struggling to draw a breath." He presented his back to me.

My teeth ground together sustaining unpleasant comments about to spill. At that moment, I was no longer able to suppress the tickling in my throat. Leaning forward, holding my side, a deep cough cleared my lungs. Flecks of blood sprayed across the white sheet. I grabbed the side of the bed reaching my threshold of tolerance.

Gran shuffled toward me. "Jake? Honey?"

Dr. Lawrence turned shouting orders to the staff in the hall. Guiding me back down to the bed, he pulled the stethoscope from his neck pressing it against my chest. Nurses rushed into the room pushing my family into the hallway.

I squeezed my eyes shut, willing my mind. *Calm, you feel nothing but power and control,* I reminded myself.

Ripping paper and clanging noises rang out from the side. I kept eyes shut trying to concentrate to ease the pain. In one quick motion, a hand moved over my right side followed with extreme pressure. My eyes opened in surprising agony. Something invaded the area. My fingers gripped the sheet twisting the material.

"You ready for the tube, Dr. Lawrence?" Nurse Mary asked.

"Yeah," the doctor replied.

Blood stained the doctor's gloved hands with the same dark hue moving along a plastic tube.

"There's a lot of blood in there," he said. The stethoscope went around his neck. "She's not getting enough air in that lung. The gang's still here so let's go ahead and take her to the OR so I can get a better look at what's going on." He left quickly.

Gran entered trying to soothe the shock of the situation and hide her own worry. "Honey, it's gonna be fine."

Bill remained close to the door. A concerned frown furrowed his forehead. He ran fingers through his gray hair appearing helpless while monitoring the nurses rushing around the room.

Gran wrapped an arm around a sobbing Katie. "Don't be mad at me, Jake, for telling. You better be okay or I'm taking over your baby," my sister said.

The baby she spoke of was my '69 refurbished black Camaro. I smiled trying to lighten the situation whispering, "You're *not* getting my car."

Before long, two women wearing the same green attire as the doctor entered connecting IV lines and ushering my worried family from the room. I took the rough hand belonging to my best friend, gave a squeeze, and tried desperately to ask him to take care of my family.

Bill said, "You know it, kid, but you'll be fine, and when you're better we're going to talk about this."

In life, there are many uncertainties but the one thing I knew with all surety was Bill's love for me. We never spoke the words but I understood. He showed a tough guy image on the outside but inside he was a man who loved completely and unconditionally.

The three left me at the mercy of the nursing staff. Mary appeared with syringe in hand.

"If it's pain stuff I don't want it," I declared, quickly stopping her progress.

One of the nurses dressed in green said, "Dr. Lawrence ordered it."

I still refused.

"Doctor Lawrence won't be happy about this," Mary sighed, placing the syringe in her pocket. She cut away my clothes, replacing them with a hospital gown. She expressed her gladness to meet me and I reciprocated with a nod.

I laid on the gurney passing through the hall of the ER spotting the nurse who first wheeled me into the hospital. The same look of disdain glowed on her face. I believe I was justified with my simple one fingered good-bye waved in her direction.

The freezing surgical suite made me shiver. I clenched my teeth tight blocking out the pain which came from shifting from one bed to the other. The same nurses who delivered me to the operating room moved about connecting monitors and relocating tables.

Dressed in new, full surgical garb, the surgeon stood beside me reading the chart on a nearby table. "Refused pain medication," he said.

A different male voice came from above my head. "Miss Conner, are you allergic to any medication?"

I shook my head.

The same voice spoke to the Egomaniac standing beside me. "General or sedation, Dr. Lawrence?"

I saw the mischief in the dark eyes above the mask covering what I knew to be a wide grin. "I've got to make a bigger cut and look around in there. So champ, would you prefer I do it with or without anesthesia?" he inquired, in a condescending tone.

I heard a short laugh above my head with the surgeon delivering the order of sedation. The drugs warmed my body. With a last ditch effort to fight the sleep overtaking my brain, one thought entered my mind regarding the doctor. The man was an ass.

4

"Jake, wake up."

I fuzzily peeked through lashes blinking several times trying to comprehend my surroundings. Bright light forced them closed. The smell of disinfectant and the surgeon standing overhead were the last memories swirling around a hazy brain. The irritating smell was gone replaced with the sweet scent of honeysuckle perfuming the air.

I rolled to the left sensing something close. I squinted trying to see what lay beside me. Confusion weighed heavily. The object came into focus. What the heck, I thought seeing a tombstone by my head.

I levered on one arm pushing upward to a righted position. It took several blinks to clear my mind affirming it didn't play tricks on me. My fingers slid across the coarse letters engraved on the granite spelling the name Bridgette Marie Conner. How did I get to the cemetery? I must have died.

"Jake? Come on we're going to be late."

I raised my chin tilting back to see who called my name but failed to do so. Sunlight forced a cupped palm over my forehead. A slender hand eased my arm away tugging upward. Upon standing, my heart leaped in my chest seeing the woman before me.

Long blonde hair hung loosely over her shoulder. Warm blue eyes radiated love with a smile creasing her lips. She was beautiful just as she had been shortly before her death.

A trembled voice spouted the wishing word, "Momma?"

She gave a nod. "Of course, it's me, baby."

Every ounce of sorrow held inside for over twelve years spilled down my cheeks. I swept arms around her slender waist clinging in fear of letting go, she might disappear.

"I missed you so much." I wept.

She brushed the moisture from my cheeks pressing her soft lips against my forehead then clucked me under the chin. "Enough of the waterworks. Come on, silly, we got to go if you plan on skating before I have to go to work."

During my youth, I lived for the chance to roller skate. It was one of the few activities which brought plea-sure into my life.

We strolled hand in hand across the grass toward a station wagon parked on the street. We owned the same type car when I was a child. Climbing behind the steering wheel, she reminded me to buckle up. Her fingers touched the keys in the ignition and eased a smile in my direction. "I love you, Jake."

For so long, I yearned for her presence and hearing the sweet voice recite poetry. I must be dead. It was the only explanation. I'd miss Katie, Gran, and Bill. The sorrow of never seeing them again would be great. However, to see my mother and to hear her, it was worth death.

"I love you, too," I said.

She was about to turn the key when something hit the driver side glass. I jumped feeling a strong desire to wet myself.

"Going somewhere?"

A slow turn toward the window revealed the wide hands splayed against the glass. Shoulders lowered showing a face I prayed never to see again. He was pure evil, an unholy soul searching for a victim. My mother and I satisfied his demented hunger for a while, until she said no more.

His fist hit the glass again, only louder and rocked the car. "Answer me. Where are you going?"

My mother's fingers trembled on the keys producing an eerie chime when the metal pieces connected against one another. The smile on her face disappeared.

"Drive! Just go," I bellowed.

She gripped the steering wheel shaking her head. "Brad's my crown of thorns. You don't need to wear it anymore." A tear slid past the apple of her cheek. "I'm sorry. I'm so sorry for everything. Go, Jake, hurry."

His fists hit the window, cracking the glass. I slammed a shoulder against the door desperately wanting out of the car. "I can't get out, Momma."

Her lips never moved, but I heard her voice in my head. "You're stronger now. You can do it."

"Please, God, please." I pushed with all my might. It didn't budge.

"Ahh," I cried in frustration. "Open. Open. Open!"

"Jake? Jake? Hey, kid, you okay?"

"Open," I yelled.

"Jake? Wake up."

The vision of a blurred male hovered above. I grasped tighter on the railing beside me shaking the metal in jerking waves. "No!"

A slight roll brought a torturous tug. I fought the hands attempting to pin my shoulders until I recognized Bill's voice. "Careful, Jake, don't pull out the chest tube."

I was out of breath and sweating profusely. Overwhelming thanks passed through my nerve endings. "It's just a dream," I whispered.

Bill gave my shaking hand a squeeze. "Are you okay?"

I nodded, wiping beaded perspiration from my brow. The garment blanketing my torso rode high on my hips. A good tug covered an exposed rear. "What time is it," I asked, untangling the wires flowing from the neckline.

Bill scooped fingers through his thick hair checking his watch. "One o'clock. What the heck were your dreaming about?"

I fussed with the covers, bit a trembling lip, and stared at the wall across the room. "I don't remember."

Gran and Katie were nowhere in sight. Bill sat down in a chair beside the bed reading my mind. "They left a couple of hours ago. Katie has finals in the morning. You were pretty out of it."

He stretched arms high over his head. "I offered to take Katie to my place so Chelsea could stay, but I think she was worried I'd lock the chatterbox in a closet."

I gave a halfhearted smile. "You would, too."

Bill ran a hand through his hair. "Probably."

"You need a haircut," I said.

"Yeah, yeah, plan on doing that tomorrow. Right now I'm more concerned with you."

"I'm all right. What happened, I mean, what did the doctor do?"

"You had a little nick on your lung. He said you should be ready to go home in a couple of days."

An older woman with silver hair entered the room and stopped on the opposite side of the bed from Bill. She pushed buttons on a nearby machine. When she finished, she winked. "How are you feeling sugar?"

I admitted being tired. Her fingers lay on my wrist while watching the clock that hung above the bed.

"Your blood pressure's high," she said. She raised the

sheet checking the bandages then moved toward the door letting me know she would return with something to ease the pain.

I felt apprehensive about going back sleep and continuing the disturbing dream. "No, I'm fine, I don't need anything."

She turned, placing hands on her narrow hips. "Now, now, I know you're tough, but you have to let us take care of you."

We argued briefly, finally agreeing to disagree on the subject. With a sigh, she concurred. "Don't let the pain get too bad. It'll be hard to ease if you wait too long."

I nodded. She walked out the door.

The mattress was uncomfortable. I changed positions feeling the twinge of muscles and nerves coming back to life. Would I be able to control the building discomfort without medication? I was determined to try.

Bill fell asleep filling the room with nasally sounds. I spent the next two hours combating the ache mixed with memories conjured by the dream until I remembered something Bill once said. The past can't hurt you unless you chose to live there. I moved on, but impromptu moments somehow visited occasionally.

"Damn drugs."

I repositioned hoping a change might keep the thoughts at bay.

Several times Nurse Nancy, I came to know her name, entered the room offering medication. She was a welcoming distraction. Still, I refused the painkillers. Bill continued sleeping never hearing her entry and exit or the brief communication we shared.

"Miss Conner," she said on one visit.

"Jake," I corrected.

"Jake, this is ridiculous. Your blood pressure's too high. You're sweating and your clothes are damp. Stop fighting the pain, and let me give you something."

I assured her I was fine. She gave up adding a threat of, "Dr. Lawrence is not going to be happy about this."

Good ole Dr. Lawrence. The man irritated me with his disapproving tone over my former profession not to mention the cutting remark he made about the use of anesthesia. If refusal annoyed him, then so much the better.

A yellowish hue danced on the blinds hinting of a rising sun. Under normal conditions, I would start the second mile of a five-mile run before the sun rose above the trees. The quietness of the country roads with crisp morning air combined with the lulling of birds roosting was my favorite time of day.

I was lost in desire for the outdoors when the lights overhead came on abruptly. Bill woke with a start leaping from his chair. I shaded my eyes to see who flipped the switch.

Standing in the doorway wearing a knee-length white lab coat over his scrubs was Dr. Lawrence. Without his surgical cap, black hair was secured behind his head. No furrows of ire on the smooth, shaven face. Just a smile broadening with advancement toward the bed.

"Well, well, well, Jacqueline," he said.

"Jake," I firmly corrected.

"Jake. You're refusing pain meds once again. Not good."

He towered over me grasping the corner of the sheet pulling it back. His fingers moved my gown to the side carefully tracing the edge of the bandage. He replaced the covers and took a seat in the chair previously occupied by Bill. Leaning forward, he fumbled with the IV line between his knees.

"Your blood pressure's dangerously high. Stress on your body will compromise your recovery," he said.

I gazed in his direction dismissing the man through tightly held lips. "I'm fine, I don't need anything." From you, I wanted to add.

He drew a deep breath. "Did you have a bad experience with pain medication?"

I bit my lower lip. "It's not that bad. I can handle it."

Bill, fully awake, put in his two cents. "Stop being a hardheaded jackass and take the drugs."

I shook my head. "I'm fine, really."

The doctor let out a long sigh. Good, run along find someone else to annoy. He didn't. Instead, he flashed a wide grin. "There comes a time when we have to do what is best for the patient no matter how much they protest. Don't you agree, Bill?"

How did he know Bill's name?

"That's right, Doc." My supposedly best friend agreed.

The surgeon took something from his pocket keeping it below the bed blocking my view. I strained to see what he was doing. The smile on his face grew with my curiosity.

I opened my mouth to ask what was going on when a hazy fog crept into my brain. All of the muscles in my body relaxed. I shook my head trying to clear the dizziness. The doctor stood with a syringe in hand.

He drugged me. I couldn't believe it. He drugged me after I declined the medication. I started to speak but only, "You…," came out before the drugs took their toll.

It was some time later that I woke finding my grandmother in a chair across the room submerged in a book. My rustling the stiff sheets drew her attention.

"Hey, baby, you awake? You need something?" She asked, while slipping the book into her large purse.

Strands of hair escaped my long braid during the drug -induced coma. I pushed the pieces away managing to find the switch to position the bed upright. Rolling stiff shoulders and allowing a twinge of ache to show on my sleepy face, I answered my grandmother. "I'm fine Gran. Bill go home?"

"He'll be back later with Katie. She's insisting on staying the night with you."

I growled. "I'm not staying another night. I'm fine. Get this thing out of my side. I want to go home."

My grandmother knew me well and never took my mean disposition personally, but used the moments to guilt me into wishing I had kept my mouth shut.

She made her way across the room. "Well, Jake, there's the door. Go ahead. Don't matter a bit we worried ourselves sick praying God spared your life."

She straightened the covers. "Poor Katie, tried to study 'til two this morning but couldn't concentrate thinking about you. But that's not important, you know, if she passes her finals or not, just as long as you get your way."

I shifted positions. "Why do you do that?"

Innocence beamed from her. "Do what?"

I rolled my eyes. "Never mind. I'll stay, but they better let me go home tomorrow."

She kissed my forehead. "Of course, sugar."

During my extended sleep, the hospital staff switched shifts. A young, pixie like woman, approached the bed. Being so small, I was sure she required standing on a stool to reach me.

"Miss Conner," she began.

I quickly corrected her.

"Jake, are you having any difficulty breathing?"

"No, I'm fine."

"How's the pain?" she asked, checking the tubes coming from my body.

Something about the look on her face when she asked this question made me think word got around about my previous refusals.

"Really, I am fine," I replied.

She trailed a finger over her lips deep in thought. "Can we make a deal?"

Curious, I questioned the deal. "Depends?"

"Dr. Lawrence ordered pain medication every four hours. I know you don't like them so I am offering you a choice. Instead of Demerol, I can give you something not as strong and in a pill form."

A little voice inside said take the deal or face the egomaniac returning with a syringe in his hand. I agreed to her compromise.

I slept most of the day waking long enough to allow a staff member to collect x-rays. A few hours later, the chest tube was removed. Nurses assisted with standing allowing me to venture into the bathroom. It's hard to pee when you have a stranger standing in the doorway waiting in case you need help. Nonetheless, it felt good to be up moving around relieving some of the stiffness.

Bill called every few hours checking in. The last call, Gran spoke to him saying, "Yeah, she's fine, full of herself only meaner." Then, she paused. "Nope, haven't seen him, I will, if she tries I'll turn her over my knee. See you later." With a laugh, she said her good-bye hanging up the phone.

"What did you mean turn me over your knee?" I asked

She turned the page of the newspaper she was reading. "Oh, Bill said I need to play referee between you and Dr. Lawrence when he makes his rounds." She clamped her lips together shaking her head. "I don't understand you, Jake. He's such a nice man."

Great, my own grandmother was becoming a member of the Dr. Lawrence fan club.

"He's a jerk," I snapped.

She ignored the comment and continued reading while remarking on several articles. Feeling the numbness settling in my butt, I decided to get up and try to move around. I swung shaky legs to the side of the bed. The bathroom was my destination, and I needed no help.

Gran peered over the top of the paper and gave me a long look. "You know, Jake? Dear Abby says a person who refuses to ask for help is a fool craving disaster."

I took the hint, gave in without argument, and let her walk me to the bathroom.

Bill came in around six with Katie.

"You look a lot better sis," she said. She leaned close. "That good looking doctor come by yet?"

I gave a sour look. "Ugh, hopefully he forgot about me."

The bag carried on her shoulder bulged with an assortment of magazines. I wondered how long she planned to stay. She flopped down in a nearby chair and removed her shoes replacing them with a pair of slippers resembling pandas. "Hey, Carter called. Left a message said he's coming to town next month," she announced.

I shivered with dread at the remote possibility of seeing Carter Neal. I met the middleweight boxer while training in Chicago. I didn't have much to say to him ever, but it seemed enough for the self-absorbed man to try cozying up by arranging his fights in the same city and weeks as mine. We would be a great team if we billed our fights together, he professed once. Carter wanted a partnership and more. I wasn't interested in a business or personal venture.

He didn't get it. My desire to box was about the sport not the money. I liked my privacy. Maintaining the status required turning down endorsement deals and interviews. It was worth it in my opinion.

Taking a magazine from the bag, flipping through the

pages, Katie sat upright with excitement. "Ooooh, yeah," she started. "Weird message was on the machine."

We all waited for the rest of the story.

"He said something like, been a long time, then kind of laughed and said can't wait to see you or something corny like that." She gave a laugh. "What a loser, can't even dial the right number."

Katie never stopped to draw a breath, continuing on describing her day and softball practice. I shook my head remembering the talkative teenager was spending the night with me. An hour later, Bill and Gran said good-night. Bill held the door looking over his shoulder. "Want me to have the nurse bring you something?"

I shook my head. "I'm fine. Hardly any discomfort."

He broke into a grin. "No, I'm talking about knocking you out so you don't have to listen to that all night," he said, pointing to Katie reading an article aloud.

A quick wave to the reprobate left me alone with my younger sibling. As soon as the door closed, I asked, "Did you bring me some clothes?"

Katie pulled a pair of shorts and tee shirt from her bag dangling them from a distance. "How bad do you want them? Like, oh, I don't know, maybe I give you the clothes and you let me drive your car to school next year?"

I wrinkled my nose. "Oh, I don't know like, give me the shorts, or I'll make you ride the bus 'til you graduate?"

"You would," she huffed. "I swear you're no fun."

With her help, I replaced the hospital gown that rode up all day. After a couple of hours listening to Katie read installments from the multiple magazines scattered on the floor and another round of pain medication, sleep took over.

"Hi."

I woke hearing his voice. It was back.

"Hello, Dr. Lawrence," came the return greeting from my sister.

His glasses rested on top of his head. He approached with arms crossing his chest holding a clipboard. "Sorry it's so late. I got caught up in an emergency. I've had reports you've been cooperating with the staff today."

I nodded, remembering his last visit. "I guess that means you won't have to drug me yourself."

He chuckled. "Okay, let's have a look." He pushed the sheet aside revealing the tee shirt and shorts. "You don't give up, do you?"

"Not in my vocabulary," I replied sharply.

After a quick exam, he lowered the black rimmed glasses and began writing.

Katie, no longer interested in a softball magazine, said, "So, Dr. Lawrence, you're new. How long would you say you've been in our small town?"

Still writing, he answered, "About two months."

He looked up at the blonde teenager gesturing with his pen at the magazine. "You play softball?"

She nodded. "High school and summer league."

I watched the exchange in amazement. My sister's charismatic personality allowed her to talk to people with such ease. I envied her boldness at times but realized one of us must be the voice of reason.

Dr. Lawrence continued writing. "I have a son starting his junior year here in the fall."

"Oh?" she said. "Is he into sports?"

"Football," the doctor said.

I took the opportunity during their conversation to sate my thirst with a cup of water from the nearby table. My mouth was full when Katie asked, "Is he as good-looking as you?"

The liquid settled on my windpipe. The coughing episode brought my hand to a throbbing side.

"You okay?" the doctor asked.

I nodded, lowering my hand.

He massaged my side checking to see if anything dislodged during the choking episode. I trained my eyes on Katie sending her a warning to cut it out. A mischievous smile spread across her face.

Satisfied everything to be in order, he answered Katie's forward question. "We have similar features."

I rolled my eyes. God, please, just let him leave before anything else came out of her mouth. I was not that lucky.

"Final question, promise," she swore holding her hand over her heart.

I wanted to place hands around her slender neck and choke her to silence. I mouthed the words, "Shut up Katie," which she ignored.

She raised an inquisitive eyebrow. "Boxers or briefs, Dr. Lawrence?"

The doctor laughed. Heat rose in my cheeks wanting to crawl under the covers. I didn't take a chance on his reply nor Katie asking more outrageous questions.

I changed the subject. "When can I go home?"

He placed a hand on the wall looking down, un-doubtedly enjoyed my embarrassment. "Maybe tomorrow afternoon, if you're still improving."

I balked and gave a growl.

Dr. Lawrence turned to leave. "I'll be back in the morning to check on you. Then we'll talk about going home."

Thankfully, he left without providing as answer to my sister's last question.

I glared at Katie in utter disbelief. "Good Lord, what's your problem?"

She settled back in the chair laughing. "Oh Jake he's cute. Did you notice the name on his coat. Huh, huh?" she chided.

"What the heck are you talking about?"

"D. H. Lawrence, MD. What are the chances of your doctor having the same name as your favorite poet? He wasn't wearing a ring either. It's kismet, I tell you. Pure divine, heavenly, written in the stars, meant to be, kismet, and he's really into you, I can tell, although I can't say why you're meaner than a snake."

I narrowed eyes in her direction. I moved my tongue along the inside of my bottom lip grazing teeth. Katie knew better than to mess with me when it came to my personal life. It didn't matter that I had no personal life but it was off limits to her or anyone else if I did.

"I'm not mean to him," I said.

She started to open her mouth, and I stopped her. "I just refuse to be talked down to, and let me tell you something those magazines haven't taught you, Ms. Authority on Men. He probably don't wear a ring so women will hit on him, and why they would is beyond me. He's an ass, and I'm not interested in an egomaniac with a God like complex."

She slung back the reply, "Takes one to know one, Jake."

I flipped her off and rolled to my side letting sleep overpower me.

The next morning Gran arrived before Dr. Lawrence conducted a final assessment of my health. My grandmother was what I called old school and lacked the appreciation of Katie's antics. Her presence meant my sister could no longer torture me about the doctor.

I found it amazing Dr. Lawrence's definition of morning and mine were so different. He made his rounds near noon. After a series of x-rays and lengthy instructions, release came a good while later.

We stopped at Hope High School on the way home

dropping Katie off to attend softball practice. The remainder of the ride was quiet with only a quick phone call to Bill assuring him I was fine.

Once the farm came into view, a relief of utter joy washed over me. I climbed the few steps to the porch which spanned the front of the two story white house. Inside, I made my way up the stairs to my bedroom. I stretched out on the soft bed glad to be home.

After a quick nap, I woke to the mouth-watering scent of pot roast. It wasn't just any pot roast. It was Gran's pot roast. After staying in Vegas for so long, eating in restaurants, and then experiencing the hospital food, I felt starved for home cooking.

The smell drew me from the bed. I went downstairs following the delicious aroma ending with Gran in the kitchen stirring a pot on the stove.

"Smells so good," I said.

She chuckled. "Miss my cooking, did you?"

"Yes, Ma'am."

A plate of cornbread fresh from the oven sat on the counter. I pinched off a piece of the crust. Gran slapped my hand. "Bill's picking up Katie from practice, and they should be here shortly. You can wait."

I left Gran to fuss over preparing the meal. I went into the living room observing the answering machine blinking with messages. Pressing play, the first message was one left by Carter.

"Freak'n jerk."

I quickly erased it. The next three were for Gran. The fifth message played.

"Been a long time," it began with a laugh. "You can run, but you can't hide, I'll see you soon, can't say the when or where. We'll cross that bridge when we get to it."

It was the message Katie spoke of the night before. I played the message again. Instead of hearing the caller, I heard the past. "Where you going? Huh? Where the hell do you think you're going? Nowhere. Right!"

I shook my head. It's not him. It's the drugs and the dream. It's not him. I stared at the play button itching for the courage to push it again. *Get a grip Jake,* I chastised myself silently. *It's the last couple of days, stress, hurting and the drugs messing with your head.*

Gran called out from the kitchen. I tapped fingernails on the button. *It's not him,* I reasoned, *it can't be him. He's in prison.* I hit the delete button removing the fifth message.

5

Confinement to the house for close to two weeks tested my sanity. Gran questioned every movement and added a scolding commentary to anything resembling an occupation. She caught me once eyeing the mower and promptly hid the gas can and keys.

I slipped out the back door a few times with apples in my pocket, spending time with Sluggo, the solid black filly I bought Katie for her thirteenth birthday. I was unsure if I purchased the horse because Katie wanted it so bad or the fact I dreamt of one as a child.

I developed a clear understanding how caged animals must feel. The floors from my bedroom to the living room to the kitchen held a little more wear and tear not to mention the keypad on the remote from flipping through channels. One thing for sure, I missed the gym and the grueling workouts.

I was in the middle of one of my aimless wanderings when the phone rang. Hearing Carter Neal's voice on the other end made me wish I had let it go to the machine. After listening to thirty minutes of everything happening in his world, I was ready to hang myself. He described life with such glory. One would think he remained the reigning champion. He lost that title the year before and was obviously still in denial.

He reminded me of his trip to Hope and wanting to talk with Bill hinting of possibly buying a gym in Chicago. Bill's professional opinion meant a lot to him. I found it absurd considering my trainer never made a secret of his dislike for Carter. The animosity was just another one of the unsolved mysteries surrounding Bill Monroe.

I called Bill later. He found the comments amusing. "I wouldn't partner up with that boxer wanna be if I was freezing to death and he had the only lighter," he said.

After the calls with Carter, then Bill, I strolled to the kitchen where Gran was wrist deep in a bowl of grated cheese. A smile came to my lips watching her work the glob conjuring a memory of another time she made a cheese ball appetizer.

Three months after Katie and I moved to Arkansas, I came down stairs suffering with my first hangover. Gran asked where I went the night before. I told her it was none of her business. She threw the ball of cheese hitting me in the side of the head and informed everything about me was her business.

I gripped Gran's shoulders and laid a cheek against her soft graying hair. "What's up, Gran?"

"Card night, you wanna play? Adell's not coming, she's got a meeting or something."

Adell Williams, the biggest gossip in Hempstead County and the area alderwoman. Although she and Gran had been friends since childhood, Adell carried herself a few feet above everyone else. She continued carrying a grudge against my assault on her baby Jesus.

After I started working at Jackson's garage paying off my debt, she pulled into the station getting out of the car with keys in her boney hand. One good shake let me know she didn't leave them in the car for someone to steal. She continued with the gesture over the years. After a while, I added my own fun by getting out of my four-wheel drive truck or Camaro, shaking keys letting her know I had my own.

"No thanks, Gran, I don't feel like playing cards

tonight," I said.

Gran spun around. "Oh come on, Jake, you've got to be going stir crazy. I've never seen ya in the house this much."

This was true, but I knew better than to play poker with the gray-haired Mafia. They cheated.

"You guys play poker once a month and go to church every Sunday. Don't you feel the least bit guilty," I asked.

"Nope, I put ten percent of everything I win in the collection plate," she said.

Raking a finger around the bowl for a bit of the cheesy remains, I inquired who was picking up Katie from practice. Gran placed plastic wrap around the symmetrical mass and said Bill volunteered.

"I bet he did," I whispered, thinking of Shirley Dobb's house located between Washington and Hope.

Bill discreetly spent time with the woman widowed many years ago. Why they kept their relationship low keyed was beyond me except for the fact Bill preferred to avoid people's gossip.

I went into the living room flipping on the TV catching the local news. Before long, three of Gran's five poker buddies, Alma Jensen, Tollie Fergusen, and Liola Graves, arrived within five minutes of each other making their way into the house. Each took a turn inquiring of my health.

It wasn't long before Cora Mae Jackson shuffled inside. The straight talking black woman was the mother of Tom Jackson and my favorite of Gran's friends. At the age of seventy, Cora Mae, every morning, made her way into Washington working at the tavern cooking for locals and tourist.

She took a seat on the sofa beside me while the others ventured into the kitchen. "How ya do'n girl?"

I rolled my eyes and exhaled loudly. "I'm about to

lose my mind, Cora Mae."

"Get Chelsea to bring you by and spend the day at the restaurant. Get you out of the house."

In a loud voice, I announced, "I plan on driving to the gym tomorrow."

My grandmother appeared in the doorway separating the two rooms. "No, you're not, young lady. Doctor Lawrence said no driving 'til he says so. You've got an appointment with him in the morning, take it up then." She went back into the kitchen.

I chuckled, thinking no matter what Dr. Lawrence said, I was driving after my appointment—if not before.

Cora Mae leaned in, speaking low. "I saw him at the Food Mart last week, that Dr. Lawrence. He's one fine look'n man."

She leaned back against the sofa, looking over her glasses. "That ole Tucker girl, the fat one always wear'n low ride'n jeans, look'n like a homemade roll with too much yeast popping out the sides, well she's at the register and all up in his face."

Cora Mae looked me up and down. "You're a pretty gal. You ought'a fix yourself up when you see him to-morrow."

"I don't think so."

Cora Mae leaned forward, resting hands on her knees. "Did that gal hit ya too hard in the head?" She rose from the sofa slowly maneuvering toward the kitchen. "Girl, if I was a few years younger, you wouldn't have a chance."

Shaking my head, I chuckled.

An hour later, Bill pulled into the drive with Katie. She rushed in through the screen door, pouting, slammed the door, and took the stairs two at a time. A loud bang from her bedroom door followed. Bill opened the screen and stepped inside, rubbing his neck.

"What's wrong," I said.

He motioned me outside. "See for yourself."

From the porch, the cratered fender around the head-light on the passenger side of Bill's truck stood out like a sore thumb.

"What happened?" I asked with dread.

Placing a hand on one of the post for support, he explained while trying to control laughter. "Well, it seems trees are jumping out attacking vehicles with their limbs."

I took a seat in the swing. "What?"

Bill relayed the story of how Katie drove his truck ending with a run through the ditch and clipping a limb to avoid hitting a cat in the road.

My sister possessed the superb skills of an athlete and student, but when it came to driving, she was the worst. I let her drive my car once last summer in the pasture before the new custom paint job. I thought it safe, being a wide-open thirty-acre meadow with nothing to hit. She hit the fence post while driving into the pasture resulting in a dent concaving the passenger door.

I offered to pay Bill for the damages. He wouldn't hear of it. We chatted for a few minutes before he decided to go home. I knew where he was going, and it wasn't the little house on East Second.

"Tell Shirley hi," I said.

He squinted and got into his truck, and drove away.

I went into Katie's room to console her bruised feelings and listened to her version of the story as she added how Bill gripped the dashboard and yelled at her.

"That man's a mean old fart. I saw the cat and was go'n around it. About the time I passed it, Bill screeched and meowed like I hit it."

I turned my face away so she couldn't see the giggling about to erupt.

"I looked back 'cause he made me think I ran over it," she huffed. "It's his fault I ran in to the ditch."

I couldn't hold it in any longer and burst into laughter.

"It ain't funny, Jake."

After gaining control, I said, "I'm sorry, but it *is* funny. The two of you need to play nice."

"I'm nice," she spouted. "I'm always nice. He's the one that starts it every time."

"Oh, really? If I recall, it was you who duct taped Bill's mouth last Thanksgiving. Ripped one side of his whiskers from his face getting that crap off," I said.

Katie dismissed the episode. "He was snoring!"

She went on ranting over Bill and the details of a bad softball practice for a good while. After enough drama, I kissed her good night and went to bed.

The next morning around eight, I came down stairs. Katie was already dressed, bent over a bowl of cereal reading one of her many beloved magazines. With the school year officially over, I found it surprising her up and about so early. "Mornin', baby girl, where's Gran?"

She gave no reply.

I pulled the headphone from her lobe. Music blared from the earpiece.

She jumped spilling some of the bowl's contents. "Dang it, Jake, you scared the crap out of me!"

I repeated. "Where's Gran?"

"Throw me a towel, will ya? Cora Mae called needing some help at the tavern. Somebody called in sick. Some big luncheon or something. I don't know." Katie went about cleaning up the mess. "She said Bill's coming to pick you up at nine."

I silently grumbled. I was more than capable of driving myself to the doctor's appointment. "Why are you up so early slugger?" I said going over to the phone pushing the numbers connecting to the gym.

She tossed the cloth onto the counter. "I took Sluggo

out for a ride."

"Gym," Bill answered.

"Morning, sunshine," I said. "No need to come out it's been two weeks I can drive myself."

It didn't work. He let me know he was not facing the wrath of Gran. We argued back and forth. Katie jumped up and down begging me to let her drive to the appointment.

I fanned her off. "Bill, I'm fine. There's no need for you to drive all the way to Washington, back to Hope, back to Washington, then back to Hope again." I turned away, trying to ignore the bouncing teen in front of me.

"Please, please, Jake," Katie whispered.

I thought for a few seconds. She had her permit. It would make me a nervous wreck. I could detour her around town via the bypass to get to Dr. Lawrence's office. I decided to let her drive.

"Hey, Bill, Katie's going to chauffeur so just stay there, and I'll see you later."

A howled laugh resonated through the phone. "Katie's driving? I'll see you at the ER."

Placing the bowl in the sink, Katie took off up the stairs squealing in delight.

"God help me," I muttered, hanging up the phone.

At nine thirty, we walked out the back door. Katie headed toward my baby, the nineteen sixty-nine, black Camaro. I stopped the teenager before she made it to the car.

"Don't think so." I waved her toward the truck.

I hesitated before handing over the keys. "Please, be careful."

Katie loaded a rap CD into the player. I turned the volume down. "Don't you think this might be a little distracting?"

She turned the music back up and shifted the truck

into reverse punching the gas pedal at precisely the same moment the rapper screamed, 'Girl you better back that ass up.'

Now, it was my turn to grab the dash. Katie giggled, put the truck into drive, and rushed down the driveway. My sister turned onto the pavement with the tires squealing, hitting the asphalt.

Stretched fingers maintained a death grip. "All right. Pull over, I can't take this," I shouted.

"I don't understand, Jake. I didn't wig out when you did the same thing a month ago."

"Katie, do you know the big difference between me and you?"

"I can define the word fun and you can't?" she said.

I pulled out my license and held it up. "I have one of these, and you don't."

My sister mimicked my words, slowing the truck to an acceptable speed.

The young driver in training delivered us to the appointment on time and without incident. We were the only two people in the waiting room.

"Jake Conner," the voice of Shelley Thompson rang out.

Shelley's daughter, Ali, and Katie were best friends. The two played softball together since the age of six. Shelley and I struck up a semi friendship sharing a seat beside each other during the games.

"Hey, Shelley," I greeted, walking toward her.

Katie stood, about to follow.

I smiled, holding up a hand. "Oh no, I don't think so. I can't deal with worrying about what's going to come out of your mouth."

She pushed her bottom lip out looking so innocent. "I'll be good. I promise."

I gave her a skeptical leer.

"I won't say a word about how good looking he is, you have my word as a softball pitcher," she swore, placing a hand on her chest.

I cuffed a laugh. "Well, since your vowing under the commandments of the mound, I guess I have to trust you."

There wasn't anything in the exam room sacred. Katie opened, closed, and pillaged everything in the room. After waiting twenty minutes and at the end of my patience, Dr. Lawrence entered wearing the green surgical scrubs. He read the chart and greeted with a quick hi.

Convinced he intentionally let me wait for the extended time, I clamped my lips tight, waiting for him to get on with the removing the few stitches in my side and brow.

"Two weeks post op from a lung puncture caused by fighting, we should be ready to go. All right Jake, take off your shirt and lie back. Let's see if I put you back together," he said.

Chewing on my lip, I removed the shirt, watching the dark head shake in some disapproving way. He raised and gave my sister a smile. "Hi. Katie isn't it?"

She nodded. The doctor engaged in conversation with her about last weekend's softball game which it seemed he attended.

He retrieved several items from a nearby drawer. "My nurse has a daughter who plays on your team. She's been after me to watch a game for a while. I have to say I am impressed. You're good. The whole team's good."

"Ali and I played together since tee ball," Katie said.

I laid on the table nearly naked from the waist up listening to the two chat all the while wanting to yell, "Excuse me, patient here. Could we get on with it?"

He examined my side working each stitch loose then moved to the brow. I let my eyes trail up. Katie and Cora Mae thought him handsome. He wasn't bad looking.

I studied him for a moment trying to figure him out. Deep tanned skin, gorgeous dark eyes, firm jaw line, a smile that drew a person in. A smile, a smile, good Lord I lingered too long. The edges of his mouth rose. I looked away, feeling a little flush of pink rise on my cheeks.

He listened with the cold stethoscope instructing me to breathe deeply. "You can sit up, and put your shirt on. We need to get an x-ray."

Dr. Lawrence stuck his head out of the room calling for Shelley. After a few instructions, Shelley led me down the hall with the doctor trailing off to another room. I managed a glimpse inside the nicely decorated office. Dr. Lawrence turned around catching me in the act. I frowned, and entered a room on the opposite side of the hall.

I returned to the same exam room and stood by the table, waiting for the surgeon to come back. He entered requesting Katie go to the waiting room. Before she closed the door, she called out sweetly, "Dr. Lawrence?"

I raised my hands, forming a noose, dropping them when the doctor looked up from the chart.

"Boxers or briefs?" she mused.

I forced her out the door.

"Jake, I didn't say a thing about how good looking he is." She laughed.

I pushed the door shut rather forcefully, bracing a hand on my hip. I swallowed hard, hoping the gesture cooled the heat on my cheeks.

I came about slowly. A few minutes of awkward silence hung in the air before I lifted my gaze to meet a wide grin.

"She's a character, isn't she?" He said.

I said nothing in return but placed attention on a poster behind him.

"Any shortness of breath or pain," he asked, writing on the chart.

"None. I'm fine."

He tilted his head to the side. "Would you tell me if there were problems?"

I kept quiet, waiting for him to move on to the next question. He tapped the folder with his pen.

I cut a dismissing glare in his direction. "If I thought there was a problem, I'd say something."

He grinned, shaking his head while writing in the chart. "Everything's healing nicely. Take it easy. You'll need another x-ray in four weeks and if everything looks good I'll, release you to go back to normal activities."

That's it, I thought, turning to leave.

"Jake, I'm serious. No working out, no lifting, and absolutely no fighting. Give yourself time to heal."

Dr. Lawrence said the word, "fighting" with a hint of disgust.

The man's an irritating jerk. He has no clue about me. It was time to address his condescending attitude.

"You don't really care for boxing do you? Or is it the word 'female' in front of it that messes with your head?"

He laid the chart down and took off his glasses cleaning the lens on his coat tail. "Have I offended you in some way, Jake?" He held them out checking the vision quality.

I snorted. "Let's see? Other than making my former profession sound like I'm nothing more than a bar room brawler, I would have to say no you haven't offended me in any way."

He relaxed. "If I come off in that way, I do apologize. I admit, I'm not a boxing fan and find the sport extremely dangerous considering the point is to knock your opponent unconscious."

I pursed my lips, gave a sarcastic nod, and confirmed Dr. Lawrence was clueless when it came to boxing or me. "Outside of martial arts, it's probably one of the most disciplined sports there is. It's no more dangerous than football or hockey. At least with boxing you know you're going get hit and can protect yourself," I said sharply.

He tipped his head slightly, rose, and walked past me. "Good answer, but I do believe they wear padding and a helmet in those sports. See you in four weeks."

I snarled, walking out the door behind him, gathering my sister from her chair.

"Want me to drive?" Katie asked.

Getting into the driver side, I mumbled, "You're already driving me crazy."

We left the doctor's office plowing down Main Street toward the gym.

"So did he say everything's fine?" Katie asked

"No, everything's not fine. He said the stress from a mischievous younger sibling is hindering my recovery."

I heard "pfft" coming from the other side.

"What? What was that all about?" I said.

Katie checked her nails. "I don't get it. That man is into you. I can tell by the way that he watches your face. All you have to do is smile at him and bam," she said, slapping her hands together. "You got him, like a Venus flytrap. How can you look at Dr. Lawrence and not think that guy's fine? Jeez, Jake, dark hair, dark eyes built like a..."

I cut her off. "Is that all you think about? Boys and lip stick?"

She giggled. "No, I think about softball too. Don't you think he's just a little bit attractive? When he was leaning over you checking your head, didn't you just wish those lips would ease on down and find yours?"

I stopped a few spaces away from the gym entrance and laid an arm across the back of the seat, eyeing my sister, determined to get the message across that I had no interest in Dr. Lawrence. "He's a jerk. The only thing I would want to do to those smooth lips is punch them."

Katie let out a howl of laughter. "Oh, my God. You did think about it."

"I did not."

"Yes, you did. Well, you may not have thought about kissing him but you noticed his smooth lips? Must have been staring real hard to notice that, Jake." Katie jumped out of the truck waiting for a car to pass before walking to the bank across the street.

I slammed the truck door. "No, I didn't. I assumed he had smooth lips."

Katie cackled in laughter scampering toward the bank, called over her shoulder, "Sure, you did."

I went inside the gym frustrated by the whole conversation. Bill sat behind his desk eating a sandwich from the City Bakery, with a spare laid out in front of him. I always found humor in the irony of Bill opening a gym located next door to a bakery.

"Hungry?" he asked, offering me the spare sandwich.

I shook my head, and took a seat on the sofa against the wall adorned with pictures taken of Bill and the boxers he trained over the years, including me.

"Where's insurance nightmare?" he asked, wiping his mouth.

"Across the street getting some cash. She must be out of lip gloss."

I filled him in on the doctor's visit.

"Better do what he says."

I gave a salute.

Placing the half-eaten sandwich on the bag next to the whole one, he reached behind his chair swinging a box around, landing on the desk, and sliding it toward me. "Found it yesterday on the floor by the door. Guess they left it without a signature," he said, chewing on the sand-wich.

I opened one end of the box. I was sure it contained a sample of something someone wanted me to endorse which I planned to decline. A glint of humor appeared in my eyes thinking about Diane Strauss, the underwear model. "I hope it's a nice leather thong," I said. This brought a chuckle from Bill.

Turning the box on end, a packet used by photo labs slid out. I opened the envelope and went through the pictures.

Picture after picture contained the same young woman with long blonde hair. At first, I thought it was Katie. It took me a minute to realize the subject of the photos was my mother. Some were of her, alone, one with me standing beside her. I came to the last picture. I stared for a few seconds before recognizing the man sitting on a motorcycle with arms wrapped around my mother. I closed my eyes tight in an effort to stop the sounds echoing from the past. "Come here."

I dropped the pictures on the sofa, shot to my feet, and moved away from the reminders.

"What's wrong, Jake?" Bill asked.

I couldn't say anything, only pointed to the pictures. Bill came around the desk and picked them up.

"It's my mom and Brad," I answered when I found my voice.

Bill examined the photos. "Who sent them?"

"I don't know."

Bill took the box from the sofa. "There's no courier label or return address. Someone must have left it."

I paced the room telling Bill about the message on the machine.

"The one Katie was talking about when you were in the hospital?"

I nodded.

I kept very few secrets from my trainer. Bill had seen

me at worst and pried the truth of heinous moments at the hands of a sociopath. "I dreamed about him and Momma when I was in the hospital, you know when I woke up after the surgery. I think she was trying to tell me something."

Bill thumbed through the pictures.

I stopped moving, resting hands on hips, letting shock turn to anger. "Do you think he got out of prison?"

Bill laid the pictures on his desk. "Jake, you need to calm down. These don't mean it's him. This smells like a stalker."

"Who would want to stalk me, and where would they get the pictures?"

Bill shrugged. "I don't know, Jake. You and your mom moved around a lot. Maybe they got left behind, someone found them, and started digging."

"Do you think Brad got out of prison?" I asked, hoping Bill gave me the answer I wanted.

"I don't know. Maybe, but that don't mean he's stalking you."

I thought for a few minutes. "It's got to be him."

Bill returned to his chair. "So you think a parole board frees him, he gets out, and the first thing he thinks about is leaving a cryptic message on your machine, gathering up some old photos, driving to Hope, and leaving them in the gym just to screw with you. Come on, Jake. "Does he even know where you're living? Nah, it's someone who's after something. Think about it. You won your third title and retired. The timing's just a little too convenient."

Bill went back to assaulting the sandwich. "You're missing the obvious thing. You're a pretty girl, successful. Maybe it's an obsessed fan."

I received strange cards and letters over the years mailed to the post office box set up in Hope. Bill was right. It could be an obsessed fan. The photos could have been floating around. I fingered the end of my long braid.

"I don't know, Bill. Why would someone do this and not send a note?"

I massaged my temples. "There just so much crap going on in here. I was fine until that damn doctor pumped me with drugs."

Bill chuckled. "Dillon saved your life, sweetheart, so get over it."

"Dillon? Who the hell is Dillon?"

"Dr. Lawrence"

"Whatever." I stood and walked a few paces away thinking about the call and the pictures. "All right, I have a stalker, but do you think its possible Brad got out of prison?"

"Jake?"

I looked up meeting the concerned trainer. "Don't go back there. It's a nut job who's got a thing for you. You need to be careful and tell me if anything else happens. Then we go to Harvey."

I nodded, furrowing deep. "I'm just...I don't know, Bill. Everything is off right now. It's like chaos took over turning my life upside down. I feel lost, not sure what to do with myself."

"It's a big adjustment going from a set schedule to retirement. And, yeah, there's a lot been going on with the injury and all. You just gotta breathe Jake and let it go," he said soothingly."Look, kid, if it'll make you feel better, I got some buddies who can find out if Brad got paroled."

"Thanks, at least I'd feel better with proof he's still locked up."

Katie's voice rang out talking to one of the patrons. I quickly gathered the scattered photos stuffing them back into the box handing it off to Bill. He placed it in the metal cabinet behind the desk. The last thing I needed was for Katie to see the pictures and ask questions. There was a lot about my life she wasn't privy to, things I intended to keep that way, things she would never know.

Katie pointed to the sandwiches on the desk. "What's up, old man? Eating for two now?"

He gave her a long look. "Hit anything lately?"

She squinted her eyes and stuck out her tongue.

I took a cleansing breath trying to hide the stress on my face.

"What's wrong," she asked me.

"Nothing. Just tired. I'll talk to you later, Bill."

The rest of the day, I spent alone thinking about the photos, and the phone call wishing I hadn't deleted the message so I could play it again to determine if it was Brad's voice.

Later in the evening, a light pain crept into my side matching the headache built over the day. Tired and wanting solace, I gave, in taking one of the prescription painkillers. My eyes grew heavy, feeling the drug take effect. I fought the clouding fog for a short time before dozing off.

The dream started out wonderfully. I was at the softball park watching Katie delivering a pitch.

"Strike," the umpire shouted.

"All right Katie one more, come on you can do it," I yelled.

My sister prepared to release the ball again. She stopped and turned her head. I craned my neck trying to see what held her attention. The sound of a motorcycle in the distance grew louder. The rider drove the bike to the edge of the field and stopped. He dismounted, walking through the gate, he strode toward my sister.

His face was exactly as I remembered. Lips twisted into a cruel sneer looking directly at me while pointing to my sister. Why would he be interested in Katie? He didn't know her.

He moved closer to the mound. I ran to the fence screaming for Katie to run. She froze. My fingers gripped the wire, shaking the fence, screaming loudly, "Run, Katie. Run, hurry, he's coming."

She turned away. I kept pleading for her to run while shaking the fence. She came about but it wasn't Katie's face. It was Momma. The dream ended with the change.

I sat up in bed running a hand through my hair rolling hips to the side. I reached over and turned on the lamp. A framed picture taken of Katie right before Momma died sat on the nightstand. I held it, scanning the image. I traced her small face, thinking it better to have a stalker than to know Brad was behind the phone call and photos.

6

The feeling of accomplishment when handed a college diploma overwhelms the toughest of people. I was no exception. The journey began with a promise made to an aging woman eight years prior. It ended on an unusually hot day in May waiting in line for the call of my name to receive the hard-earned degree. Only one person was missing to make the day perfect.

The line moved forward. I closed the gap and lowered my chin, remembering a time when I was young sitting at the kitchen table, working on homework while Mom cooked supper. The assignment required using spelling words in a sentence.

"Momma, I can't think of a sentence using hope," I had said.

She replied, "We hope with our minds and believe with our hearts."

I nipped the inside of my lip wondering what she would have thought of a daughter who stopped hoping and believing. I was an acceptor of what is, what had been, and what would never be. Wondering and wanting were foolish inclinations leading to bitter disappointments.

"Jacqueline Marie Conner."

My head snapped upward, caught off guard by the deep booming voice. Across the vast audience, Katie and Bill shouted praises. The packet containing years of hard work passed to my hands. A sense of a portion of my life ending came to mind. School finished, boxing career over, and the next phase of my life to begin. Was I ready to trade boxing gloves for grading tests?

After the ceremony, classmates and college friends hugged each other extending their happiness of the time spent together with goodbyes putting away the years that bound them. For me, there were no exchanges other than courtesy handshakes. The time I spent on campus was limited to classes and then I'd scurry away for training or fly off to a match. No time for friendships.

After the mandatory photography session in graduation ensemble, I removed the garb revealing the light blue cotton dress chosen by Gran for this auspicious occasion. The day she brought the dress home with matching shoes, I protested.

"Jake." She sighed, "I don't ask much from you, and you are the first college graduate in this family…"

Before she finished the guilt trip, I gave in.

Katie curled and teased my long dark hair, arranging the locks in a pile on top with tresses hanging down to my waist. I preferred a pair of nice slacks, dress shirt with a ponytail, but I had to admit, the results were very nice.

I handed the graduation attire to Gran.

Mr. Dickerson, the Dean of Students, approached. "I had my doubts of your managing the demands of boxing and attending classes, but you did it. You should be very proud of yourself," he said.

After a quick handshake and thanks, I joined my family waiting to go home. A quick look over the shoulder brought on a little melancholy moment thinking of the memories spent walking from class to class. With a final exhale, the four of us climbed inside the Cadillac and drove toward Hope.

The desire to rid myself of the shoes and dress made home sound good. At the intersection, instead of taking a left, Gran turned right which led to the gym.

"You're going the wrong way," I said.

"No, I'm not," she smiled with slyness.

I widened eyes upon seeing cars lining the street in front of the gym and across the way overflowing into the bank parking lot. A huge sign hung over the awning read, CONGRATULATIONS TO THE GRADUATING CHAMP

"Oh, my God," I swore under my breath.

I slumped in the seat, eyeing the mass of people gathered on the sidewalk. I didn't enjoy attention drawn to myself, and this was the ultimate humiliation.

When the car came to a stop, Tom Jackson was the first to my door. The six-foot-three two-hundred-fifty pound man forgave an unruly teenager for stealing his truck and crashing it. That was Tom, all heart and smiles. Some of the best days were spent in his garage. He taught me a lot about respect for other people but mostly respecting myself. After Bill and Gran, Tom was the one I looked up to as an example of the person I strived to become.

"Get on out here, girl," he said with much enthusiasm. A hug from huge black man brought a wince. "Sorry Jake forgot your still smartin' from the rib thang," he said.

I stood on tiptoes hugging the wide shoulders. "It's okay. Tell me you're not a part of this?"

He howled a laugh, "Everybody gotta pay for their sins, Jake. This is your'n for stealing my truck."

I patted the big chest and moved on through the gauntlet of congratulators. Inside the gym, tables of food lay in wait with a very large cake from the bakery resting in the center, YOU DID IT KID, lettered on it.

"Bill's doing," I said, through a fake smile.

I looked for a place to escape the attention. The office was a few feet away with only one thing standing between the door and me.

Adell Williams approached in her swaggered high-heeled steps. Not one black and gray hair was out of place. I waited for some disapproving words to spout from the bright red lipstick-covered mouth.

She stood a few inches shorter but enough in height to be face-to-face somewhat. With hands on her slender hips she said, "Well, well, well, the county felon with a college degree."

I waited knowing what to expect. She revealed the keys to her car and gave them a firm shake.

I threw my hands in the air. "Yeah, Miss Adell, what can I say? They taught me how to hot wire cars as part of the curriculum."

She squinted, wondering I suppose, if it were a possibility. Without warning, she coiled her arms around my shoulders drawing me close. She spoke in a low sweet voice making sure no one heard. "You made something of yourself, and you're good to your grandma. I'm proud of you, Jake."

She released me and walked away, leaving me stunned by her words and actions. I wondered if she had taken a hit from the gin bottle kept hidden in her garage to explain the tender moment

Congratulator after congratulator blocked each step toward the office. After a while, I gave up avoidance. I scanned the room searching for my family among the growing crowd. Gran sat with her friends minus Cora Mae who was nowhere in sight. Katie disappeared with Ali the moment the car came to a stop. Bill, who naturally stood near the tables of food, was deep in conversation with Sheriff Jones and Tom. He looked up long enough to gaze on Shirley Dobbs standing across the other side of the table.

The woman was very attractive with her large green

eyes, light brownish blonde hair with touches of age. It tickled me to watch the odd pair pretend each other didn't exist. One observing closely saw the lingering looks shared between them. Bill caught me staring and shot a scowl across the room. I grinned and turned away.

There had to be at least fifty people crowding the gym. I passed from face to face. Then an unexpected figure caught my attention. The man stood at the far end of the room dressed in dark jeans and a black dress shirt with fingers on his chin speaking to a short, red-headed woman. No scrubs or glasses were present. His dark hair was secured behind his head in a ponytail. I gave the tall body a once over. I pondered how I became so lucky to have Dr. Lawrence at my party. Who would invite him? I looked around. Katie shifted her stare between the doctor and me. I narrowed my eyes and clamped my lips together curling a finger for her to come over.

My younger sibling reluctantly crossed the short distance. "I did." She answered before I had the chance to ask.

Outraged, I said, "Why would you do that? He's my doctor not a friend or part of the family."

She scuffed her shoes on the floor. "I told him about the party at the game last week. I thought it might be nice, you know, him being new and not knowing many folks. Besides I think he's really into you."

I scowled. "Stop. Don't push this, Katie, and don't embarrass me. I'm serious." Noting the hurt on her face, I muttered, "Besides, he probably came to make sure I didn't fight anyone over the cake."

"Jake, I've talked to him a lot after the games. He's a nice guy," she said.

I waved her off, clearly showing no desire to continue the conversation.

I kept an eye on the doctor from my peripheral vision.

He engaged in conversation with a young man who was the same height only slightly slimmer. The face was more rounded. Black hair cut just above the collar of his white tee shirt had a messy just-out-of-bed look.

Katie spotted the hunky boy. "Oh, Jake, is that his son?"

"I don't know. Pretty, isn't he?" I admitted.

The pair walked toward us.

"Well, Miss Socializer, here's your chance to find out," I said, nodding in their direction.

Katie whirled around whipping a mirror from her bag, checking her face and hair. She smacked lips together and smoothed her strands. We're so different, I thought, while shaking my head in wonder. I wasn't sure where Ali, came from but she appeared next to Katie giddy and begging for the mirror.

Dr. Lawrence stopped directly in front of me. I felt him looking me over from toe to head before coming to rest on my face.

"You look absolutely, uh, nice, Jake. Oh, congratulations," he said, holding out his hand.

I took the offering. The young man standing beside the doctor cleared his throat.

"Sorry, this is my son, Josh. Josh, this is Jake and Katie Conner and Ali Thompson."

The younger Lawrence was even more handsome up close.

"You're Jake Conner, the boxer," he more stated than asked.

"Guilty."

"Wow, I saw the exhibition on the sports channel last year. You're awesome. You went two rounds with Carter Neal. Popped his nose good," he said.

It was for charity, of course. No serious damage to either Carter or me. I thanked him with a grin wondering what dear old dad thought about the female boxer sparing with a man on live TV.

"Are you enjoying our little town, Josh?" I asked.

"Not sure. I just got here about four hours ago."

He flashed a smile in the direction of Katie and Ali who stood speechless for what had to be the first time in their lives. A nudge from my elbow brought Katie out of the trance.

"Hi, I'm Katie, and this is my best friend, Ali."

Ali chimed in. "Hi Josh."

Katie immediately dove right into conversation about sports. I kept my attention on the teens, pretending the doctor didn't exist. The three went off to introduce Josh to a few teenagers leaving me alone with Dr. Lawrence.

He scanned the crowd avoiding eye contact. "So you've been good?"

I bit my lip, uninterested in anything he had to say. "Yeah, feel great. Following the code and yourself?"

He displayed high cheeks. I could have sworn he was blushing.

"Something wrong?" I asked.

"I'm just a little surprised."

"Surprised I am doing okay?"

A chuckle escaped exposing perfectly aligned teeth. "No, I mean yeah, I am glad you're fine. I just didn't expect…" he trailed off giving a wave up and down.

"Oh, I see. You didn't think I'd clean up this good."

"No, not that. I didn't mean it like that," he stammered looking away. He gathered himself and tried again to explain. "You look more—" he started.

I interrupted. "More feminine, more approachable, less intimidating, which one?" I was enjoying unnerving the man.

He gave a slight nod cutting a glance in my direction with a daring lift to one side. "Yes to the first two."

He lowered his shoulder, leaning in with a smug smile, broadening to a full-blown grin. "And for the third, you've never intimidated me. Congratulations on your graduation." With this, he walked away wearing the same look of satisfaction worn the night he snuck the drugs into my IV.

Dr. Lawrence approached Bill who slapped him on the back with the familiarity of two long lost friends. Both glanced over, with the corners of their mouths turned upwards.

Bill and I needed to have a long talk.

"What an ass," I said.

From behind, Cora Mae announced, "Yep, I like that firm round bootie, and he's good-lookin' to boot."

I spun around. "Cora Mae I…"

"Honey, I told you fixin' up a little would make that man notice and I was right. He noticed." She walked away before I could defend myself.

My face felt hot. I ducked inside the office, exhaling in frustration. I kicked the leg of Bill's desk. "Shoot," I exclaimed and took a seat on top.

"Jake? There you are," a voice called.

Mrs. Morton, the high school guidance counselor and wife of the current principal stood in the doorway. Her short, gray hair edged her face displaying a sweet, demure person. She was always nice to me. When I sat on the other side of her desk during my senior year, she said something I took to heart and never forgot. It doesn't matter where you've been, what counts is where you're at and where you want to go. When word spread of my impending graduation and boxing retirement, she campaigned for my hiring.

I stood and took her hand. "Mrs. Morton, I'm so glad you came."

She gave mine a pat. "John and I are so proud of

you."

She wrapped an arm around my waist guiding me outside the office, halting in front of a short, red-headed woman. The same woman Dr. Lawrence spoke to earlier.

"Jake, this is Teyla Martin, John's new secretary," Mrs. Morton said. "Teyla, this is Jake Conner, the pride of Hope, Arkansas.

"Nice to meet you Teyla," I said.

She looked me over rather oddly. Maybe she had the hots for the doctor and was measuring me up. I would gladly explain my lack of interest in the man. She made me uncomfortable, and it began to show.

"I'm sorry," she apologized. "It just that you look so familiar…I mean, I know I've probably seen you on TV or in a magazine."

I doubted it considering the few interviews ever allowed during my career. I agreed anyway.

Katie made her way over with Josh to join our little group with Ali lagging behind. "Hi Mrs. Morton," Katie said.

"Katie Conner, I swear you get taller every time I see you. Are you ready for school to start?" Mrs. Morton asked.

"No, ma'am we just got out."

The short redhead looked funny sandwiched between my sister and me.

"You're sisters?" Teyla asked.

Grinning, Katie said, "Yeah, but I am the better looking one."

Katie introduced Josh to everyone. The conversation focused on the newcomer. I took the opportunity to excuse myself moving over to Gran and Cora Mae.

I was halfway across the floor when Bill announced, "Folks, can I have your attention for a minute?"

The room grew silent. He took my arm, positioning

my body between him and Gran.

"Years ago, a tall teenage girl walked through that door," he said, pointing toward the entrance. "I can still see her dragging her feet, wearing headphones, a smart mouth with a huge chip on her shoulder."

I ducked my head, avoiding the guests' faces.

"I saw a kid in trouble that needed some guidance or a good butt whipping," he continued.

A brief hum of amusement went throughout the group.

"By the end of the first week I wanted to strangle the little witch."

I lowered my lashes feeling the blush rising on my face.

"But she learned to take the negative and change it into something positive. Her grandmother and I are very proud of the woman she's become."

I felt his rough fingers under my chin bringing my head upward to look into his eyes.

"Anyway, I just want to say congratulations, Jake." He drew me into his embrace hugging me tight. I was stunned. Bill's not the type to publicly show emotions. The roomed engulfed with applause.

It took a moment for me to collect myself. I smiled at Bill, saying loudly enough for everyone to hear, "I don't believe little *witch* were the exact words you used."

Laughter burst through out the room.

I faced my guests feeling emotional. "I'm very fortunate to have a great family, including this guy right here. I just want to thank everyone for their support and putting up with me all these years. It means a lot."

Clapping erupted throughout the gym.

I got out of the way of Cora Mae and Gran cutting and serving cake. I spied the group standing in the back of the crowd close to the entrance. Josh, Katie, and Ali stood on one side of Dr. Lawrence with Teyla Martin on the other side. He bent over the short woman saying something to her.

I was fixated on the Martin woman's face. Her manner was pleasant enough, but it was something about the way she seemed to study me that was disturbing. Dr. Lawrence spoke to his son then lifted his hand waving goodbye. Not to be rude, I waved back watching the pair walk out the door.

The party ended around ten. During the ride home, Katie gave me the details on Josh. He was seventeen, a football star at his last school, and Ali is in love with him. Curiosity got the better of me. I asked about his mother. Katie replied Josh did not mention his mother.

I thought, *She probably got tired of the ego maniac surgeon and left him.*

We arrived home with each saying goodnight going our separate ways. I reached my room pulling the dress and shoes from my weary body replacing them with the comfort of a tank top and shorts. Standing by the window, the moon gave vision on the nearby field. Many nights, I stood in the very spot, looking out, reminiscing or psyching myself up for a fight.

Something moved in the shadows. With the recent events, I felt a little unsettled. Sluggo walked out, beneath the overhead night-light, grazing on the fresh hay Katie put out earlier. I breathed a little easier.

It was after midnight, and I couldn't sleep. I watched the beautiful animal wondering all the while if it were possible for me to manage the saddle for a late night ride. Not brothering to change, I slipped on my boots and made my way down stairs grabbing a couple of apples from the counter before heading toward the barn.

The high, pole mounted light gave the yard visibility. Sluggo saw me and moved in the direction of the barn. I opened the barn door leading to the pasture and went back inside, climbing on one of the stalls, whistling to bring the horse inside. I rewarded the mare with one of the apples. Doctor Lawrence warned about lifting. I elected to run the bridle, just throwing a blanket on the horses back instead of the fumbling with the saddle.

Stepping from the stall, I straddled the horse and left the barn riding through the nearby fields and sparse forest. I rode for an hour thinking about my life. For twelve years, I was Jake Conner, boxer. I was starting over as Jake Conner, the schoolteacher. It sounded boring, but then again, it was better than nothing. Changes were coming. I hoped I accepted them better than the last time my life changed so drastically.

7

$\mathcal{A}$ certain degree of difficulty accompanied adjusting to a life with so much time on my hands. In the past, I knew what to expect. Train, fight, and attend school. Days lagged on a quest for something to occupy my time.

The Parker home maintained the most well manicured lawn in the county. Mowing the oversized yard, hanging out at the gym, and Jackson's garage, plus the softball games kept me from going completely out of my mind. Fortunately, the knife-wielding doctor never showed at the games I attended.

I was watering one of Gran's many flowerbeds bordering the house when an older model green Honda Accord pulled into the driveway. Josh Lawrence emerged from the driver's seat wearing blue jeans and a rather snug tee-shirt showing off his muscles. He was indeed handsome and understandable why Katie and Ali flocked to him. I tossed a wave.

"Hey, Miss Conner," he greeted, walking toward me.

"Call me Jake."

He trailed behind, taking in the rehydrating of hydrangeas.

"Katie tells me your teaching history this fall," he said.

I nodded, moving on to the sweet peas climbing the nearby fence. "You going to be in one of my classes?"

"I hope so."

We went around back to the roses blooming close to the portable carport covering my Camaro.

"Whoa, is that a sixty-eight?" he asked, his eyes wide with wonder.

"Sixty-nine," I corrected. I turned off the hose and invited him for a closer look at my baby.

He opened the driver's door scanning the interior with the enthusiasm of a kid mesmerized by a shiny new toy. "Sweet," he murmured smoothing the leather seats. It was obvious he wanted to sit behind the steering wheel.

"Go ahead, get in. I don't mind," I said.

The excited teen climbed in, whistling. "Man, this is one slick set up." He almost drooled running his hand over the dashboard and grasping the chrome shifter. "Did you find it like this or restore it yourself?"

"Bill and I come across her about five years ago rusting in an old barn outside of Philly. She was in pretty bad shape. Tom Jackson did most of the work, but I turned a wrench or two," I boasted.

"Don't breathe on it too hard, Josh. She'll have a coronary." Katie strolled across the yard, gulping a bottle of water, coming to rest her rear against the front fender.

Josh righted. "Man, this car is too cool. Thanks for letting me sit in her, Jake."

I nodded watching the pair walk away. Katie smiled irreverently. "You're lucky she let you sit in it. I swear she has some serious issues when it comes to that car."

"If it was my sweet ride, I'd have issues, too," Josh said.

The pair disappeared around the corner. I returned to watering the plants. Josh seemed to be a quiet but very polite young man which made me wonder how he and my sister became such fast friends. Shaking off the thought, I went about my business.

Later I cornered the house stepping onto the porch. Katie sat in the swing reading a magazine.

"Josh gone?" I asked.

She chewed on a piece of gum and popped it several times. "Yep. His dad called. You remember Josh's dad, right? You know the one with the smooth kisser."

I tossed a narrowed glare and went on into the house.

Before bed that night, I went into Katie's room to catch up since we hadn't spent much time together over the previous week. She was stretched across the mattress flipping through a magazine.

"What's new in the world of mascara?"

"Not much." She rolled to her back. "Think Gran'll let me ride to Hope with Josh sometime?"

When cows fly, I thought, then said, "Don't know. You and Josh spend a lot of time together."

"Yeah he's a good guy. We have a lot in common."

I raised a brow. "Like what?"

"We love sports, we like the same music, and we both have no memories of our mother."

I hated the sadness in her voice. I stretched out on the bed beside her. "What happened to Josh's mom?"

"She died when she was trying to have him."

"That's sad," I said.

Katie tossed the magazine to the side and rolled to her side. "What was she like? Mom?"

I chewed on my lip, preferring the subject about our mother went away. "You know. I've told you a million times."

Katie shook her head, "No, not a million times. You don't talk about her. Why?"

I rubbed my forehead and sat up. "I'm kind of tired. I'll see you in the morning."

I left the bed and made it to the door before Katie said, "Did she love me?"

The question spun me around. "She loved us more than life itself."

"Then tell me, Jake. What were her dreams? What

was her favorite color?"

I turned my back to her. "Come on Katie, I'm tired."

"Run along, Jake, keep your precious memories to yourself," she snapped.

Katie was right. It was selfish not to share the memory of the woman who gave birth to us, but it hurt too much to talk about it or worry one answer might lead to other questions. "Pink, that was her favorite color."

I made my way down the short distance of the hall to my room recalling the theory surmised after the party about the doctor's wife leaving him. I felt bad for thinking such a thing after learning Josh's mother passed away during childbirth. I was fortunate to have had my mother for fifteen years.

The following afternoon, I ventured into Washington, or Old Washington, as the locals referred to the small town populated by less than two hundred people. The place had seen decades of a changing world. Anyone paying attention saw the history seeping from the building and spilling onto the streets. But then again, it took me a while to appreciate what existed in my own backyard.

It resided on a patch of highway unnoticed by most folks traveling through. Registered as a state park, Washington reflected an early settlement with a major passage between Missouri and Texas for travelers before and after the civil war. The little town boasted extensive history of early frontier characters. Cora Mae once provided that Davy Crockett and many other western folk heroes passed through the town at some point.

A person could sit on the old courthouse steps seeing flip-flops and cell phones on one corner while on the other, men and women dressed in eighteen-hundred's style clothes, and led tours. Whenever I needed a place to relax, I found myself lazing about the grounds, forgetting troubles and worries.

I pulled my baby into the lot across from Williams Tavern, one of the preserved buildings converted into a restaurant maintaining the ambiance of the time. A cool glass of iced tea and a seat on the front porch was a favorite way of killing time. I reached out for the door. It swung open revealing Cora Mae Jackson in her long skirted period dress on the other side.

"Well, honey, you're too late for lunch," she said.

Hands placed in my jeans pockets, I scooted a booted foot across the porch. "Not really hungry. Thought I'd wander away from the farm. Getting cabin fever."

Cora Mae took a seat on the bench beside the door. I joined her.

"Hard, ain't it?" she said.

I raised a brow. "Jailed on the farm? Yep."

Cora Mae took a snuff can from her pocket, tucking a small amount of the powdery tobacco in her bottom lip. "Nope, I'm talkin' about tryin' to figure out what to do next?"

I kicked legs out and crossed my arms. "Oh, I know what I'm going do next. Just not sure I want to."

Cora Mae worked the tobacco in her mouth. "Then why do it?"

I shrugged. "I love history, and it's a living."

"I reckon it is," Cora Mae said. "Purty day, ain't it?"

I nodded, rising from the bench, gazing at the back of the blacksmith shop a block away. "You think when people first settled here, they knew this is where they wanted to be?"

"I suppose or they got tired of ridin' and figured this was good a place as any," Cora Mae replied.

I gripped the porch rail watching a group of kids following a guide down the street. "It's so peaceful here. I don't know how anyone could leave it."

The porch planks creaked when Cora Mae rose, walking over to the side of the porch to spit off the edge. "You thinkin' about leavin'?"

I shook my head. "No. I'm just trying to figure out why Momma ever left."

"She was like most young'uns thinkin' there's more out there than this place," Cora Mae said.

"Was Momma happy here? I mean when she lived here, you know, as a little girl, was she happy?"

"I'd knowed Bridgette since the day she was born. She was always happy. Come on let's walk my old bones gettin' stiff," Cora Mae said, limping to the edge of the porch.

We stepped off the porch, strolling along the wooden sidewalk, passing through the gate of the picket fence lining the frontage of the building.

"Bud's going to leave, if you're not here when he pulls up," I jested.

She stopped moving and wore hands on her hips. "That man knows he better wait. Last year, he run off and left me at the Jonquil Festival. I had'a ride home with Adell. I hid that old goat's fishin' poles for a week. He'll wait."

We moved along the shady sidewalks. "Why you askin' about your Momma?" Cora Mae asked.

I stopped in front of one of the old buildings and watched tourists listening to the guide describing frontier life. I ran a finger over the wooden fence. "Everything's changing, you know. Finishing college and retiring. She's been on my mind lately."

The elderly woman laid her hand on top of mine, patting gently. "You're gonna be jus' fine, Jake."

I met the elderly eyes. "I can't stop wondering what she was like when she lived here or what she'd think of me…how I turned out."

Cora Mae smiled. "Bridgette was the sweetest little

thing, always smilin', kind of a cut up like Katie, but I see her in you. Your Momma would be proud of you."

I moved ahead of my grandmother's oldest friend, disagreeing. "I look nothing like Momma or act like her."

"That's where you're wrong, you have her heart," she said.

I did not take the comment seriously.

I could tell Cora Mae ceased moving when the sound of her shuffling feet grew silent. I turned to investigate. Cora Mae leaned her weight against one of the old lampposts.

"The one thing I can say about your momma. When she loved, she loved with all her heart, just like you. Yes ma'am I see how you are with Katie and Chelsea. Both ya'll just alike, you and Bridgette, move heaven and earth for the people ya'll love."

With a hearty chuckle, she continued. "Lordy, I remember one time, I speck Bridgette was about seven, in the middle of January. Herman and Chelsea stopped by t' visit. Bridgette wondered off and found a puppy in the pond behind the house."

A smile spread across the aging face. "She jumped in pulled that critter out, both of 'em soakin' wet and freezin'. I thought Chelsea was gonna skin her alive. Bridgette said, Momma, dogs are God's creatures, too, and they need love just like us. She kept that dog until it died of old age, I reckon."

Cora Mae was right about my mother's love. She tried to move heaven and earth until the day she died. Before I could ask her to tell me more, a honking horn interrupted. Cora Mae's husband, Bud, yelled out the window of his old truck. "Come on, Cora Mae. Tom's awaitin' me."

The older woman shouted back. "Shut up, old man, 'for I break that dang fishing pole."

Taking my hand, she gave it a squeeze. "Come on by the house sometime. We'll talk more."

I promised, then watched the bickering pair drive away. On the way home, thoughts of my mother plagued me. I decided to stop by the cemetery and parked at the entrance. Walking slowly, I inhaled deeply of the freshly cut grass. I came to the family plots reading the name HERMAN PARKER, a grandfather I never met. From the stories Gran and others told, he was a kind man. Next to him laid my mother.

I stared at the headstone bearing her name. She was patient, and had an uncanny ability for memorizing poetry. She made birthdays special and managed to turn the multiple times we moved into an adventure. I bent down touching the small basket of silk flowers adorning the head stone. Gran always kept new arrangements on both graves. I glanced to my grandfather's resting place seeing no new flowers in sight. Turning back to Mom's, I caught sight of an envelope pushed down inside the bouquet of daisies. I pulled out the homemade post card of a gray house.

Flipping the paper over, I found the words HOME SWEET HOME typed in large letters. What was the meaning? I examined the picture closer. It was at the bottom left hand corner where my eyes grew wider seeing the end of the walkway with the letters BC, drawn heart, JC, drawn heart, then a broken corner where I knew the initials KC were suppose to be.

My hands shook remembering the day the landlord poured the concrete allowing Mom to write our initials. "Now, our names are here and this is home," she had said. Although the color changed, there was no doubt the house was the same as the one occupied in St. Louis. It was the last house we lived in together.

I sat down next to Mom's grave holding the card

remembering that period of my life. They were some of the best times, yet one of the worst. Katie's toddler words begged for Mom the day Gran came to pick us up. No one was able to console her, not even me.

I scanned the cemetery trying to understand why someone wanted me to remember. Was it about remembering or something else? Who ever had done this probably didn't understand the implication or my lack of appreciation for such gifts.

I placed the card in my pocket and grabbed the arrangement tossing it over the fence. If Gran found the card, it meant explaining why I've kept the possibility of a stalker from her. If Katie found it…it meant confessing more than an obsessed fan. One question leads to another which eventually brings the truth. Our mother loved us, we had a happy life, and she died too young. That was the only truth Katie needed to know.

I left the cemetery and sped toward the gym.

Several patrons worked out in the weight area with one red head walking the treadmill. Teyla Martin raised a hand. I gave a slight raise of the fingers acknowledging her.

Bill lounged behind his desk reading a magazine. I didn't greet him but flung myself onto the sofa.

Bill closed the magazine. "What's wrong?"

I leaned over, tossing the card on the desk. "That was in a flower arrangement on Mom's grave."

I picked at a small hole in my jeans. "It's the house in Missouri."

Bill flipped the card over. "We need to call Harvey."

I got off the sofa and walked to the door, crossing my arms, concentrating on the patrons. "And tell him what?"

"Jake, who ever left this is getting too close," Bill said.

I rested against the jam. "Did your guy find out about

Brad?"

Bill reached for the phone. "Not yet, but I'll give him a call."

The call was short and cryptic. "He's working on it and he'll call me when he knows something.

I remembered agreeing to pick up Katie from Ali's house at five. "I want to keep this quiet until we eliminate Brad. I gotta pick up Katie. Call me if you hear anything."

I walked out of the office with Teyla Martin waving again. I ignored her and left. Stalker, fan or someone just plain mean, it didn't matter. I wasn't going back there. I couldn't go back to that place. I worked too hard to leave.

8

Late June marked the beginning of a hot Arkansas summer. On the day of my final doctor appointment, I woke early to get in a jog. I turned onto the old logging road traveled many times over the years. The overgrown path was a familiar place, a refuge used in the past to psych myself up for the next fight. There was still plenty to think about, just not the things that I wanted to ponder.

The future translated into a seat behind a desk, noisy teenagers, and a clock ticking away minutes of my life. Added to the sentiments, someone wanted to take me on a trip down memory lane.

I didn't understand it. What had I done to make someone act out in such a cruel way? What did they hope to gain from it? Flying under the radar to stay out of the limelight was my reasoning for keeping intruders and crazies away. I received fan mail which I answered impersonally. Maybe that was the cause of this whole fiasco. Limited information created curiosity.

The further I ran, the more animosity toward my new career and a psycho fan bubbled to the surface. I slowed my troubled legs. The old walnut tree stood majestically near the edge of the ravine. I walked around the thick trunk seeking the serenity to quell building anxiety. A few cursing words escaped me, and echoed through the forest. I perched a foot on one of the large tree roots kneeing several inches out of the ground.

It was quiet except for the occasional birds chirping overhead. A look down the trodden path reminded me of where I had been. When I first started training, I ran the path cursing God for my troubles. After years and miles running through the forest, I thanked him for letting me find a place of peace.

I smiled thinking of Katie. At five years old, she rose early, sometimes demanding to go on the morning runs. Her small legs were no match for my long strides. I chose to walk with her. We took our rest under the old walnut tree.

"When I grow up, will you still be fightin'?" Katie asked one day.

I recalled my answer. "When you grow up, I'll be too old to fight."

"Good," she said. "Then we can run just because we want to."

Somehow it never registered that when Katie grew up I would still be young. I shuffled last year's fallen leaves with my foot. "Just because I want to, but what the heck do I want?"

I left the tree behind, running the remainder of the path, putting behind doubts about my future and the glory days that would be no more.

An hour later, I ran the length of the driveway in time to see the gray Cadillac pulling from the garage. Katie's and Gran's planned shopping trip gave a sense of relief knowing my sister would not be anywhere about begging to go with me to the doctor appointment.

Gran rolled down the window and called out, "We should be back around two. Are you sure you don't want to go? We can wait."

Oh, I was sure. If the two made it back in the time frame planned, it would be a first. My grandmother and sister can shop, and do so for many hours.

"No, thanks Gran, I'm just going to the doctor and then the gym."

After a quick shower, I grabbed the keys to the Camaro from the buffet. The house phone rang. The doctor's office called informing of an emergency and needing to reschedule the appointment for the next day. I agreed to the appointed time.

For the past couple of weeks, I felt great. With the change in the appointment, I choose to declare myself healed and avoid seeing Dr. Lawrence altogether. When Gran inquired about the appointment later in the evening, I simply replied, "Everything's fine."

The next morning, I remembered the changed appointment. Although I felt a little guilty, it wasn't enough for me to give in. I decided to stick to the plan and miss the scheduled visit.

I drove Katie to Ali's house before venturing on to the gym for a much-needed work out. Even though boxing was over, maintaining my skills was important to me and gave the pretense that I still played in the game.

After dropping Katie off, I went to the gym, parking across the street in the bank's lot. Bill was in the back of the gym lounged in the entrance of the area housing the boxing ring. I walked up behind him stretching my neck to see what held his attention. A little girl ran circles inside the ring.

"New protégé," I mused.

I startled Bill.

"Could be," he smiled, adding, "Holly's kid," pointing to the woman in her mid-twenties, climbing endlessly on the Stairmaster behind us.

"Mind taping my hands after I change?" I asked.

Bill was skeptic. "Doc give the okay?"

"I am healed and released into the wild," I said, walking away toward the dressing rooms.

Once spandex replaced jeans and tee shirt, I entered the office laying my car keys on Bill's desk. "Speaking of the doctor," I said, "you two seem to be getting real chummy."

Bill dug through the contents in a drawer. "Cut him some slack. He's a good guy. Comes by every evening to work out."

Good information, I thought. Avoid the gym in the afternoons.

I splayed fingers watching Bill work the tape. A deep, frowning line creased his forehead.

"What's wrong?" I asked.

Bill smoothed the tape staring at me. "My guy called. He's out. Been out for six months."

My heart sank. A part of me desperately wanted to believe it was my own paranoia causing the worry. I rubbed my temple trying to conceal the amount of stress injected by the announcement. "How could they let him out? He's supposed to serve twenty five years."

"He's served a lot of it, and it was probably time for him to come up for parole. If no one showed up to protest his release, that's how he got out," Bill said.

A mixture of rage and fear pounded my chest. "Tell me it's not him?"

"He's been out six months. Why would he wait so long to start messing with you? Don't do this, Jake. Don't go there. You worked too hard to get your head out of that bad place. You're letting whoever sent the pictures and the flowers accomplish exactly what they wanted. They got you rattled," Bill said.

I nodded. "Why is this happening? Why now?"

Bill caressed my cheek. "I still say it's all a little convenient with the timing, but you got to remember the past can't hurt you, kid. Let it go. Whoever's behind this will show their face and when they do, trust me, they'll pay for it. I'll make sure of it."

Bill finished taping my hands with silence between

us. I wanted to hit something hard to clear my head. I needed to work out frustrations on the bag. I swung at air, jogging a few steps.

Bill walked to the office door gazing out at the patrons and shouted, "Hey, Doc, you're here early."

"Oh, crap," I muttered, ducking below the window. My appointment had been two hours ago. I had to concoct a plan to sneak out avoiding a confrontation and the possibility of Dr. Lawrence busting me in front of Bill.

"Jake, what are you doing?" Bill asked.

I jumped up. "Umm. Tying my shoe."

"Hmm for a minute I thought maybe you might be hiding like you missed your appointment."

My mouth fell ajar. "How did you know?"

"He called looking for you just before you got here. Sounded concerned you missed your last appointment."

Irritated by the thought of the two becoming friends and discussing my health, I grabbed the keys from the desk hissing, "I guess you told him I was on my way here?"

Bill grinned. "Somebody's got to save you from yourself."

"See ya later, buddy," I slung. I rushed past Bill toward the front door avoiding eye contact with the doctor. I caught sight of him standing by the free weights. He was dressed in his scrubs with arms folded, watching my escape while shaking his head.

Bill called with laughter in his voice, "Jake, where you going? I thought you were going to work out."

Without looking back, I replied. "Later, Bill."

My trusted friend's robust laugh echoed throughout the gym.

Five feet from the door, I ran into kryptonite. Carter Neal's six-foot firm body filled the doorway. My eyes closed in despair having forgotten he was coming to town.

His arms opened wide, drawing me inside. "Good to see you, honey."

Carter was a handsome man with his light brown hair and smoky eyes. He would be a catch for some young girl if she didn't mind his self-centered in-love-with-me personality.

"Hey, Carter, when did you get into town?" I asked with false bravado and pulled away.

I glanced over my shoulder trying to locate Dr. Lawrence. He stood next to Bill who laughed and nodded in my direction.

"Just now. You look great. Are you fully recovered?"

"Yeah, how long are you in town?" I shifted about, monitoring the conspirators standing a few feet away.

Carter squeezed my hand, moving us further into the work out area. "Just for the day. God, it's good to see you, Jake."

I pretended to listen to his nonstop chatter. Annoyance set in after ten minutes of listening to endless feats of the commercials and endorsement deals. I edged my way toward the entrance. "I hate to just run out like this, but I really got to go. Bill's inside waiting on you."

Carter caressed my arm. "I really miss you. I want to catch up. Have dinner with me?"

"I..."

An arm went around my waist.

"Sorry, honey, I'm ready now."

My eyes widened.

Dr. Lawrence extended his hand to Carter introducing himself. "Dr. Dillon Lawrence."

"Carter Neal," came the confused reply. "You two?" Carter asked pointing back and forth between the Doctor and me.

The doctor tightened his hold. "We've been seeing each other, oh, what would you say, sugar lips, a couple of months?"

I moved my head away from Dr. Lawrence fighting the urge to let a string of profanity fly. Choosing between the two, the doctor seemed the lesser of the evils. I kept my mouth shut but, jabbed the surgeon in the side loosening his hold on me.

Dr. Lawrence sighed moving behind me and wrapping both arms around my waist laying a cheek against my hair. "Isn't she just the sweetest thing?"

A broken-hearted sag crossed Carter's face. "I'm happy for you, Jake."

Dr. Lawrence guided me to the entrance spouting, "We've got to go, hon. I have patients waiting. Nice to meet you, Carter." With an arm still clinging to my waist, Dr. Lawrence led me across the street to my car.

"All right, back off!" I squirmed out of his hold.

He took the keys from my hand, unlocked the driver's side door, and got in under the steering wheel. I gave an exasperated huff searching for words. What did he think he was doing? It was my car.

He cranked the engine. "Get in, precious. He's still watching."

I climbed inside, protesting. "You're not driving my car."

We moved in reverse. "Buckle up." He chuckled while speeding across the lot, turning onto the street.

The car came to a stop at the traffic light, allowing an opportune chance of switching drivers. "You've had your fun. Now pull over," I demanded.

He turned right onto Third, then left onto Main.

"Where are you going?" I shouted.

Never losing the-cat-ate-the-canary smirk he answered, "To your appointment."

I fell back against the seat, folding my arms over my chest releasing an angry growl. The trip ended in front of his office. We climbed out at the same time. I rounded the car, extending my hand.

"Keys?"

He walked to the office door.

"I need my keys," I yelled.

"When I have my x-ray," he returned.

I grumbled, refusing to move an inch watching him enter the building. I stood there, tapping my foot on the pavement. The office door closed. He wasn't joking. I ran across the lot trying to catch up with him.

Once inside, I followed behind the doctor repeatedly asking for my keys with the doctor replying each time, "When I have my x-ray."

He disappeared inside his office.

Shelley took over. "Okay, Jake, let's get a picture."

Defeated, I trailed behind her.

Shelley went about setting up the equipment. "Where did he find you?"

"Gym," I growled.

"We had a bet," she said.

I drew my brows together. "What bet?"

"Whether or not you would show for your appointment." Shelley led me in front of the x-ray machine lining my back against the wall.

Curiosity got the better of me. "Doc in on the bet?"

"Yep, he told us point blank he'd win. Take a deep breath and hold it." Shelley walked into a cove then reappeared.

"The man's a little over-confident, don't you think?" I said.

"You're here aren't you?" she chided.

When finished, I blocked her exit. "What's his game? Is he this involved with all of his patients?"

She backed away with her mouth slightly open, stifling a laugh. "Nope, but then he's never had a patient who worked so hard fighting medical care. I believe his exact words were she is the most stubborn person I ever met."

I muttered under my breath how much the egomaniac irritated me while walking down the hall to the doctor's private office. Dr. Lawrence was preoccupied with a folder lying on his desk. He didn't look up or acknowledge my presence.

"Reading up on your next fugitive?"

He laid his glasses on the desk. "No, this patient actually wants my help." He tossed the keys to my car, adding "By the way, it drives good."

A light knock on the open door brought Shelley with the x-rays. After doing the flip and search on each picture, Dr. Lawrence rounded the desk with stethoscope in hand. "Okay, let's make sure you're still breathing." He took position behind me slipping the cold object under my shirt. "Take a deep breath."

A chill went down my spine feeling his breath on my neck. He stood close. Too close. Don't you think he's the least bit attractive? Katie's voice sounded in my head.

I leaned away placing distance between our bodies.

"Any discomfort or trouble breathing?" he asked, moving the stethoscope around to my chest.

The tips of his fingers brushed my skin. A wave of butterflies fluttered inside. I lowered my lashes hiding the uncomfortable state. "Everything's fine."

"Standard answer, huh? Everything's fine." He took a step back. "Lift your shirt."

I snapped my head upward. "What?"

He towered over me, flashing white teeth. "I need to check the incision."

Judging by the sweat breaking my brow, my face had to be completely red. I raised the right side of the shirt. He squatted down eye level and traced the fine line across my rib cage with the smooth pads of his fingers.

He pressed against my side. "Any discomfort?"

I swallowed the nervousness in my voice. "No."

He rose and laid a hand on my cheek. I allowed my eyes to lift, meeting his. The man held me hypnotized for some reason. He moved my jaw to the side.

"The scar right here," he said retaining eye contact and brushing the line of my brow. "It'll fade over time."

Staring into those dark eyes and hearing the soft voice, I found myself wondering what it would be like to kiss him. I pulled my face from his grasp, berating a lapse in control. I knew better than to allow such thoughts. They led to no good place.

He walked away and took a seat behind his desk. "Everything feels in place and sounds fine. X-ray looks good."

I was a complete idiot allowing myself to feel foolish notions for a split second. I started to leave and stopped at the door. "Do you need a ride back to the gym?"

"I'll have Josh pick me up or catch a ride with Shelley," he said.

I hesitated for a second then said, "Thanks for every-thing."

"You're welcome, and I'll see you Saturday."

I peered over my shoulder. "Saturday?"

He gave a nod. "When you come over for dinner."

I did an about face, fully perplexed. He sat back in his chair, folded hands in his lap, wearing the grin of confidence I had seen so many times. "Come on. After waiting all morning for my patient to show up only to discover she blew me off, having to chase her down, and let's not forget I saved you from an old boyfriend, I think the least you could do is come to my house for dinner."

The smug jerk.

"Carter was never my boyfriend," I said.

He kept the irritating grin on his face. "Not what I heard."

I narrowed eyes. "Then you heard wrong."

"Okay, maybe I got it wrong. He was your boyfriend or wanted to be your boyfriend or something. You can explain it to me over dinner."

I gritted my teeth. "There's nothing to explain. I don't owe you an explanation, and I'm not coming to your house for dinner."

"Fine, I'll pick you up at seven at your grandmother's place. We can go to a restaurant in town," he said.

Right, come to Gran's so I can't be rude or refuse to entertain his company. I would never hear the end of it.

"Look, Dr. Lawrence, I know you're probably a nice guy, but let's face it. We both know I'm not Debbie Dater," I said, hanging my quoting fingers in the air.

He chuckled. "Debbie Dater, I've got to remember that one. So Saturday, which one, my house or a restaurant?"

I stretched my arms wide. "What have I said or done to make you think I want to have dinner with you?"

He clasped his hands above his head. "Oh, I know you don't want to have dinner with me. You think I'm an egotistical ass with a God like complex. I want to prove you wrong."

I closed my eyes reeling upon hearing my own words fall from his mouth. Oh, how my sister would pay for this. "I'm not going on a date with you in town, at Gran's, or at your house. I'm sure there are plenty of giggling girls who want to go out with you. Find one, because I'm not it." I took a step toward the door.

"Oh," he said loudly, "I am sure there are women who would say yes, but somehow I don't think they'll be as fascinating as you."

Teeth ground against each other. I came around to

face him with nostrils flaring near rage. "I'm a challenge? Is that what you think?"

He exhaled lowering his arms. "No, I don't think that way. From what I hear, you graduated with a 4.0, maintained a full-time boxing career while taking care of your grandmother and sister."

He rose from the chair and tapped a pencil on the desk. "And I think under all the, I need no help from anyone, winning charm of yours, is a smart, loyal, caring, person."

I wondered between Bill and Katie how much they told Dr. Lawrence. I narrowed eyes and gave my best tough boxer glare. "I am what you see. So there's no mystery."

"I think you're good at hiding behind those gloves. Why is that," he asked.

"I don't want to have dinner with you," I said flatly and turned to leave.

A loud booming laugh rang out behind me. "Now who intimidates who?"

The last words from his mouth worked the devilish side of my mind. Oh, to put him in his place would be so much fun. I came about faking a smile. "Dinner at your house Saturday? What time?"

He smiled. "Six-thirty okay with you?"

I nodded with a glint of mischief in my eye. "Sure."

I walked out the door, plotting against the surgeon. After a dinner with me, he'll wish he'd left the rib in my lung.

When I arrived home, I charged through each room of the house, bellowing for my sister. Gran poked her head out of the dining room. "What's all the yelling about?"

"Where is she? Where *is* that meddling little schemer?"

"Upstairs on the phone with Ali."

I climbed the first two steps of the staircase. "Katie!"

Gran scurried after me. "What did she do, Jake?"

"She's been running her mouth to that ass of a doctor. Katie? Get your butt down here."

Katie appeared at the top of the stair. "What the heck are you yelling about?"

I breathed hard and gripped the rail. "What did you tell him?"

She tried to play innocent. "Tell who?"

I took another step. "You know who. What did you tell Dr. Lawrence?"

Her eyes grew large, and she took a step back. I charged up the staircase, chasing her down the hall. She ran to her room, squealing. The door slammed right before I got to it.

I slammed a shoulder against it."What did you tell him?"

Gran slid in front of me. "Don't break down the door, Jake. Katie, open up."

"Not until Jake goes downstairs."

I paced the hall with my hands on my hips. "I'm not going anywhere. What did you tell him?"

"He asked me if you were dating anyone. I told him no and he was wasting his time cause you don't like him," she shouted from the other side.

I stopped in front of her door leaning a hand on the wall. "I think you said a little bit more than that. He knew word for word what I said about him being an egomaniac ass. How do you suppose he knew that?"

My grandmother sighed. "Why did you say that in front of her? You know she doesn't have a filter between her brain and her mouth. She needs to learn to stop running her mouth. I swear, Katie, you say one more thing to him, I will wring your neck. You hear me?"

Before she could reply, I stomped off to my room,

slamming the door.

I wore a hole in the carpet pacing the room, more mad at myself than my sister. I couldn't believe it. I agreed to have dinner with Dr. Lawrence. What was I thinking? Wiping the smugness off his face, that is exactly what I thought. I flopped down onto the bed stretching an arm across my forehead. I was so stupid for letting myself fall into his trap.

I didn't want to go out with him or any man for that matter. From what I had seen in my life, they were all alike except for Bill. Behind the facades and honey-filled words, they all had hidden agendas.

Rolling to my side, I rested my head on an arm. What was happening to my life? Retiring was supposed to make things simpler. It had gotten harder. Every since the last fight, I was an emotional train wreck struggling to keep memories at bay and goaded into a date. I rubbed my forehead trying to figure out how to get control of the chaos.

Pushing off the mattress, I walked to the dresser and picked up the photo of Katie sitting in my lap. My sister was only nine months old when Mom took the picture. I ran a figure over her smiling face.

"You're lucky, Jake. You have Katie. Always remember that," my mother once said.

I never forget how much I loved Katie nor stayed mad for very long. Her outlandish behavior dug spurs in my rear but never enough for me to regret having her in my life.

Later in the evening while sitting at the table at supper, Katie appeared in the doorway sticking her head inside. "Can I eat or are you still mad?"

I waved her to sit down. "You know I can't stay mad at you and besides payback's are a..." I stopped upon glancing at Gran who sat at the end of the table. "When you least expect it, dear sister, expect it," I said.

She sat down on the other side of the table, spooning potatoes onto her plate keeping her attention trained on me. "So how did you know I said anything to him?"

"Because he asked me out this afternoon."

Gran's and Katie's eyes lit up speaking in unison. "And?"

I shifted eyes between the two. "And what?"

Katie slumped in the chair. "Did you say yes?"

I couldn't tell them the whole story. If I did, Gran would know I lied to her about the final appointment. I rose from the table and took my plate to the sink. "He was insistent. I agreed to have dinner at his house Saturday. But I have a feeling it's not going to be a pleasant meal."

Katie stabbed a fork into the green beans on her plate. "You gonna be mean to him, aren't you?"

I didn't answer but gave a broad grin, leaving my family to finish supper alone.

9

"Jake, you riding with us," Gran called from the other side of the bedroom door.

I slipped boots on answering, "No, go ahead, I've got to go by the gym. I'll meet ya'll at the ball park."

Friday night, softball game. Saturday, the day of reckoning with Dr. Lawrence. For twelve years, I managed to escape the clutches of the male population. Dr. Lawrence baited the trap by using his special brand of sneaky tactics which I fell right into, letting him snare me into the date.

I blamed Bill and Katie, mostly. They supplied the doctor with information about me. How much remained a mystery. I already confronted my sister. Now it was Bill's turn.

I drove away from the farm questioning what I had done to attract Dr. Lawrence. My sunny disposition was not an encouragement. His reasoning of fascination as the attraction didn't wash with me. If history taught anything, underlying motives lay in the hearts of those who pursue the un-pursuable.

Maybe his scientific nature wanted to explore the unchartered waters of a woman immune to his finesse. I planned to prove my theory. I was not a woman Dr. Lawrence wanted to date.

I arrived at the gym to a quiet deserted place.

"Bill?" No answer. "Hey, Bill?"

The drawn office blinds raised concern. I placed a hand on the door. Giggling erupted from the other side.

"Stop that Bill."

A quick covering of the mouth stifled a spasm of laughter. Upon recognition of Shirley Dobb's soft voice, I quietly left. Once inside the truck, the pent up hysteria exploded until tears came to my eyes. There was not enough imagination inside me for picturing Bill in a romantic situation.

I recalled overhearing Josh describe to Katie the area along Patmos Road where he and his father lived. With plenty of time to spare, I decided to take advantage and do some reconnaissance. The house was not that hard to find.

My truck inched along the country road hoping for a view of the doctor's home. Trees obscured the yard with hints of a white framed house peeking through the limbs. The only way to fully see the place was by pulling into the drive. I chose not to and disappointedly elected turning around making my way to the softball park.

At a traffic light, I waited for it to change. Several motorcycles lined behind the lead car across the inter-section. The thudding of multiple pipes reminded me of Paris, Texas where Momma and I lived. A group of riders held court across the street from our house. I thought about one man in particular, one I hadn't thought of in years.

The house across the street belonged to him. I never knew his real name. Everyone on the block called him Z.

He was slim built, clean-shaven with braided hair hanging to his waist. The one thing that stood out most in my memory was the large white patch on his leather vest. Black wings embossed the midsection with the same description arching over the top in bold letters. The bottom carried a scrolling piece of material reading the name of our town.

Z lived alone except for the occasional visits from his friends who wore the same patch on their back. He was nice to the neighborhood kids. Children brought bicycles, wagons, and every sort of riding toy imaginable for him to repair. He never told them no but stopped what he was doing to help. I didn't ventured over to his house. My place was on our porch, observing.

Several mornings he aided my mother with starting our old station wagon. In turn, Momma cooked food delivering a plate to him. It was a simple gesture, but one he appreciated. Once, when he came over to change the battery cables on our car, I went outside and took a seat on the steps watching him work.

"Hi, Jake," he greeted me by name. I remained quiet and gave a weak smile. A part of me wanted to be like the other children, but distrust run deep in my veins.

The motorcycles across the intersection revved louder drawing me further into the past to the down side of our lives, the part that eventually led to fleeing the Paris home.

One afternoon, I sat on the porch watching Z work on a little boy's tricycle. He was patient and encouraged the boy to help him. I was lost in the repair job when the sound of motorcycle pipes coming down the street drew my head around. It grew louder approaching our neighborhood. I waited to see which of the many characters that came and went would appear, stopping in the drive across the way.

The roaring pipes deafened my ears the closer it came to our house. My face changed from curiosity to dread recognizing the motorcycle. I scampered into the house, alerting Mom of Brad's arrival, and took refuge in my bedroom.

My room faced the frontage. I lay on the bed eyeing Brad climbing from the bike all the while wishing Z would cross the street and make him leave. A young foolish heart hoped the biker would hear my thoughts and save us from the man entering the house. It didn't happen.

My mother avoided airing dirty laundry in public.

Later that afternoon, my hopes diminished when Z rode away on his bike. I stayed in my room quiet with the door cracked, listening for the warning that it was time for me to hide. Brad held no interested in seeing me most of the time unless it swerved his purpose. I thanked God for that little bit of peace.

I heard him in the other room ask Momma. "Where's the kid? Haven't seen her in a while."

"At the neighbor's playing," Momma lied.

"Playing? Hell, she's gettin' too old to play. Really need to think about that girl earning her keep. She'll be old enough to turn out in a couple of years."

"You stay away from my daughter," my mother said through clenched teeth.

He gave a snicker. "Oh Bridgette, I'm just kidding."

I didn't know what he meant at the time, but it wasn't good if it angered my mother. I used it as a cue to climb into the closet beneath the small quantity of clothes hanging on a metal rod and hid behind an old worn trunk.

Around eight, the fighting started. After so much exposure to a vicious cycle, I systematically knew what to do. Headphones went over my ears blocking out the noise coming from the other room.

I fell asleep and was startled when the trunk moved. My mother held a blood soaked washcloth pressed to her mouth and nose motioning for me to come out. We packed what we could with no time to spare. I followed Mom down the hall passing her room spying the man who beat her passed out on the bed. We left with very little of our belongings, never returning to the house nor seeing Z again.

A car honked from behind, interrupting the memory. I shook the thoughts away urging the truck forward. When I passed the group of motorcycles, my mouth fell ajar recognizing one driver. I was astounded. I never expected the conservative, safety-first Dr. Lawrence to be the type to ride a motorcycle. The surprising discovery quickly changed to worry hoping he hadn't seen me. My foot pressed hard on the accelerator speeding up. I watched the bikes in my rearview mirror dispersing at the light. The doctor drove over the crossing disappearing in the distance.

At the softball park, I found Gran in her lawn chair close to the fence behind home plate. I let her know I had arrived. Shelley Thompson perched on a bench a few feet away so I sat beside her.

"How you feeling Jake," she asked.

"I'm all right."

The bet came to mind. "I never heard what you and the staff lost on the bet?"

Shelley curved her mouth. "Well, you should have a very good meal tomorrow night since we paid for it."

I frowned. "Does everyone know about the dinner?"

She nodded. "We got another bet going. Dr. Lawrence's betting you won't show. I don't want to lose this time Jake."

"Oh, I plan on showing." I laughed with mischief.

Shelly closed her eyes and wrinkled her forehead. "Lord, Jake Conner, what are you going do?"

I was unsure except it involved making the doctor miserable. "Nothing that requires medical attention."

"Jake, seriously, he's a nice guy. I've worked for a lot of doctors but he's the best. Please don't be mean to him," she said, championing his cause.

It seemed Dr. Lawrence's fan club grew by leaps and bounds. I started to ask Shelley a few more questions about him.

Gran distracted me with, "Bill coming?"

Remembering the giggles from the office, I gave a

chuckle replying, "Not real sure. I think he's showing someone how to use his equipment."

A few minutes later, the game started. Shelley moved closer to home plate. Katie's team, The Heat, sponsored by a local heating and cooling business, played the Dirt Diggers. Carley Everett took the mound for the opposing team. The short little brunette knew her stuff when it came to pitching although I thought Katie better. After one strike out and two fly balls, the teams switched places. Katie took the mound.

A weird chill swept over me. I glanced over my shoulder locating the draft in the form of the new redheaded school secretary positioned on the top bench. She waved. I extended one in return. She should have been sharing dinner with Dr. Lawrence instead of me. They seemed to get along pretty darn good at the party. I went back to watching the game.

Josh Lawrence strolled along the fence and sat beside me. "Miss anything?"

"Three straight outs, middle of the first," I said.

He sat down. Out of the corner of my eye, I saw a building grin on his face. "So you're having dinner with Dad tomorrow night."

I frowned. Good lord, did everyone in Hempstead County know about the dinner? "That's the plan. You join -ing us?"

"No, giving him all the space he needs." Josh chuckled. "I'm just shocked he asked you."

The son saw the makings of disaster. The father must be blind. "It's a little weird, huh?" I said.

Josh shrugged. "Yeah, kind of, when you think about your parents datin'. I've never known my dad to go out with anyone."

I raised a brow. "He doesn't date?"

Josh shrugged. "If he does, he's discreet, and I've

never met 'em."

It was nice to know the doctor didn't parade women in and out of his son's life. Surely he dated, but why unmarried after so many years? Dr. Lawrence was becoming more of a puzzle.

"So you're okay with this?" I asked.

"Yeah, I gave Dad a few pointers like be polite and don't make you mad or he might end up getting knocked out."

I laughed. "I don't think we'll go a round. You can join us if you want, just to make sure."

Josh lowered his head grinning. "No, thanks. I'm heading to Tulsa in the morning to visit Grandpa for a few days."

He waved to a sandy-haired boy and left the bench saying, "See ya."

"Dinner with the Doc? I guess you forgot to tell me that one," Bill said.

I leaned away, tilting upward and lifting a brow. "You mean to say you and your new best friend didn't discuss this beforehand? Come on, Bill, he got information from someone."

Bill rubbed his neck. "All right, we talked about you. He mentioned wanting to take you out to dinner and figured why bother? You're going say no anyway. I told him if he wanted to spend time with you not to give you a choice, just do it."

I shook my head, biting the inside of my cheek swallowing the choice words that came to mind. "Don't you think it's strange he wants to go out with me? I mean, come on, have I given him any indication I'm even remotely interested?"

"Actually, I think you're perfect for each other."

Bill clucked me under the chin. "And sometime you ought to take a look in the mirror, Jake. You might see what the rest of the male population already knows."

I gave him a skeptical glare. "What's with you and all this touchy-feely stuff?"

"Just being nice, Jake," he responded.

"Right. I expect plotting from Katie but not you. So why are you pushing Dr. Lawrence?"

Bill stretched. "I'm not pushing anyone. He's a good guy. He asked, and I gave my opinion."

"What else did you tell him about me?"

Watching the game intensely he said, "Nothing that would embarrass you."

Shirley Dobb's giggle came to mind. I gave a sarcastic grin. "Nothing embarrassing like, say, someone who forgot to lock the gym door while having a private meeting with a patron?"

Bill furrowed his brow. "Don't know what you're talking about."

I let it go remembering Carter's visit."What did Carter want?"

Clapping over a hit one of the girls made, he replied, "He's trying to buy a gym in Chicago. He offered me a job managing the place. Can you believe it?"

Carter and Bill were never friends. Why would he offer Bill a job? Bill was a trainer who lived and breathed boxing. It was possible, regardless of the tension between them, that Bill might leave Hope if given the chance to train again. I stressfully waited for Bill to reveal his decision.

"And?" I paused. "Are you thinking about his offer?"

The question produced a grunt of disgust from Bill.

"No, I nearly decked him for asking."

A wave of relief surged through me.

"He had to know you'd say no so why did he come?"

"Because he's trying to buy Romano's gym. If he wants the gym, he has to go through me to get it," Bill replied flatly.

"What do you have to do with Romano's gym, and why does he have to go through you?"

Bill waved me over to make room for him. "The gym he wants is owned by Bobby Romano's widow."

I searched my memories for the name of Bobby Romano. I never heard Bill mention him. "Who's Bobby Romano?"

Bill whistled loudly when Ali dug a ground ball from the dirt making the play at first. "Bobby bought the gym I owned in Chicago before I came to Hope. He died a year ago."

It would have been easier to pull my own teeth than get information out of Bill. "So? What does this have to do with you?"

Bill sighed deeply, crossing his arms over his chest. "Bobby and I go way back. I'm just acting as an advisor, helping his wife."

"Oh, I see. You don't like Carter, and you're recommending she turn him down," I concluded.

Bill shot a harsh look in my direction. "I don't have a problem with him buying the gym, but he's not getting it at the pittance he's offered. He already screwed the Romanos once. He's not doing it again."

It was time to end the mysterious why-I-hate-Carter-Neal saga. "What's the deal between you, Carter, and this gym?"

Bill quickly stood. "Good job, Katie. Three up, three down."

I clapped, keeping my eyes trained on Bill, paying no mind to the game. I wondered if he planned to tell me or dance around the question, pretending he didn't hear me. He seemed to have selective hearing when it came to certain areas of his life.

Bill sat down, leaning back and propping his arms on

the bench behind him. "About sixteen years ago, Eddie Neal brought his kid around wanting Bobby to train him. Man, Bobby sunk a lot of time into Carter. He started winning, moving up in the ranks, and Bobby arranged a shot at the Golden Gloves title. A month before the fight, Carter and Eddie came in, packed up, and fired Bobby. They said they had a new manager. Bobby put everything, time, cash, heart and soul into the boy only to have it thrown in his face."

I understood Bill's resentment toward Carter. It happens a lot in the boxing world, fighters leaving the ones who brought them up.

"So Bobby dies and Carter wants to buy the gym," I said

Bill took a deep breath and exhaled loudly. "Bobby left some pretty serious debt. More than his wife, Angela, can handle. Back taxes and stuff. Carter got wind of the problems. He thought he'd swoop in, offer half the value, and Angela might be desperate enough to take it."

"And she asked your opinion," I surmised.

Bill nodded. "She called me. I told her not to sell and let me deal with Carter. So he came to see me, and if he wants the gym, he'll pay the full value and then some."

The conversation grew more complicated by the minute. I cast my vision down, daring to ask, "Why would he agree to that and offer you a job?"

At first, he didn't answer. I shifted my gaze, meeting his cold eyes. "It wouldn't be in Carter's best interest if certain people found out he tried to screw over Bobby Romano's widow." He softened his face adding, "The job offer is Carter's way of sucking up. I told him what to do with his job. I'm going to Chicago to give the place a once over and make sure he signs the papers."

I know Bill better than most. He would never allow anyone to hurt the people he cares for, even if it means resorting to using the connections he refuses to acknowledge. "You're a good man, Bill Monroe," I said. He gave me a wink, turning his attention back to the game.

After four innings, the Dirt Diggers were up three to two. The Heat advanced a runner to third with Ali coming up to bat. A line drive hit brought the runner home tying the score and Ali to first.

Katie came up to bat. The first pitch Carley delivered way inside, causing my sister to jump from the batter box. I read the snarl on her usually soft features. She took a step back, hitting the bat against the edge of her cleats.

Carley rolled her shoulders twisting a cunning grin on her lips before releasing another pitch. I saw what was about to happen before the ball left her hand. Katie tried to cover up by lowering and tilting her head to expose the helmet but not quickly enough. The ball struck her hard on the chin.

My sister very rarely became angry but when mad, she was a handful. Katie dropped the bat heading for the pitcher's mound yelling, "You did that on purpose."

I leaped from the bench rounding the fence to the dugout, pushing past Josh and the sandy haired boy standing at the fence.

"I didn't do it on purpose, Katie," the pitcher yelled sarcastically, backing away.

By now, both coaches were on the field corralling their players. My red-chinned sister continued to the mound. Carley backed a few steps toward the short stop. Katie caught up to her, towering over the shorter girl.

The Umpire reacted placing himself between the angry teenagers. "Back to the plate, or you're out of here," he said pointing to Katie.

I shouted from the side of the dugout, "Katie, shake it off. Get your head back in the game."

My sister gave a sneer then returned to home plate

picking up the bat.

The umpire warned Carley. "One more time, and you're out of here."

When things settled down, Carley released another pitch. Katie put all of her anger into the swing, delivering a standing double bringing Ali home. When it was over, the Heat won the game by two runs.

Bill checked Katie's swelling chin which proved to be very bruised. It was unlikely anything was broken considering her mouth never stopped moving while complaining about her arch nemesis.

Katie thanked the trainer remarking, "I could'a took her, Bill."

Bill laughed and placed an arm around her shoulders. "Yeah, with your history of hitting things, I have no doubt you could'a took her."

Katie gave a playful punch to Bill's side.

Josh asked Ali and Katie to ride with him to pick up some food. Shelley, not as strict with Ali, gave her daughter permission to ride with Josh. I was surprised when Gran agreed to let Katie go, too.

I liked Josh well enough but worried for Katie. Her carefree behavior concerned me. She was too trusting. I took her arm, pulling her to the side.

"Be careful and get home by ten," I warned.

She frowned. "We can't drive to Vegas, get married, and be back by ten."

I left the ball field shaking my head at the teen comedian and followed Gran to Washington.

It was around nine when we made our way into the house.

Gran dropped her purse on the buffet with a loud thud. "I can't shake this headache. You mind waiting up on Katie?" she asked rubbing her temples.

"Not at all, go to bed Gran."

She went upstairs, and I stretched out on the sofa, flipping through the channels waiting on Katie. A yawn escaped a few times while fighting off the urge to close my eyes.

At ten, Katie was still not home. I paced the living room letting all kinds of scenarios run rampant with my imagination. How could she be late the first time Gran lets her out of our sight? The phone rang. I raced over, picking up anxiously. Katie had some explaining to do.

"Hello," I said.

It was quiet for a moment before the masculine voice spoke. "It's been a long time."

Stop, my mother's voice screamed from the past. I nearly dropped the phone. It's not him, I reasoned.

"You got the wrong number," I spoke with caution.

"Don't think so."

Fear pitted my stomach stirring the bile into nausea. "Who is this?"

"Has it been that long?" He laughed. "It me, Brad. Ring any bells?"

"Don't ever call here again." I moved the receiver away from my ear.

His voice rose. "If you hang up, I'll just call back when I can talk to Katie."

I froze when my sister's name rolled off his tongue.

"Yes, sweetheart, I know about Katie except not real sure where she came from. Want to fill in the blank?" he said.

"Why…why are you calling? What do you want?" I stammered.

"I take that as a no, you're not going to tell me. That's okay. We can talk about it some other time. I been reading about you. I just wanted to check and see how you're doin' and tell you I'm proud of ya Jake. It's been so long, thought maybe we might let bygones be bygones," he said.

In a low voice, making sure Gran didn't hear me from upstairs if she was still awake. "The day I let bygones be bygones is the day I spit on your grave."

He chuckled. "Look, Jake, I know you have some hard feeling, but I just thought we might reconnect, that's all."

"Get under whatever rock you're calling home, and leave me alone," I spat out with venom.

"I think we both know where I am, and I can't leave. It's part of the parole thing, you know, staying put." He gave a demented howl of laughter. "Of course, you know. You put me here." His laugh faded. "Sorry, Jake, I need to let that one go. What's done is done, let sleeping dogs lie, and all that. Never know when they might wake up and start running in packs."

"Stay away from me, and don't call here again, or I'll go to the sheriff."

"No need to get the law involved. We'll do things your way. I won't call again."

The line went dead.

I labored with adrenaline that tortured raw nerves. My gut instincts were right all along. My fist lashed out against the sofa. I leaped to my feet, swinging a fist into thin air and cursing.

I walked to the front door then back to the sofa repeating the movement several times. I sunk down on my knees fighting to stay in the present by covering my ears in an effort to block his voice from my head. It didn't work. The memories flooded taking me back to the places I feared the most.

"Jake, where are you?" Brad's voice resonated in my head.

It was like so many times before, Brad in a rage, Momma trying to appease him. I was scared and wedged between the bed and the wall hiding like she told me.

He found me and dragged my eight-year-old body over the bed by my hair. When we got to the bedroom door, I fought against him. My foot caught on the worn carpet and stumbled into the door jamb hitting my chin. His fingers dug into my skull, raising me by my hair, then gave a shove toward my mother who lay on the living room floor.

The maddening laugh shouted, "Damn, Bridgett, this kid has more fight in her than you. Go ahead, Jake ask her. Ask her why do you make him do this to you?"

Blood dripped from my mother's nose. Her eye was swollen shut. Why didn't she fight back just once?

"No," I said trying to pull away from his painful grasp.

He slapped me. I never forgot the sting of his hand.

"Say it," he demanded giving me a shake.

"Mommy!"

"Say it," Brad hissed increasing the pressure on my arm until I thought it would break.

"*Mommy*," I pleaded.

My mother tried to push herself up. Brad dragged me closer to where she lay. He placed a boot on her back slamming her to the floor. "Move again, Bridgette, and Jake'll pay."

His fingers crushed my arm. "Say it, Jake?"

"No!" I shook my head.

He slapped me again. I tasted the saltiness of blood on my lips. My forearm twisted near deformity.

"Say it or I'll break it," he spewed.

My mother trembled. "Do what he says. Just do what he wants."

I hated him. I feared him. But for sure, I believed him. He would have broken my arm and hurt me bad. "Why do you," I choked a sob, "make him." I shook and cried so much that Brad flung me out of the way.

"Hide Jake," my mom whimpered.

I barked my shin on the coffee table, and out of the harrowing recollection. Looking around wildly, still shaky from the vivid memory, I fixated on the clock, it was ten-fifteen and Katie was late. I called her cell phone.

"Where are you?" It's after ten," I shouted.

"We're nearly home. Jeeze, Jake, cut the umbilical cord already." She laughed.

I ran a hand through my hair. I had to calm down. "Katie, it's not good to be late the first time Gran lets you out on your own," I said, easing the tone of my voice.

She assured me she would be home in five minutes.

Josh's Honda pulled into the driveway shortly afterward. Less than a minute later Katie sauntered through the door.

"Happy?" she said, dropping her sports bag and throw -ing her arms in the air.

"I'm sorry, it's just…, I worry about you. Sit down."

Reluctantly, she took a seat in an overstuff chair near the stairs slumping with her arms crossed.

I found a spot on the staircase next to her. "You're so trusting and you never take anything serious. I worry you're going to run across someone who'll take advantage of you."

She wrinkled her nose. "Good lord, Jake, Josh is a good guy. I am not stupid. What do you think? You think I'll just go off with anyone? I can take care of myself. I did pay attention every day I sat in the gym watching you."

I shook my head realizing how much Gran and I sheltered the girl. "I don't want you to get yourself into a position where you have to defend yourself. There are people who can finesse their way into your life and end up forcing you into situations you don't want to be in."

Katie broke in. "Oh, dear God, tell me this isn't the sex talk?"

"Well, when you start dating, you can be pressured into doing things that you would normally never consider."

Her hands flew to her face covering the splotches of red already present. "Ali's Mom gave us this talk two years ago. Please, don't make me relive it."

I was relieved to know Shelley, being a nurse, explained the birds and bees letting me off the hook. "Just be careful with Josh," I said.

She rose from the chair pursing her lips taking the steps beside me. "Josh and I are just friends."

Maybe for now I thought *but I've seen how much time the two spend together.*

"I'm glad you're friends but if he starts pressuring you, come to me, please," I said.

She was a few steps above me, and twisted to face me, appalled by the statement. "Josh and I are friends, good friends. I don't think of him like that, and he doesn't think of me in that way either. You don't have anything to worry about. He's into Ali."

I got up, reached out, and took her arm. "You know I love you. You can come to me about anything. I won't judge you or get mad. I just want you to be safe."

She leaned down embracing me. "I love you too, Jake," and added, "Do you want me to ask Mrs. Thompson to give you the talk before your date tomorrow night?"

I pushed her away. "I think I can handle it on my own."

She laughed all the way to her room.

I sat on the stairs wondering what to do. What if Katie found out about him?

I rose and went to the phone searching the call log.

The last was from Brad. I wrote down the number and deleted it from the records.

Upstairs, I powered up my laptop and began a reverse look up. The number belonged to a machine shop in St. Louis, Missouri. There was no doubt in my mind he was behind the pictures, the flowers, and the postcard. Somehow he managed to get them here. But how?

10

Night brought very little sleep. I tossed and turned most of it in an effort to shut off my brain. When I felt myself dozing, I drifted back to emotional crippling moments and places escaped years prior. One phone call turned back the hands of time. One voice reminded how weeds that once lay dormant waited to spring up in the peaceful garden planted by my own hand.

I gave up the bed before dawn and drove to the gym. It always helped, working out. When Bill arrived an hour later, I was sweaty and exhausted from repetitious swings at the fast bag.

"You're here early. You're not in training anymore," he said.

I stopped punching the bag and rested gloves on hips. "He called last night."

"Who called?"

I turned toward Bill. "Brad."

Bill scowled.

I met Bill at the corner of the ring. "He called right after we got in from the game."

"What did he want?"

"To check on me and hoped maybe I got over the past." I gave a short laugh hiding my worry. "That just goes to show how crazy he is thinking I'd just forget everything."

"Did you tell Chelsea?"

"No, she went to bed as soon as we got home. She doesn't know he called, and there's no reason to worry her."

Bill took a sip from the cup in his hand looking over the rim. "Is that all?"

I nudged my shoulders. "He knows about Katie and wanted to know where she came from."

"What did you tell him?"

I shrugged. "Nothing. And he didn't press it. I told him not to call again or I'd go to the cops, and he said he wouldn't."

"And you believed him?"

I tapped the gloves against the boxing mat. "I know he's still in Missouri, I checked the number. But I'm not stupid either. He's trying to get in my head."

Bill paced toward the doorway. "Come on. We're calling Harvey and getting a restraining order before this goes any further."

I stood my ground. "And tell him what? Huh? I can't go to the cops. They'll ask questions. Then Katie'll ask questions."

Bill came around. "Tell her the truth, Jake."

I raised a brow. "Are you serious? She doesn't know him. She doesn't know anything about him."

I grasped the Velcro straps with my teeth trying to remove the gloves. Bill walked over, sat his cup down, and took over the task.

"Why are you so stubborn? What are you going do if he calls, and Katie answers the phone? You're playing with fire, Jake. You need to tell her, and you need to tell Chelsea he's out," he demanded.

"I am not giving him what he wants. He wants me scared and to see how far he can push me. It's a game, Bill."

Bill worked the first glove loose. "Go to Harvey and end this."

I wiped the sweat off my face. "What will they do, Bill? He didn't threaten me. Nothing, that's what they'll do and I'll ruin Katie's life just because he called one time. No. It's a game. I made it clear I'm not playing. He'll leave me alone."

Bill ripped the second strap tossing the gloves to the floor. He placed his hand under my chin brushing his thumb across the cleft. "What did it take for him to leave you alone the last time?"

I couldn't believe he said that to me and it showed. I turned away.

"Sorry, kid, that was a low blow."

I ran my hand over one of the ropes."I can't tell Katie. I don't want her to ever know…"

Bill stroked the braid hanging down my back. "I know, but you need to take it serious. Don't let him get in your head. You worked too hard to get him out. You're, Jake Conner, the fighter, the champ. You've been through more bullshit than most people experience in their whole life, and you've survived. You didn't make it by letting people get in your head."

The words struck a chord. I turned around and patted Bill's shoulder."You're right, and I have the upper hand on him."

Bill pulled back with a puzzled stare. "How's that?"

I gave his unshaven cheek a playful tap."I'm not Mom."

A crease wrinkled his forehead. "Don't go looking for trouble. If he calls again, I want you to change your number, tell Chelsea, and get a restraining order. The cops'll run a check before they serve the papers. They'll alert his parole officer."

I gave a nod walking to the dressing room.

Bill called out. "I mean it, Jake. Don't go looking for trouble."

I walked away with one thought. I'd see Brad in hell before I let him near Katie.

11

Pacing the farm was the worst way to occupy my time for the remainder of the day. It was enough that Brad wanted to play mind games with me but with the added stress of the date with Dr. Lawrence a few hours away, the scales tipped toward a full-blown anxiety attack.

The barn represented a good place to lose myself. There was a lot to do or so I imagined. I gave Sluggo a good brushing, bringing the black coat to a glistening shine, seeking wisdom from the beautiful creature.

"How do I get out of this date, girl?" I asked.

Sluggo dipped down nibbling on loose hay.

"I could just jump in the truck and disappear," I said. I ran a hand over the hindquarters, smoothing the dark hair. "Yeah, right. Dr. Lawrence calls Gran whining how I stood him up, then I spend the night listening to her chew me out. He's got her wrapped around his little finger. He's got all of them, you know. But he just can't snow me, and that bugs him."

I stopped brushing, and waved my arms in the air. "Look at me. I am the great Dr. Lawrence, Mr. Nice Guy trying to help the..." I wrinkled my nose and huffed. "Boxer."

Sluggo turned her head toward me. I stroked the horse's nose, exaggerating my movement with a sarcastic mimic. "Oh, I must save Jake Conner from the barbaric, disgusting sport called boxing. Sickening isn't it?"

I tossed the brush onto a nearby bench. "Sluggo, my

friend, I'd run off, but with my luck, he'd comb the county looking for me. Why the heck did he do that? Hmm, why did he drag me to his office? What's he up to?"

I laid an arm across the horse's neck, rubbing her mane. "You know I bet the reason he doesn't bring his girlfriends around Josh is because they're all one night stands. Yep, wham bam, worship my greatness, ma'am."

I patted the horse and started moving hay."It don't matter," I said, tossing a bale. "I'll go the dinner, sit there and keep a straight face, staring at those half ass glasses, and get my message across loud and clear."

"Jake, what are you doin'? You need to get ready for your date," Katie said, coming into the barn.

I jumped hearing her voice. Did she hear me talking to Sluggo? I flicked my wrist peering down at my watch. "I don't have to be there until six-thirty. It shouldn't take more than forty-five minutes to shower and get there."

Katie threw her head back groaning. "I know you're not planning on going without fixing your hair and putting on a little make-up."

I pursed my lips, moving my head a little to one side. "That is exactly what I plan to do."

The intention since the day I agreed to the date was to make Dr. Lawrence regret his dinner invitation, which involved making sure I appeared unappealing as possible. I even considered meeting the man without showering, reeking of sweat and horses.

Katie slumped over a stack of straw, moaning. "Why do you do have to be so mean all the time?"

I moved another bale, ignoring the ranting.

"Jake, he's a nice guy. Why can't you give him a chance?" she whined.

I leveled one of the bales against my knee, gave it a kick, and let go watching it land on top of the stack.

"Katie, I don't know what you think'll happen on this date with Dr.Lawrence but let me make it perfectly clear once and for all. I'm not interested in him."

Sluggo neared Katie. She rubbed the nose keeping her back to me. "I've thought about this a lot. You use Gran, boxing, and me or whatever you can come up with to get out of dating. I know what's going on with you."

"Really?" I said. "So enlighten me."

"You're gay. And it's okay, Jake, I love you just the same," she said so serious.

The question floored me. "No I'm not gay," I exclaimed.

She brought her head around. "Then what is it? I see men looking at you. Carter Neal is so in love with you, it's pathetic. You won't give him or any other guy the time of day. You never date. Why is that?"

I didn't want to have this conversation. What was there to say? There were two sides to men, nice and cruel. They used nice to draw a person in just to turn cruel. I couldn't tell her what I really felt. It would lead to other questions.

I took a seat on a hay bale, resting a hand on each knee. "First of all, Carter's not in love with me. He's in love with my marquee. Second, exactly when have I had time to date over the past twelve years? Hmm? If I wasn't boxing, I was training. When I wasn't training I went to school."

Katie nuzzled Sluggo's nose. "Excuses, excuses. So what does that have to do with going out now? I mean you're retired, right? What's your excuse now?"

I wish my sister were stupid. It would be so much easier on me. "I'm not like you. Sometimes I wish I were, but I'm not. I can't talk to people like you do. I never was the high school boy-chaser, and I never wanted to be that girl. I'm a boxer. Guy's don't like women who can beat their ass."

Katie lowered her head moving a foot over a small pile of straw. "It's more than that, Jake. I know something happened to make you push people away, men in particular. Gran told me after Mom died you kind of lost it for a while, really screwing up. What happened during that time that made you so hard on people? Were you raped?"

I rose, shielding my sister of the building anger from remembering my own reckless behavior and knowing Gran spoke to her about it. I stacked hay avoiding further discussion on the subject.

"Is that it?" she asked.

I slammed a bale down, snapping, "No, Katie, I wasn't raped. God, you just don't get it. I'm not like you. I don't have to have a boyfriend to define who I am. The sooner you get your head out of the clouds and learn you don't need someone to make you feel good about yourself, the better off you'll be."

I grabbed the strings of another bale and gave a sling across the barn. Katie stomped across the barn toward the door.

"Crap!" I muttered.

I was ready with an apology when she stopped at the barn door. "I know who I am, Jake. I'm just a dumb kid who's not afraid to show people how I feel. How can anyone understand you or how you feel what you don't feel because you're never going to tell anyone anything? Yeah, I got my head in the clouds. At least I don't hide behind 'em and let life pass me by."

Katie gripped the edge of the door, pushing it wide.

"I don't know what happened to you but I feel so sorry for you and everything you're missing. Dr. Lawrence is a really good man, but you'll never know 'cause you're not going to give him or *anyone* a chance."

She walked out.

I deplore fighting with my sister. I jerked off the gloves throwing them to the ground along with a string of profanity. I sat down on the hay staring at Sluggo."You agree with her, don't you?" The horse gave a snorting neigh. "Traitor!"

I sat in the barn for a while thinking how much Katie's words reminded me of the same disappointing tone Momma used at times.

"The saddest thing I've ever seen is my daughter afraid to try," Momma said the first time I attempted to skate. I fell on my rear and refused to stand up declaring I couldn't do it. She righted me on shaky legs. "Jake, everyone spends the biggest part of their life flying by the seat of their pants. Don't be afraid. Spread your wings and see how far you can soar."

I searched the beams holding the roof. A deep sigh escaped. "All right, I hear you."

With the barn behind me, my steps led across the yard to the back door thinking on a brighter note, Dr. Lawrence was a jerk with a pre-formed opinion of the person I am. I could build on that by fixing myself up, appease Katie, and still be mean to the good doctor.

I found the brooding teen in her room. I stood in the doorway with a hand bracing the jamb. "Keep the makeup to the minimum."

Katie jumped from the bed in glee grabbing a plastic container similar to a fishing tackle box. She opened the lid revealing an assortment of bottles and brushes and began arranging the items on the vanity.

After a quick shower, I let her work her magic. I stood back examining the person in the mirror dressed in a yellow sundress with sandals.

Katie walked up behind me wrapping her arms around my waist. "You're so beautiful."

I shrugged off her compliment seeing the reflection in the glass. It was everything I detested about Diana Strauss."Yeah, I guess I could always try modeling underwear if the teaching gig doesn't work out."

This brought a chuckle from my sister. "I can just picture you on a runway with some guy saying, shake that butt, honey. Then you'd jump into the crowd and knock him out."

I gave a laugh, leaving the room.

At five-thirty, I descended the stairs ready to leave. I collected keys and found Gran in her recliner, watching the news.

"Well, do you think I can knock him out without even touching him?" I asked, dreading the answer.

Gran stared in disbelief. "Sweetheart, you're beautiful."

"You may want to pray, Gran."

She rose from the chair walking over placing a kiss on my cheek. "Honey, you'll be fine. No reason to pray."

I stepped onto the porch. "Not for me, for him."

The screen door slammed with Gran shouting, "Be nice, Jake."

12

For probably the first time in my life, I drove under the speed limit. At a traffic light, serious consideration took root to turn around and go home claiming illness. Fingers tapped the steering wheel waiting for the light to change. Turn and forget about it, my nerves urged. The boxer inside yielded, just go to his house, shovel down the food, get your point across that you're not interested, and leave.

I growled over the cowardly moment. What's wrong with me? I intimidate people, not the other way around. My natural talent for putting people off didn't work on Dr. Lawrence. He was different.

Bill and Tom were the only constant male figures present in my life. Both loud, no holds barred, personalities, knowing up front what to expect.

Dr. Lawrence was the opposite. What was it I overheard the nurse at the hospital say? "He could be up to his elbows in blood or maybe wrestling a drunk in the ER, but always steady." I also remembered her co-worker whispering with a sly smile, "Hmm. I'd like to see if I can get him excited."

Katie and Cora Mae saw what the nurses had seen. I certainly did not see the fuss over the man.

Liar, I chastised myself.

He towered over my five-ten, so he stood at least six foot or more. He kept his hair pulled back wearing those silly old-style black half-framed glasses. Dr. Lawrence was attractive, just not my type, if I ever figured out my type.

I tapped the steering wheel debating on the turn. "Good Lord, I'm acting like a sixteen-year-old girl going on her first date," I mumbled aggravatingly.

In fact, it was my first real date.

I lack the experience of a man driving up to my home picking me up for an evening of wining and dining or going to a movie. The closest thing resembling a date happened at a party during the wild six months of rebellion.

His name was Ray. I didn't even know his last name. Drugs and alcohol clouded the night but not enough to cover the memory of two teenagers bumbling around having an awkward sexual encounter. Shame riddled me the next day. I never spoke to him again. After that, it was all about boxing.

The light changed. I looked to the left watching my last chance for escape pass by. The closer my car approached its destination, the more apprehension tingled every nerve ending. I couldn't put my finger on it. It was something about the few moments he stood so close, the lingering attention at the party, and that stupid grin. He always wore a smile. It hid something. I was sure of it. It was just a matter of figuring out what alterative motives hid behind those pearly whites.

I took a deep breath and turned onto the gravel driveway leading up to a single-story, framed house. Nothing ostentatious stood out about the place. Well-kept flowerbeds lined the frontage with an inviting stone walkway leading to a small porch. I expected a far more grand home for a doctor.

Cutting the engine, I scanned my image in the mirror, "Good Lord," I muttered. "Why did I let Katie do this to me?"

Primping in front of a mirror, applying makeup opposed everything I maintained over my adult life. Katie used everything in her arsenal plus more hair products than I could name. The way she swept my long brown strands up with the clip, allowing a little poof on top with the length hanging was nice.

Surveying and dabbing with a tissue, I confirmed getting the gunk off my face and out of my hair proved impossible.

I made one final effort to remove some of the dark lipstick. A movement caught the corner of my eye. Dr. Lawrence stood on the porch near the steps. I did a double take. It was him all right, but different, very different.

My mouth fell ajar eyeing the white sneakers, khaki shorts showing deep tan calves. A navy blue tee shirt covered his chest with sleeves snuggling his biceps. Straight near black hair hung loosely ending just below his shoulders. The glasses were gone revealing high cheekbones raised by an ever present smile.

"Oh, my God." I dragged out each word.

I was like any other woman when it came to a handsome man feeling the increased pulse rate, wondering, and speculating. Gawking was not in my nature. Appreciate in silence; I gave caution to the wind because one never knows what might blow in. Was it possible a hurricane stood on the porch?

"Damn it. He's not supposed to look like this." I agonized. The words came out of my mouth leaving me to wonder why I even said them. Then thought, *You are Jake Conner a world champion boxer. Stop acting like Katie.*

Then I recalled the past communication between us and knew that once Dr. Lawrence opened his mouth delivering a condescending tone, those good looks would not matter. I exhaled slowly counting to ten before opening the door.

I kept my eyes adverted while approaching the porch.

He met me at the bottom step. "Hi. Glad you made it. Have any trouble finding the place?"

"No," I replied, fighting to keep from scanning the imposing stature once more.

"Come on in," he said.

I followed through the screened door, trailing behind trying to keep up with his long strides. A few pictures of Josh hung on the living room wall. Each represented a different age in chronological order. My toe stubbed an end table. Dr. Lawrence turned around. I straightened quickly.

"Thought we'd have dinner on the patio with the weather so nice," he said.

I quickened my step. The patio was magnificent. It boasted a fully equipped, outdoor kitchen, flagstone flooring with wooden beams looming above. Trellises covered with an assortment of ivy and climbing vines created a wall near the far end separating the patio from the rest of the yard.

Neatly trimmed Crepe Myrtles stood in various areas allowing plenty of shade mixed with late afternoon sunshine to filter on the flowers lining the house. One section appeared designed for sitting year around with a small fire pit providing warmth in the colder months.

The doctor made his way around a counter starting dinner preparations. I stared upward, questioning God. Where were the glasses and scrubs? He's not supposed to look like this.

Dr. Lawrence looped an apron over his neck that sported the phrase You'll Eat What I Cook on the bib. I stifled a laugh wondering if it were Josh inspired or maybe a 'my way or the highway' attitude.

"How about a drink? We have just about anything

you want," he offered.

"Water," I replied strolling up to the counter. My face felt hot. I rubbed my brow, wishing to turn back time and take the left at the light.

Dr. Lawrence pulled several items from the small fridge including water. "Sit down and talk to me while I cook."

I took a seat on a stool and gave the bottle cap a twist looking everywhere but at the doctor.

"I'm not much of a red meat eater so I hope you like chicken and seafood," he said.

I owned a weakness for seafood dishes prepared any way possible. Knowing my baby sister, she probably gave him full disclosure on my likes and dislikes. Playing it cool and showing no interest, I said, "Yeah, whatever you want to cook."

Gran used the basic salt, pepper with a few extra spices depending on the recipe. He retrieved several bottles from the shelf, some I had never seen before, dousing everything of substance.

I took a sip from the bottle with eyes widening in amazement watching the chef at work. The last time I saw someone peel, slice, and dice so fast it was in a Japanese restaurant. I imagined myself on the operating table, him talking to the staff wielding a scalpel through my side approaching the task in the same manner.

He broke my bizarre thought with a small laugh.

"What?" I said.

His smile grew. "I see you eyeing the knife, and I'm just wondering if the evening will end with a better understanding of each other, or me in the ER pulling one of these from my chest."

I gave him a smirk and swiveled the bar stool a hundred and eighty degrees. "I promised Gran to be a gracious guest, but it's a comfort to know we both agree on who'd end up in the ER."

He broke into a hearty laugh. "I'll remember to thank your grandmother. So tell me about Jacqueline Conner."

I hated hearing the use of my full name. I snuck a peek at the broad shoulders when he started the grill. Fingers massaged my lips debating an answer. "You know the basics, twenty seven, retired boxer, sister, granddaughter, future teacher. Not much else left."

"I think there's more than the basic chart information." He walked over to a cabinet, gathered a few items, and came back to the grill. "What do you like besides fighting?"

Perfect, the judgmental tone of the word *fighting*, just the distraction I needed.

"I never had time for much else. I trained, boxed, went to class, and took care of Gran and Katie, *and* I never dated Carter Neal," I said, matter of factually.

He chuckled. "I know. Bill told me it was a one sided love affair built in the guy's mind."

I bit my lower lip. The sneaky underhanded jerk. He knew all along that I never dated Carter. What got me, though, was Bill discussing my past with the doctor. For a man who didn't like to talk about his own, he really had some nerve talking about mine so freely.

I watched intensely for a hint or gesture that might provide a clue of the real Dr. Lawrence. He reached above the grill turning on a fan. The stretched body gave a good view of well-maintained male frame. I shifted on the stool holding my mouth tight, berating impromptu thoughts.

Doctor Lawrence left the grill moving to the counter facing me and continued chopping vegetables. "So do you like movies, reading, music, anything?" he said.

I placed distance between us by leaving the counter,, inching over to the nearby table pretending something caught my fancy. "History."

The sound of the knife connecting with chopping board followed with, "Any particular era?"

Be mean, I reminded. Come on, Doc, help me out. Say something derogatory about boxing.

"Post civil war," I said.

I cupped a hand on one hip shuffling my sandal on the floor steering the conversation away from me. "So I know nothing about you except you have a son, apparently great with a scalpel and knife, and love to drug your patients."

He snuck a laugh. "Thirty-eight, doctor, father, occasional chef, and I only drug patients who are too stubborn for their own good. Have you always been that stubborn, or do I just bring it out in you?"

Say something mean, I reminded. The point of dinner was to make it clear for him to look elsewhere for female company. "I can see why you would interpret me as stubborn. I refused pain meds and after all, you are the one with the MD on your coat. What can I say, Dr. Lawrence? God gave me a brain and the crazy sense for knowing what's best for me."

He didn't seem to be put off with my nasty attitude but smiled instead.

"Dillon," he said.

I was puzzled by his response, and it showed.

"Dillon. Away from the office and the hospital, I'm Dillon," he clarified. "I think we all need a little perspective from others, at times. That's all I did, give a little perspective. Sorry if I insulted your intelligence, never my intention." He followed the statement with a chuckle.

Why can't he frown? Mr. Always Smiling, Mr. Nice Guy, Mr. Polite, handsome, stay in shape... damnit, go home or be mean, I shouted in silence. I crossed arms over my chest.

"Here's some perspective. We both know I don't want to be here so why not just call it a night and avoid further insults."

"Do I make you nervous?" he said, chewing on his lip fighting laughter.

I raised a brow. "No. Do I make you nervous?"

He snorted. "I'm not the one wanting to leave."

I moved in for the kill, edging toward the counter. "Let's cut through the BS. Why did you ask me here because I know it's not my welcoming company or out-going personality," I snapped.

He scooped vegetables in his large hands, dropping them in a bowl. "Actually it is your personality. You're straight to the point, an over achiever when it comes to dismissing people, and I have to say, the attribute that most pulls me in, is that little shade of pink on your cheeks every time Katie asks about my underwear."

Heat radiated my face. I turned away.

"All right, let's cut through the BS," he said. "I didn't bring you here to get you between the sheets or whatever you're thinking. That's not me. And I'm sure I'd end up with a black eye if I tried."

I pivoted and pursed my lips, prepared to spout something sarcastic.

He rubbed his neck and shrugged. "I'm not going deny it. You're a good looking woman, Jake, and there is a physical attraction. But that's not why I asked you to dinner."

"Then why?" I asked.

He laid palms down on the counter, resting his upper weight. "Part of my job is reading people. It's how I determine if someone is real or faking it. There's nothing fake about you. We have a lot in common, high demanding jobs, putting our families first, a little cautious when it comes to the opposite sex. I just thought we might spend an evening together, maybe become friends. No one forced you to come to dinner. You could have bailed, but I think a part of you wanted this. It's just out of your comfort zone. I get it. This isn't easy for me either. If you want to go, feel free. No hard feelings."

There was no doubt to the sincerity in his voice. I thought about the conversation with Josh. His father left dating alone altogether or at the least kept it from his son.

Maybe a part of me wanted to come but admission translated to weakness and betrayal. Dr. Lawrence didn't sell the material used to build the wall of protection. I constructed it all on my own. Sad thing, it sure was lonely inside the stronghold.

The struggle inside went on for a short while before I let chance take the win. I sat down and sighed, "Okay, fair enough. What do you want to know, Dr. Lawrence?"

"Dillon, and I want to know how you got into boxing," he said.

I laughed. "You're actually asking me about my barbaric sport?"

Dillon turned on the faucet running his hand underneath the water raising the corners of his mouth. "I guess I am. Bill said you're one of the best he's ever trained."

I shifted on the stool. "Bill's opinion is a little biased."

Dillon dried his hands on a towel, and raised a brow. "I don't think so. He really cares about you, but he doesn't seem to be the type of person to hand out compliments to those who don't deserve them."

Tell him the truth or at least part of it. That might be something to dissuade him, my colorful criminal record.

"Okay, if you really want to know. It all started when I stole Tom Jackson's truck." I told Dillon the story and all the shameful details.

He released a robust laugh. "So you stole Tom Jackson's pickup, totaled it, and he gives you a job to pay off the damage. That is priceless."

He continued laughing. "Too funny, but I just can't picture it. Katie? Yes. Definitely. You? No way. You seem more conservative than your sister. So what possessed you to steal a truck? Rebelling?"

I frowned, disappointed that he wasn't totally repulsed by my past behavior.

"Something like that." I continued, keeping it honest and brief. "Bill taught me to box, I guess, to keep me out of trouble."

It was my turn to quiz him. "So what about you? What possessed you to become a doctor, and take on single fatherhood while managing to be a chef?"

No answer came immediately. I didn't know if he was too involved in the food preparation to hear me, or biding his time, hoping to move to another topic. Then I recalled Katie explaining how Josh's mother died. I felt like the person who just ran over a kid's puppy, wishing I had kept my mouth shut and not asked any questions.

His eyes rose to meet mine with a sincere and somewhat somber expression. "I always wanted to be a doctor, make a difference in people's lives saving as many as I can and comfort those I can't." He placed the chicken on the grill.

"Single fatherhood was never in the plan. My wife died giving birth to Josh. Strange, huh? Even with the advances in modern medicine women still die in childbirth."

Why, oh, why, couldn't I have left it with tell me about being a doctor? I felt horrible.

"Mastering the kitchen became a necessity." He added more food to the grill. "I wanted my son to eat something other than fast food and snack cake. We are a health-driven family, you know," he said, flashing a grin.

I shifted positions, picking at a piece of lint on my dress feeling bad about stirring up memories of his deceased wife. "Josh said he went to school in Tulsa last term. Are you originally from Tulsa?"

He moved the food around on the grill. "I was born in Broken Bow, Oklahoma. Both of my parents were full-blooded Choctaw Indians. My father died when I was five. My mother moved the two of us to Tulsa. She started hanging out with some unsavory characters. Eventually gained a drug habit."

I appreciated his candidness and wished I could reciprocate. One question led to others that I could not answer. I understood his plight and said, "That must have been terrible."

He closed the lid of the grill, placing two strong hands on the counter. I studied the doctor's features. Tan face, smooth skin with light lines around the eyes and mouth probably from raising high cheekbones forming the grins he seemed to wear quite often. The dark iris of his eyes meshed with the pupils creating difficulty distinguishing where one color ended and the another began. I saw something different. A familiar distant pain I knew all to well.

He winked. "Surprised, huh? Bet you thought I was born with a silver spoon in my mouth."

I bit the inside of my lip feeling guilty, knowing he pegged my thoughts.

He sighed. "It wasn't all bad. I was very lucky. We lived next door to an old bachelor named Sam. He bought me my first bicycle and taught me how to ride. I stayed at his house most of the time. Then one day I woke up and my mother was gone. I guess I was about seven when she left. I went over to Sam's and never left, and I never saw my mother again."

I didn't know how to respond. Quietness engulfed the patio. Bill's words came back to me about Dr. Lawrence and I being perfect for each other. I understood what he meant with similar backgrounds. We were abandoned in our youth in some fashion but fortunate enough to have someone to cling to for love and support.

Dillon pushed away turning his attention back to cooking. "What about you?"

It was selfish thinking my own life the worst possible situation. I shocked myself when I said, "My mom died when I was fifteen."

Dillon nodded. "Bill told me that's why you and Katie live with Ms. Parker."

"Yeah. It hurts whether they die or just leave. They're gone all the same, right?" I furrowed trying to understand why I opened up to him. "Sorry I shouldn't have brought that up. Can we talk about something else?"

Dillon eased a look my way. "Don't be sorry. That's what friends are all about, sharing. Let's talk about my amazing cooking skills. Ready to eat?"

I smiled and nodded.

Dillon collected food from the grill and arranged on plates. The smell of the cuisine was mouth wateringly delicious. He motioned toward the table under the awning. "Let's eat. I'm starving."

The sun sank behind the house casting shadows from the Crepe Myrtles. Taking my cue, I sat down in the offered chair. Dillon set a plate in front of me going back to retrieve his own. He pressed several switches on a nearby wall turning on lights hidden in the awning with a soft flow of music filling the air.

I did not recognize the music or for that matter understand the lyrics. They were in Spanish. My dinner companion saw the confusion. "A Hispanic nurse I worked with many years ago introduced me to the music. I really like this band, in particular. If you don't like it I can change it."

I took a sip of water. "No, it's nice. I thought Mexican music was Mariachi bands. I really like this. It sounds like soft rock but in a different language. Do you speak Spanish?"

"Just enough to understand some of the lyrics."

I took a bite of chicken. The smell promised what the taste delivered. I savored the flavor before swallowing. The man could cook. "This is wonderful." I said.

He extended his thanks.

Lightening the mood from earlier, Washington became the topic of conversation through the remainder of the meal and afterward. I explained briefly the history of its importance during the civil war and some of the people who passed through over the years. I went on relating Washington's influence for my choice of teaching history.

"So you're trading gloves for teaching," he asked.

I nodded. "I love history, and, hey, I get the summers off."

"I'd like to take the tour of Washington one day," he said.

I agreed it to be a good idea. "You should talk to Cora Mae Jackson. She knows more about the town's history than anyone."

He thought for a moment then laughed, "Cora Mae, the older black woman at the graduation party?"

I couldn't believe he directly recalled my grand-mother's best friend. "Yeah, do you know her?"

"No, but she came up to me at your graduation party and told me, oh how did she put it?" he said, sitting back searching, for words. "Oh, yeah. She said, Doc, if you're smart, you'll ask that girl out."

I turned red, and wondered what other information Cora Mae supplied. "Did she say anything else?"

"She said you liked my ass or you thought I'm an ass—not exactly sure which one she meant, but I do know it had something to do with me and an ass."

I wanted to die. I peered upward, grimacing, with the urge to set the record straight. "I don't think she gave the correct interpretation."

His eyes creased around the edges, presenting a chuckle. "I think she did, first impressions are important and my manners were lacking, and there certainly are times I can be an ass, especially if I have a stubborn patient."

First impressions can be misleading. There was no ego or judgmental superiority sitting across the table. He was a person like me, struggling to overcome the cards life dealt. He's a good man, Bill, Katie and Shelley's voices rang in my head. I wanted to believe so much it was possible for someone to be this nice without an ulterior motive.

My cheeks grew warm. "Well, I think I'm beginning to understand you better, and you're becoming less of an ass, if it's any consolation."

He accepted the half-apology. "Does this mean I can relax, and bring the knives out of hiding?"

I laughed aloud. "I think my first impression left you with the wrong idea about me. Sure, I'm cautious and somewhat of a control freak, but I can admit when I'm wrong."

He leaned forward resting his elbows on the table, folding his hands together. "Caution's not a bad thing. I can relate to control issues, but you, Ms. Conner, were stubborn when I first met you, and I think you can still be just as stubborn."

We broke into a round of laughter. It was nice talking to him. The longer we conversed, the more comfortable I became. I let myself get too comfortable. Every time he flashed that wide grin, it cast a spell over me taking my mind to places it shouldn't go.

The ringing of his cell phone interrupted the moment. Glimpsing down at the caller id, he apologized.

"Dr. Lawrence." His voice sounded so serious and different from a few minutes ago.

I glimpsed at my watch. Nine o'clock. The time flew by. After a few words including medical terms I could not understand, he closed the phone with a sigh of disappointment.

"You have to go," I said.

"I'm sorry, Jake. There's a kid in the ER with an appendix about to burst."

We rose with my offering to clean up before leaving. He declined the help. He quickly turned off the music and lights. We made our way through the house with the doctor stopping to gather his wallet and car keys from a small table in the dining room.

Once outside, he walked me to the car. My hand went to the door to open it. I lowered my head for a moment then raised it, staring up at the man. A part of me wanted to leave with no more words exchanged letting the evening end. A strange curiosity came over me wondering how his lips would feel on mine. I scolded myself for such weak thoughts and held out my hand. "Thank you for dinner, It was nice, Dr. Lawrence."

He took my hand. "Dillon, and I'm sorry I have to go. I really enjoyed this."

I returned with a smile, "It was nice, and thank you again, Dillon."

Climbing into the car, we gave each other a final wave. I drove away with the doctor following close. He went straight toward the hospital. I turned watching his car through the driver's side glass.

I felt a change come over me. The mixed feelings

wanting to know more about him and protecting me from the possibility of getting into a relationship was perplexing. I witnessed firsthand how relationships weaken a person. Dillon was a weakness I did not want to allow into my life...or did I?

I drove toward Washington questioning who I was and how I let this happen. Dillon Lawrence seemed nice enough but behind the smile was there another person lurking?

My phone rang showing Gran's house number. Concerned something was wrong I answered with urgency. "Gran?"

A snicker came through the other end. "Do you know what time it is? It nearly ten, where are you?" Katie broke into laughter.

"Ha, ha, I'm on my way home," I said.

"Jake, it's not good to be late the first time Gran and I let you out of the house." With this, she hung up.

When I arrived home, Katie half laid and half sat in a chair eating grapes.

She moved her head back over the arm, peering up at me. "So tell me everything."

I went to the kitchen retrieving a bottle of water from the fridge with Katie in tow. "Not much to tell. He can cook," I said.

She followed me to my room. "Come on, Jake. Details."

I pulled off the dress, changing into my shorty nightshirt. I shrugged, "You were right. He's not so bad."

She became excited with the announcement. I told her about dinner and some of the conversations.

"Are you two getting together again?" she asked, with a sense of hope in her voice.

I walked across the room, pulling the clip from my hair, running a brush through the long strands. "No plans.

He was called to an emergency before it got that far, and besides it's best to leave well enough alone."

Aggravated, she walked out the door saying, "Mean as a snake," and left me alone to face the night.

I lay in bed thinking of Dillon Lawrence, the photos, and the phone call from Brad. Ever since the last fight, my life seemed to be more complicated. Rolling onto my back, I grunted in annoyance. I should have never stopped boxing then maybe none of this would have been happening.

13

Two days passed uneventful. No phone calls from Brad. None from the doctor, for that matter. Maybe both realized I was not the person they wanted to tangle with. A part of me hoped that was the sentiment for Dillon Lawrence, but the other part of me was intrigued by the conversations with the man. The ease in which we talked surprised me yet frightened at the same time. I worried that behind the smile and sincerity lurked an alternative personality.

It was late afternoon. I needed to go to the bank and get in a good work out. Katie had softball practice. As usual, she took forever to get ready. How she spent an hour perfecting a ponytail only to hide it under a baseball cap amazed me.

"Katie, hurry up," I shouted.

"Go ahead," she said, from behind the closed bathroom door. "I forgot to tell ya I'm catching a ride with Josh and Ali."

How she managed to talk Gran into so much freedom boggled the mind. I was uncomfortable with her out in the world without me by her side, protecting. She was a trusting soul. To her, the world was a safe place and everyone's intentions good. Deep down, I truly believed Josh good but lingering doubts nagged.

"What time's practice over? I'll swing by the park and pick you up," I said.

The bathroom door opened widely. "Josh'll bring me home."

"Gran say it's okay?"

Katie closed the door laughing. "No, Josh's waiting down the road until I climb out the window and shimmy down the tree."

She joked yet the fact she actually thought about how to escape undetected bothered me. "Be careful and get home right after practice."

"Gran said be home by eight."

I went downstairs calling for Gran. She was in the kitchen. "Did you tell Katie she could ride with Josh and stay out 'til eight?" I asked over the roaring of the mixer.

Gran turned off the noise. "Yeah, she'll be with Ali, and I told her if she's late, don't ever ask again."

I shook my head. "Fine. I'm going to the gym. You need anything from town?"

"Nope. Got to go over to Liola's to pick beans later."

I walked out the front door and met Josh.

"Hi, Jake."

"Hey, Josh. Katie's still getting ready." I remembered his trip to Oklahoma. "How was the trip?"

Josh sat down on the porch swing. I chose the wicker chair. He tilted his head to the side with a staid expression."Grandpa fell Sunday morning. He broke his hip. I hated calling Dad especially after I found out he'd been in surgery all night. He left straight from the hospital," Josh said.

At least it explained why the doctor hadn't called. I was sure I inadvertently accomplished my original goal sending the doctor running in the opposite direction. "I'm sorry to hear that. Is he going be okay?"

Josh kept his gaze down, rocking the swing on his heels. "Yeah, he's not the type to let things get him down. Dad said it'll take a while for him to recover in the rehab center. He's hoping to talk Grandpa into moving to Hope with us. I don't ever see him leaving Oklahoma."

We sat quietly for a few minutes. I felt Josh staring at me.

He grinned. "Dad said he had a good time Saturday. He needs to have some fun. All he does is work and hang out around the house or ride his bike. He mentioned giving you a call when he gets back. I'm sure he planned to Sunday, but with Sam's accident it slipped his mind."

I cast my attention on bees swarming the flowerbed, feeling compelled to leave before the conversation grew. "I hope your grandpa gets well soon." I stepped from the porch and turned back to Josh. "Make sure Katie's home by eight."

He nodded.

Katie bounced out the screen door, slamming it loudly."Havin' a heart to heart with your future step-mother?"

One would think by now there was absolutely nothing Katie could say to shock me. I wanted to crawl under the porch hearing her commentary. I bowed my head shielding my face from Josh's view.

He surprised me with his snappy comeback. "Come on your nephew'll drive you to the game. See you, Jake."

The two made their way toward the car. Josh edged closer to Katie, inhaling deeply. "You're not one of those aunts that's going to smell like cats when you get old, are you?"

Katie pushed him away. "Better be nice. I may be the only thing standing in the way of mommy dearest shipping you off to military school."

The pair left me mortified with their banter.

As soon as I got to the gym and began working out, Bill immediately came into the boxing area nosing in on my weekend.

"So was I right or was I right?"

I threw a punch at the bag, weaving my head. "About

what?"

"Doc Lawrence. You two have a good time?"

I bounced around on toes delivering another swing at the bag. "He's still breathing if that's what you're asking."

Bill gave a deep rumble from his chest. "Come on, you know you had a good time. You're just pissed 'cause he turned out to be a nice guy. Admit it, you were wrong about him."

"He's not a total jerk. Satisfied?" I said, dancing around the bag.

Bill couldn't let it go. "So are you going to see him again, or did you scare the hell out of him?"

"I have no plans of seeing him again. It's best to leave well enough alone." I said, throwing a hard right.

He shook his head in disappointment. "Hard ass."

I gave a grunt, planting a fist on the bag. "That's kind of like the pot calling the kettle black, isn't it?"

Bill walked around to the other side of the bag holding it steady. "He's a good guy. He's good for you."

I cut an icy glare in his direction. Bill expelled a deep sigh. "Boxing's over, kid. You need to think about settling down and starting a family."

I stopped punching the bag. "Oh, really? So let me get this right. You think I should spend more time with the doctor because he's husband material?"

Bill read the ire growing in my voice and turned his head, muttering, "A husband wouldn't be the worst thing."

The words sent me reeling, close to rage. How dare he try to run my life when it was obvious he couldn't run his own. I gave the bag a hard punch from my left fist. Bill braced himself. I followed with a right jab.

"Maybe I want to be like you, Bill," I exclaimed, throwing another right."Maybe I want to string a guy along for what, fifteen or twenty years? Sneaking around, hiding, grabbing a bit when I can."

A combination left and right landed against the bag forcing the trainer to hold on tighter. I stopped punching and threw a harsh look at the man on the other side. "Tell me, Bill, when you going make an honest woman out of Shirley Dobbs? Heck, we can have a double wedding. Or is using her, what does it for ya? That's what every man wants, right? Either use 'em, abuse 'em, or lose 'em."

I went too far. Bill's cheeks splotched a bright red hue with the hazel eyes growing cold. "Don't you ever throw me in that mix again. I'm not Brad and neither is Dillon. It'd probably best if he leaves you alone 'cause you don't want to get your head out of the past."

He released the bag and walked away.

A ton of bricks weighed down on me. I attacked the one person who always stood beside me. "Damn it!"

Bending over to catch a breath with hands on my knees, I called out, "I'm sorry, Bill. I didn't mean it. It's me. I don't know how to deal with this."

He came about. "Deal with what, Jake?"

I shook my head and waved in the air. "Everything. It's all changing."

Bill grabbed a stool and took a seat. He searched the ceiling, drawing in a deep breath and blowing it out. "I know it's not easy for you, Jake. Taking it out on me shows you still have that survival instinct. Hell, you're right. I shouldn't be telling anyone else how to live his or her life. I just want you to be happy. You deserve to be happy."

"I am happy."

Bill snorted."Bullshit. You're just good at pretend-ing."

I sat down in front of him and hugged my knees. "I don't know what's wrong with me. I feel just like I did the first time I came in here except I'm not angry, just confused. I don't know what I'm supposed to do, Bill. Every day for twelve years I trained, fought, went to school, and took care of Gran and Katie. I didn't have time to think about anything else."

I eyed my best friend. "I know Dillon Lawrence is a good guy and it scares the hell out of me. How do I move forward when I don't know where I'm going? I can't get the past out of here," I said rubbing my temple.

Bill rubbed my shoulder. "You can't get it out, not completely. You just got to remember it can't hurt you. It's over and done."

He leaned forward clasping hands between knees, searching my face. "When you first told me about Brad, I understood, but it's time to let it go."

Bill reached out capturing the braid hanging over my shoulder and tugged. "You can't keep throwing the entire male population into the same mix with the Brads of the world. Dillon's not going to hurt you. Stop worrying about what you should do or not do."

I stood placing gloves on my hips. He spoke the truth. Whenever I look at a man with the exception of Bill, I could see hidden agendas, plotting, waiting to blind side me. I didn't want to become an unsuspecting victim, drawn into their web of pain.

I went back to the bag and ran a glove across it. "What if you're wrong about him?"

Bill appeared in front of me. He spoke softly with love clearly in his voice. "What if I'm right?" One of his callused hands caressed my cheek. "Kid, I've seen you walk into a ring with more confidence than anyone I ever trained. Don't doubt yourself now."

Bill left me alone with a lot to think about. I wrapped my arms around the bag relaxing against it. I was so tired. Tired of punching the bag, tired of fighting the past, and tired of fighting to keep people away. Maybe Bill and

Katie were right. It's time to start trusting and living life instead of running from it. I wish I could convince myself it was the right thing to do.

14

The weekend brought the Fourth of July on Sunday. Washington celebrated by adorning buildings with decorations keeping in the red, white, and blue theme. Spectators observed many different crafts demonstrated from candle making to blacksmithing. Many folks took advantage of the tours of the historical building running every hour.

The small town did not boast fireworks due to the risk of a fire outbreak. Instead, officials set up an old-fashioned town social beside the historic courthouse. A wooden dance floor lay over the grass in anticipation of dancers taking advantage of the musicians preparing to play once the sun sank cooling off the humid Arkansas air.

Tom and Bud Jackson sat in their horse drawn buggies in the street separating the courthouse from a building once occupied by a pioneering lawyer. I found a place on the porch of the old hotel watching Josh and Ali ride away in Tom's carriage. Katie climbed into Bud's with the boy who sat with Josh at the softball game a few weeks prior.

He was cute with sandy blonde hair peeking out from under a white cap and appeared to be the same age as Josh. Katie saw me staring. I lifted a brow of concern. She waved then disappeared when the buggies pulled around and crossed the street in the direction of the blacksmith shop. I made a mental note to quiz her later.

A voice called my name. Adell Williams stood to the side of the hotel with a group of her society friends. "Jake, you plotting to steal one of those buggies?"

I wished her neck were inside my hands. I forced a smile replying, "Not today, Ms. Adell."

Laughter undulated with the local alderwoman leading the pack away.

"I think the penalties for horse theft are harsher than grand theft auto around here," came from behind.

I whipped around. Even with hair pulled tight behind his head, Dr. Dillon Lawrence was handsome in his jeans and plain white tee-shirt. A smile crept across my lips for a moment before fading. The short red-haired school secretary, Teyla Martin, stood at his side with a camera hanging around her neck. A twinge of jealousy waved. I wrinkled my nose scolding such behavior.

"Taking some good shots?" I said, pointing at her camera.

"I got a real good one of that old Magnolia tree a few blocks away. Mrs. Morton says you're a history hound. It's the largest Magnolia in the state, right?" she said.

I confirmed her information correct. An awkward moment passed. I shifted my weight uncomfortably then remembered the injured grandfather. I raised meeting Dillon's dark eyes forgetting, for a moment, the question that entered my head. "How…how's your father? Josh said he had an accident," I stuttered.

Teyla injected, "Oh, your father had an accident? What happened?"

Dillon's gaze lingered on me. "He fell going out the back door and broke his hip." A smile creased with a light chuckle escaping. "He's trying to persuade me he doesn't need to move to Hope, so that tells me he's going be fine."

I was lost in his hypnotic stare until Teyla drew me back to reality. "Are you ready for school to start next month?"

I ran a hand across my cheek, trying to smooth away

the trance and shrugged. "Yeah, I suppose so. I think we have a workshop on the twenty-fifth, don't we?"

"That's right," she said.

"I'm sure it'll be interesting going from fighting in the ring to fighting teens to learn," I said.

She nodded agreement. "I think you'll be just fine. Most of the kids'll probably be afraid to tangle with a former boxer."

I surveyed Dillon's face for a disapproving reaction to the mention of my former profession. None came.

"I want to get a picture of the hotel. Do you mind standing beside Dillon," Teyla asked.

I really didn't want to pose. "Maybe you should take one with just Dr. Lawrence," I said, taking a step away.

A hand grasped my elbow guiding me backward.

"Oh, come on, smile. In case you've forgotten, my name's Dillon," he said.

I gave in.

After the photo, Teyla excused herself wanting to take a few more shots of the other buildings. "I'll see you later Dillon. Thanks for being my tour buddy."

She strolled to the nearby lot where a woman demonstrated candle-making.

My boots shuffled toward the steps. "New friend, or are you just a player?"

A light laugh rumbled close to me. Too close, in fact. If I had turned around, my face would have hit his chest.

"New friend, I guess. Met her at your graduation party and ran into her at the gift shop. We were on the same tour."

I distanced myself from the doctor by moving down the steps. "Maybe she likes you. You should cook for her."

I heard a chuckle from behind. "No, I think she's batting for the other team."

I turned around puzzled. "Huh?"

Dillon placed hands in his pockets stepping off the porch. "She asked a lot of question about you. Like are you single, do you have any kids. I think you have a new admirer."

I snorted, "Maybe she wants the four-eleven on her competition." My eyes grew to saucers when the words came out of my mouth.

"So I'm the prize catch." Dillon grinned.

I blushed. "That didn't come out right."

"Never had women competing. Kind of puts a little giddy up in my step," he said.

"I'm going to check on Cora Mae, to see if she needs some help closing the restaurant. Enjoy your evening."I scurried off in the direction of Williams Tavern.

Dillon caught up to me. "Mind if I walk with you?"

The point of walking away was to escape humiliation. I thought, *yes I do mind*, but I just shook my head.

"I had a good time last Saturday," he said.

I hoped he wouldn't bring up the dinner. I kept ahead of him slightly. "It was nice, thank you."

"Sorry I didn't call you. I had to leave pretty early Sunday. I should have called after I got Sam settled," he said.

Did he think I waited by the phone with bated breath? I rolled my shoulders, replying, "I didn't expect you to call."

"You didn't. Why?"

"You asked me to dinner, I came, we ate, and that's that." I crossed the street stepping onto the wood plank sidewalk.

"Is that your subtle way of saying it's never going to happen again?"

My gut instinct wanted to snap, no, I'm not ever going out with you again. I answered with, "I'm just saying I didn't expect you to call."

"I really like this place. You can feel the history. You live close by right?"

I was thankful he changed the subject.

"A mile southwest."

"So I guess you've toured all of the buildings probably a hundred times."

"A few," I replied.

"Looks like folks are setting up chairs. You planning on hanging around and listening to the music?"

"Yeah."

"Do you like music?"

"Yes."

He laughed. "Okay, since you're so chatty, let me guess, you like hard core mosh pit head banging music."

I targeted my vision on the tavern a few yards away. "I guess you have me pegged."

He ceased walking. I gazed over my shoulder and wondered why he stopped. He wore a wide grin shaking his head.

"What?"

He clasped his hands over his head then lowered them to his side. "I thought we were beyond the snappy short answers."

Cora Mae Jackson's voice rang out. "Well, Lord have mercy."

I broke away from his penetrating stare in time to see the elderly woman rounding the building struggling to carry three lawn chairs. Dillon and I rushed to her side, taking the bulky items.

"I'm glad to see the two of you. That good-for-nothing man of mine was suppos' to help me," she said, handing over the chairs.

The three of us walked across to the courthouse lawn setting the chairs upright. The carriages arrived at the same time delivering the four teenagers. Cora Mae yelled to her husband and son. "Ya'll need to stop fooling around and park those buggies. I've been waiting for some help with the chairs."

Bud shouted back. "I'm tryin' to hurry up, old woman."

"That old fool's crazy. He don't know who he's talkin' to," she said, taking her seat. "I may be old, but I can still whoop him."

This brought a hearty laugh from Dillon.

I spotted Teyla taking pictures of the buggies and teens before heading toward the parking lot. I felt a little sad for her. She was new and alone yet if she were batting for the other team, I didn't want to encourage it.

Katie passed by. I took her arm and moved away from the crowd. "Who's the new friend?"

She shifted adoring eyes toward the boy standing several feet away. "Clint Anderson just moved here from Texas. Real gangster, Jake. Cattle rustling, stagecoach robbery. I think he's planning on getting me a job in a saloon."

I released her and handed over the keys to Gran's Cadillac. "Ask Clint to help you with the chairs. Then we can all sit together."

Katie gave a wicked grin. "I'm not sitting with you and Gran. We'll be close by in case you wanna watch me work my mojo. Might learn something, Jake." She wiggled her brows motioning her head toward Dillon Lawrence.

I gave her a playful push. "Just get the chairs."

Dillon tossed his keys to Josh, ordering the same.

"Sit with us, Dr. Lawrence. Plenty of room," Gran said.

He smiled at me. "Only if you call me Dillon, Mrs. Parker."

"Pull that chair over here by me, Doc. I'll tell you all ya need to know about everything unless you want to sit by Jake," Cora Mae said, with a flirty bat of her eyes.

He winked at the elderly woman. "She is single, and your husband might not appreciate me taking up all of your time."

Cora Mae smiled. "Oh, go ahead, Doc. We'll talk some other time."

Dillon and I unfolded chairs. I turned my face away from Gran and Cora Mae. "Did the three of you rehearse that?"

Dillon chuckled. "Nope. Great minds think alike."

We took our seats listening to the first group playing bluegrass music. I scanned the area keeping an eye on my sister. Katie, Clint, Ali, and Josh lay on a blanket several yards away.

Several times, Katie caught me staring. After several songs passed with no conversation, a shoulder bumped mine. "I don't think she's going anywhere," Dillon asked.

I huffed with humor. "Never know about Katie."

Dillon crossed one leg resting his ankle on his knee. "I look at them and think, man, to be that age again, no worries, not a care in the world."

"I never had the luxury," I whispered.

Dillon gave a nod. "That's right. You were in the boxing ring. Didn't have time to be, what did you call it, Debbie Dater?"

I released a short laugh. "Right."

"So how about we recapture our youth, go out to dinner, a real restaurant or maybe a catch a movie?" Dillon said.

"Good to see you, Doc."

We both turned finding Bill with Shirley Dobbs in tow. Bill extended a hand shaking Dillon's and introduced Shirley.

Shirley waved in my direction. "Hi, Jake."

It was the first time they appeared in public together as an official couple. I waved back. "Hey, Shirley."

I raised a surprised brow at Bill. He nodded and held Shirley's chair for her to sit down.

The sun disappeared behind clouds shading the night from the rising moon. Lights illuminated the dance floor casting a soft glow. Our group of family and friends chatted listening to the music through two different bands. Dillon sat to my left conversing with Bill and Shirley. I listened to Gran and Cora Mae commenting on the old days when the festival was larger with more activities.

"Young folk just don't know how to have a good time anymore," Cora Mae said.

Gran agreed. "If it's not that headache loud screaming music, video games or some of those stunt shows, they don't want no part of it."

I shook my head listening to their version of how bad the new generation was becoming.

The next group was younger. They played renditions of songs heard on the local pop stations. Although some of the older crowd felt annoyed by the music, the teen crowd enjoyed the change.

I felt a presence close to me. "So do you dance?"

I formed the word, "no," but never managed to get it out of my mouth.

My eavesdropping grandmother said, "Why yes, Dillon she does. I spent good money driving her to Texarkana for ballet lessons once a week for two years."

The revelation surprised the doctor. "Oh, really?"

I searched the ground wishing people would stay out of my business.

Katie and Clint made their way onto the dance floor. Her chin lifted upwards giving way to flirtatious blue eyes captivating her dance partner. I studied the couple for a while, envying my sister's innocence and trusting soul.

The song changed to a slower pace. A hand brushed mine, grasping and pulling me upward.

I protested. "Trust me, Dr. Lawrence, you don't want to do this." I balked.

He was unaffected by my hesitance. "I think we can manage, and the name is Dillon."

I glanced back to the area where we once sat noting the approval shining on Gran's and Bill's faces. The toe of my boot hit something hard. I stumbled going from grass to wood. The doctor caught me around the waist, steadying my feet. My palm landed on his upper arm. The contact surprised me. I let go quickly.

He kept his hand on my waist urging an unwilling dance partner to stand in front of him. I wasn't sure what to do. I reached out to rest a hand on his shoulder but drew it back before touching him. He grasped it and placed it on his shoulder. We started moving slowly. My eyes went directly to the floor, concentrating on footwork and feeling awkward.

"Ballet lessons?" he said.

"It improves balance."

"So what do you think?" he questioned.

"I think it helps," I replied.

"No, not about ballet. Dinner or a movie? Yes, no, maybe?"

I stumbled slightly.

The wide hand on my waist caught me and edged our bodies closer. Warmth hit my cheeks feeling his chest inches away.

He bent his head to my ear. "Relax, I'm not going to bite."

The breath on my cheek sent a shiver down my spine. I drew my face away, listening to a hint of amusement escape his lips. Intimidation was my field of expertise.

Now I understood how it felt to be the recipient of such tactics.

I became a little miffed knowing he enjoyed watching me squirm. Taking control of the situation, I deliberately stepped on his foot. This brought a healthy laugh from the doctor. He pulled me closer.

I froze when our bodies touched. He took on the task of dragging me around the floor. Fingers massaged the back of the hand held in his. It was too intimate.

I drew in the scent of his cologne. God, he smelled good. The beat of my heart quickened sending more heat to an already flaming face. I tried to distract my mind unsuccessfully. Finally, my feet found the beat of the music and glided across the floor.

My eyes attempted to betray me wanting to peer up to find the stare I knew bore down. I couldn't let him see the visible unchartered emotions of desire present. It would be the worst weakness I ever allowed someone to witness.

"Jake?"

The way my name slipped from his mouth with the gentleness of a caress beckoned my head around lingering each movement until I found his face. A small lift of his high cheeks delivered a peaceful smile lulling me to a place wondering what if. What if he's genuine? What if there were no hidden agendas? What if I gave in and let myself take a chance on him?

"You're a pretty good dancer," he said.

I became lost in the dark pools that had a way of holding me hostage. Everything inside begged, walk away before it's too late. I didn't listen.

For the remainder of the dance, neither of us spoke but held each other's attention and forgot others moved about the floor. When the song ended, I stepped away knowing something wordlessly transpired between us.

"Thanks for the dance," he said, leading me back to

our seats.

I managed a nod choosing to remain quiet.

I sat in the chair next to him the rest of the evening trying to understand. Things were happening inside me, frightening things. All my adult life I lived by strategically blocking emotions I considered weak. Giving in to mental and physical distractions had no place in the heart of a boxer or my life, for that matter. For me, everything was about experience, strength, and control. All three took a good thrashing. This was not me, not Jake Conner, the world champ.

It was after ten when the party broke up. Dillon insisted on helping carry the chairs to Gran's car. I objected making it clear my capabilities. He ignored my protest and took them anyway.

Bill and I lagged behind the others. "Okay, Jake, let's have it. I know you wanna say something about me and Shirley."

I was not about to say a word. I knew it would bring comments from Bill about Dillon and me. I shook my head letting a sly grin build. "No I think we should save our comments for another time."

I discovered Katie, Clint, Josh, and Ali were riding together to the farm. It wasn't easy watching her get into the truck without me there to look out for her. I made a move toward her, then stopped. She would be okay, I reasoned. Ali and Josh were with her.

"Dad?" Josh called out while getting into the back seat of Clint's extended cab truck. "I'll be home later." The doctor waved his approval.

Saying good night, he turned to leave. Gran stopped him. "Dr. Lawrence, the kids are going to hang around for a while. I'm tired. Why don't you stop by and help Jake chaperone?"

I wanted Gran, Bill, and Katie to stop pushing. A

small part of me wished he would say yes, a part prayed he wouldn't. In the end, he agreed to stop by the farm.

During the ride home, Gran's phone rang.

"Call me in the morning," she said.

"Who was that?"

"Katie. She's spending the night with Ali."

I pressed the brakes. "What? They are supposed to come to the house."

Gran said nothing. I kept shifting my concentration between the road and Gran. The light came on in my head. This wasn't about a change of plans letting Katie spend the night with Ali. It was a set up. Dillon followed us to the farm expecting the four teenagers. When he arrived with no kids in sight, what would he think?

"What are you doing, Gran?"

"Nothing."

At least I knew where Katie got that coy, Who me? look.

I drove on, fuming over the humiliating situation. When the car stopped inside the garage, Gran hopped out and rushed to the back door. "I'm tired. See you in the morning."

"Wait. Gran…"

I unbuckled the seat belt, hitting my knee on the dash trying to exit the car to catch up with her. She was in the kitchen and up the stairs before the driver's side door shut. For a woman of sixty-nine, she sure could move fast. I limped from the garage into the yard, rubbing my aching knee.

A car entered the driveway turning out its lights. I hobbled to the front porch, cursing.

The doctor emerged from the shadows into the lit area. "Where's the kids?"

I wanted to strangle the woman upstairs for setting me up to be alone with him. I sunk onto the steps hanging my head. "Katie called, and there's a change of plans. They're at Ali's. I'm sorry."

He took a seat on the porch beside me with some distance between us. "Oh. So what's wrong with your leg?"

"Hit it on the car. I'll live." I said.

An uncomfortable, thick tension filled the air. I decided to break it. "Did you get a chance to tour all of the buildings?"

He nodded with a brief run down and his enjoyment of the historical facts.

"You should try the diamond mine next," I said.

He shifted in my direction. "One of the nurses at the hospital told me about it. Maybe we could go together sometime."

It had been many years since I dug for the diamonds in the freshly plowed fields located in the neighboring town of Murfreesboro. Gran took Katie and me the second summer we spent on the farm. Every year prior to my busy career, we made the annual digging for diamonds pilgrimage a ritual.

"Maybe." I stretched my arms resting them on my knees.

It was quiet again. We sat on the porch serenaded by the clicking of crickets and the distant croaking of a frog in the country night air. Sluggo grazed close to the barn and gave a snort.

"You have a horse?" Dillon asked.

"I bought Sluggo for Katie's thirteenth birthday. Come on." I stood, motioning for him to follow.

Passing though the barn door, I flipped on an overhead light. I made my way across the straw-scattered ground, pushing open the adjacent door.

Once outside, I whistled for the horse. The clouds scattered allowing partial light from the moon to shine on the dark beauty coming toward me. Dillon stepped from behind me rubbing the horse's nose.

"She's a fine-looking animal. She ride good?"

"Yeah, gentle. Do you ride?"

"Long time ago."

The horse grew tired of the attention and pulled away, nudging the ground. We watched her for a while.

Dillon inhaled sharply. "It's quiet around here."

"I come out here sometimes at night just to think," I said.

"About boxing?"

I smiled. "No, about a lot of stuff."

I felt him move closer to me.

"Jake, I'm going take Bill's advice."

I raised my chin toward him. "What advice?"

"Don't give you a choice. Just do it." Dillon placed a hand on my jaw and leaned down, brushing his lips against mine.

A mixture of panic and yearning came over me. Everything I experienced over a lifetime warned me to push away. Bill's words echoed in my head. What if I'm right? I took the huge step out onto the proverbial limb by returning the kiss.

The moment began and ended in the same way, slow and gentle. Dillon raised his head from mine and took a step back.

I felt perplexed. I didn't realize a frown was present until the doctor took an additional step backward.

"Do you want to punch me now?" he asked.

"No."

I took a few steps away, staring out onto the dark pasture. End this now, experience said. I feel sorry for you missing out, Katie's voice reminded.

"I'm not sure about the etiquette or what you expect from me," I said.

Dillon stayed in his place."I have no expectations. But I want to be honest."

I turned, looking into the dark where I knew he stood. "About what?"

He walked into the stream of moonlight. "I told you I wanted to be friends. I do, but truth is I want to be more than friends."

The next words out of my mouth could have put an end to the whole thing, but they didn't come. "I've never had the boyfriend experience. I made one stupid, inebriated mistake when I was a teenager. I've regretted it ever since. I can't promise you anything but I'm willing to try."

He sighed."Fair enough. No pressures, no expect-ation. I'm on call for the next two weeks straight. Would it be okay if I called you? Then when I'm off rotation, we go out to dinner or maybe a movie."

Say no, sense and sensibility cried. I ignored it. "Yeah, I'd like that."

"It's getting late. I need to head back to Hope," He said.

I walked him to his car. He didn't try to kiss me again, but said his goodbyes, leaving me to think about the can of worms I had just opened.

15

A good bit of Summer had already passed. Each day pivoted my life in a direction I never imagined. Although the surrounding world evolved, my mind had a difficult time catching up. A few short months ago, I was in complete control of my life and emotions. I didn't allow daydream fantasies. My beliefs were simple. What's in front of me was real, anything else, dimwitted and foolish inclinations. I was, Jake Conner, boxer, sister, granddaughter, and student. I didn't date. I saw no man in my future nor wanted one.

I betrayed myself by letting one man in particular seep into my thoughts. It happened more at night when the house was quiet while lying in bed lingering between the dusky haze of consciousness. He crept inside my head with images of the ever present smile speaking my name in a whisper. Every day, a constant battle raged between the strong desire to allow Dillon Lawrence inside my closed off world and the berating refusal pulling my feet back to the earth.

It would have been easier to combat the tug of war if he never called. But he did. True to his word, the phone rang several times over the days following the Fourth of July weekend. We managed to stumble our way through light conversations.

My sister added to the pain. Every time Dillon called, she made a point to torture me with sly comments until I got mad or Gran demanded she stop. One afternoon, I walked through the back door hearing Katie speak into the phone. "You know, Dr. Lawrence, since you're calling the house in a non-professional manner I think you can answer the question you keep avoiding. Boxers or briefs?"

A few seconds passed then Katie giggled. "Oh, come on. I won't laugh. Which one?"

I grabbed the phone out of her hands wanting to thrash the little brat while apologizing to Dillon.

During the time, Angela Romano also phoned Bill letting him know the papers were ready to sign exchanging ownership of the Chicago gym to Carter Neal. I volunteered to manage Bill's gym for the two days he was gone.

The first morning fell on a Thursday. Gran and Katie planned to leave later in the day to attend a softball tournament held in Little Rock over the weekend. I had hugged my grandmother the night before, instructing her to be careful during the trip.

I made it to the gym before six preparing for patrons arriving for their morning workout. With a bottle of water in hand, I kicked back in Bill's chair reading the local paper.

The music blared throughout the place. I moved my head to the beat noting nothing new for the little town of Hope.

Between six-thirty and seven o'clock, the place grew crowded. I recognized a few faces and spoke to them. Josh and the boy named Clint were among the patrons. Neither saw me approach. I took them by surprise greeting from behind.

"Hello, boy's, getting ready for football season?"

Clint took a few steps back. I thought his reaction strange. We were never formally introduced, but he moved away in obvious fear.

Josh laughed at his friend's retreat. "She's all right Clint, Katie exaggerated."

I furrowed my forehead holding out a hand. "Nice to meet you Clint. What did Katie tell you?"

Clint cautiously grasped my hand. "Just that you're very protective."

Josh laughed loudly. "Insanely protective. She told him you'd beat him up if he stepped out of line."

"Well, that little angel," I mouthed sweetly, between firm lips.

A mischievous plot brewed inside with a grin growing across my face. It was time to get even with my sister for all the abuse dished out over the summer. I located my phone in the back pocket of my shorts and flipped it open. "Let's have some fun with dear little Katie, shall we, gentlemen?"

They grinned with eager participation and followed me to the office with the plan explained. It was seven thirty.

Katie's sound asleep I thought, chuckling to myself. I rang her cell phone, putting her on speaker.

She answered in a groggy voice for all to hear. "Hello?"

I handed the phone to Josh and began screaming at Clint. "You good for nothing little punk. Think you can take advantage of my little sister. I'll show you, Clint."

I smacked a fist into my open hand close to the phone. The young man acting along responded, "Stop. Stop!"

Josh put his mouth close to the phone. "Katie, she's gonna kill him."

Stifling bouts of laughter, we heard Katie's voice franticly screaming, "Oh, my God. Oh, my God. Make her stop. Stop it, Jake!"

I grabbed the phone. "I'll stop when you stop."

All three of us were howling with laughter. Colorful words escaped my sister on the other end of the phone. I turned off the speaker holding the phone against my ear. She whined, "You know I have a long drive to Little Rock and have to play. You're mean Jake. Just plain mean."

"Like I said, pay backs are a bitch, dear sister. Oh, and don't use me to bully your boyfriends," I said and hung up.

It took a while for the three of us to stop laughing. The two teens left around nine with things slowing for the rest of the morning.

The girl I recognized as Holly, came in with her daughter around one o'clock. She was a cute little light brown-headed girl with dimples in both cheeks and a big smile.

She walked up and said, "Hi."

I bent down. "Hi, I'm Jake. What's your name?"

She twisted her rear. "Sadie."

"How old are you, Sadie?"

"I'm four," she said, holding up a hand to show me four little fingers before running back to her mother.

I watched her for a while thinking about Bill's words of starting a family. Katie was so young when Mom died, I felt I already raised one child.

After closing the gym, I went home to a quiet, empty house and watched a little television. Around nine, Dillon called.

"Josh said Bill's out of town, and so are Katie and Mrs. Parker. I'm just checking to make sure you're all right."

It was exactly what I feared would happen, letting a man in just a little. Someone wanting to run my life.

"I'm fine and yourself?" I answered, somewhat irritated.

"Tired, actually. Did a couple of back-to-back surgeries," he replied, ignoring my tone. "I'm off tomorrow night. I was wondering if you wanted to grab dinner and a movie since you're on your own, or we could go for a drive on my bike. I've been itching to ride."

My first thought was to decline and end further pursuit, convinced it would only end badly. Lately, the voice of reason was drowned out by something inside pushing me to ease up. I recalled Gran left food in the freezer.

"Okay, but I really don't feel like going to a restaurant. I have to lock up and won't be home until eight, so why don't you come to the farm and I'll cook this time?"

Laughter engulfed my ear. "You cook?"

I sat on the sofa wondering how he knew I couldn't cook. Katie, that little pain in butt, or Bill, must have been the informant.

"Fine," I said, with a little scowl. "You got me. I can't cook. Gran left pot roast in the freezer. I'll heat it up."

He agreed to the plan. "Sounds good. It'll give me a chance to ride my bike. See you at eight."

I turned out the lights, making my way up the stairs. How did I go from a boxer to a doctor's wanna-be girlfriend? If I were twenty years older, I could blame it on menopause. As it was, my only excuse was hormonal stupidity.

The second day managing the gym turned out to be much like the day before, slow and uneventful. Several times, anxiety coursed through my veins anticipating the visit from Dillon scheduled for later in the evening. At one point, I laid on a weight bench working my upper torso trying to burn up nervous energy.

At seven P. M., I started closing, trying to hurry and get home before my date arrived. I picked up a stray water bottle inside the women's dressing room and tossed it into the trash bin. I caught my reflection in the mirror. A disappointing shake expelled, "Diana Strauss has more self control than you ever thought about having. You are so stupid. End this crap tonight."

The sound of the front door shutting caught my attention. I moved to the doorway sticking my head outside shouting, "We're closing."

I picked up the few towels scattered about and tossed them into a nearby hamper. After a quick scan, the light went out, and I left the room. Passing the men's dressing room, I slipped a hand inside flipping the switch off before rounding the corner entering the area housing the boxing ring.

A shadow moved on the far side. I froze immediately realizing a person stood on the other side of the ring against the wall.

"We're closed," I said.

"I told you I wouldn't call again."

My mother shouted in my head, *Hurry, Jake, and hide*.

I took a step back feeling panic rising inside my chest. It was a hallucination. He wasn't real, I rationalized. But he was real. Every inch of the man with a black booted foot braced against the wall was real.

He pushed off stepping into the light. Brad hadn't changed much over the years. He was still a tall, stocky built man in shape, light mustache. He had blonde, thinning hair, with the same harsh look about him.

He released an all-too-familiar, evil laugh. "I'm a man of my word, Jake. I didn't call. What, no hug?"

I reverted to the kid hiding in the closet, afraid of the monster across the room. I took a few steps to the side. "You…you broke your parole coming here."

He laughed loudly, strolling toward the ring. I edged closer to the doorway leading into the workout area.

Run, Jake, hide, my mother's voice warned.

Running wasn't an option when it came to dealing with a natural born stalker. I swallowed hard pushing images of my beaten mother from my thoughts.

"Leave," I said.

He ducked his head but kept his eyes on me. "I'm not here to hurt you, Jake. I'm just checking to make sure you're okay."

Why didn't I listen to Bill and call Harvey?

"Leave now and I won't tell anyone you were here."

It was a lie. The cops were the first people to call.

"Why, that's so generous." His lips drew into a smirk.

What was I doing? A trained fighter didn't back away. They didn't retreat. "Just go and don't ever come back here and never contact me again, or I will call the cops and get a restraining order," I said, gaining courage.

"Time's made you hard, Jake, but looks like you've done well for yourself, all things considered. That's good." He moved closer.

I felt in my back pocket for my phone and remembered it lay on Bill's desk. I inched along the wall hoping to make it to the doorway. "Why did you send the picture and the flowers? What do you want, Brad?"

He gave a sick laugh that turned into black disdain. "You know me well, don't you? I'll tell you Jake, I can honestly say I didn't leave the state of Missouri 'til this morning. You should know by now, I have my ways."

His fist landed on the fast bag. I flashed to a scene with the same fists hitting my mother connecting with her beautiful face.

Stop it, please, she had begged so many times.

I fought to stay in the present. There was nothing between the door and me. The option to run was still there if I took it.

"What do you want?"

He curled his lips into a revolting grin. "I kept up

with you over the years. Saw all the pictures in the magazines. Boxing Sensation, Jake Conner, Wins Again. I wondered just how good is she? I got out just in time to catch your last fight on TV. What was the payout? A million and you've won it three times?"

"So?"

"That's what I want, my share."

"You're share of what?" I said, feeling my temper rise.

He took a step toward me. "I spent years rotting in that prison because of you."

He was insane. We both knew why he was locked up, and he deserved what he got and more.

"You put yourself there. They should've never let you out." I moved backward, touching the wall behind me easing a step to freedom.

His eyes narrowed. "You were always a pain in the ass, always screwing up my life. Don't know why I thought this would be easy."

My face was red and full of heat. "Your life? *I* screwed up your life? Do you really want to go there, 'cause I sure can set the record straight."

"The only thing I want to set straight with you is the fact I spent all those years behind bars because of you, and now you're going pay. I want one million for my trouble."

"You put yourself in jail, and you should have died in there. I owe you nothing," I shouted.

He snarled, "Yeah, you do. Get my money, or I take my disappointment out on that little girl you're calling sister and I think we both know how far I'll go."

All sense of fear disappeared hearing his threat against Katie. The thought of her in his head was enough to push me over the edge.

"I'm not that scared little girl anymore, Brad. You're not getting one cent from me, but I promise you this—go near her, and I'll kill you," I spat out with pure hate.

Brad shifted his head to the side. "Where she come from? Hmm. Is she yours?"

The exit was right behind me. I could have run but didn't. My blood boiled wanting to hit him. I clenched fists ready to make my stand. "Katie is none of your business."

His hand tightened at his side, and he closed the distance. "Get my money, or she will be."

I stood in full boxing mode, feet apart bouncing on the balls of my feet. My hands positioned ready to defend. He was less than five feet away with three inches in height on me. Arm reach would not be a problem. I spared with a few men taller than Brad.

He stopped his progress and started howling in laughter. "Oh, you gonna whoop my ass, Jake?"

My mouth was set so tightly, pain shot throughout my jaw. I hated him. He caused more misery in my life than any person should experience. "I don't want to fight you but I will. You're not getting any money so you need to leave."

He nodded never taking his eyes off me. "If that's what you want, I'll leave for now but who knows," he said, with a disdainful shrug. "I may decide to stick around town, and get to know sweet Katie."

I went blind with fury, losing control, forgetting everything Bill taught me. A high pitched scream flew from my mouth while swinging a left fist toward his face. It caught him on the chin, snapping his head back. I prepared to throw another punch when he whipped around returning one of his own connecting against my cheek. I tripped backward feeling another punch to my stomach and fell to the floor.

He hovered above me, delivering a swift kick to the ribs injured months before. The sharp pain crippled my body. He knelt down placing a knee in my chest, and his hand at my throat, squeezing my windpipe.

"You're the only problem I ever had. Bridgette and me would have been fine, but, no, you just had to keep on and on. You're the reason she's dead. I ought to just finish you right now."

I fought the hand on my throat until the pressured eased.

"I want my money."

He stood upright with the sound of the soles of his boots sliding a few steps away.

"Be smart like your Momma, Stay down. The next time I see you, you better have my money."

He was out the door. The sound of a motorcycle cranked and pulled away.

I lay on the floor remembering how many times I had seen my own mother in this same situation.

We never feel sorry for ourselves, Jake, she would say every time. I closed my eyes fighting back tears.

I rolled to my good side holding ribs tight drawing in a painful breath trying to rise to my knees.

"I'm not Momma," I whispered, forcing my body upward and staggering to the office I got my keys.

I locked the door behind me. I reached the car grasping onto the top for support while listening to the distant sound of the motorcycle and trying to judge the direction. Climbing inside, I slammed the shifter into gear knowing I had to find him and end his reign of terror. He wasn't coming near Katie nor would he ever treat me with the same methods he used on my mother and get away with it.

I searched the convenience store parking lots before racing toward the motels close to the freeway. I gave up after forty-five minutes realizing he could have driven to the other exits or possibly gotten on the freeway leaving town altogether. Katie and Gran were in Little Rock and safe for the moment. That was all that mattered.

I remembered Dillon coming to the farm. I called his phone to cancel the date. He wasn't answering. I cursed aloud speeding toward home.

On the stretch of highway in front of the municipal airport, cars halted.

Great, I thought.

If Dillon were already at the farm waiting on me, how would I explain my face? I was sure a bruise had formed on my cheek by now.

I pressed the brake letting road rage take root. No one was moving.

It was light out, but the sun faded fast. An ambulance and several police cruisers lined the highway a few feet from the intersection. I craned my neck to see what was going on. I got out, investigating, noting a car's hood and grill folded into the motor. There were two motorcycles, one upright on its stand near the turn and one lying twisted across the road. My heart sank thinking of Dillon. He mentioned riding his bike to the farm.

I squeezed between people gathered around the emergency vehicles. I saw Dillon on the ground. He appeared fine. He was lending his medical expertise to another person.

"How long before the chopper gets here?" he asked a portly paramedic looming above him.

"Five minutes out."

A state trooper blocked my view. I moved to the side, getting a full view of the person on the ground. My eyes trailed up to his face cringing at the amount of blood coming from his mouth and nose. Staring at the face, my eyes widened. On the pavement, lying in his own blood was Brad. He must have been on his way to the farm.

All my troubles would be over if he died. The past

would be over, Katie safe, and I would never have to worry about him again. Please God let him die.

A deep thumping bass sound filled the air indicating a helicopter circling low overhead. I inched closer.

Dillon, calm as ever, looked to someone I couldn't see. "Do you have epinephrine on board?"

The other person must have replied he did.

"Get it. His pressure's dropping," he said with a commanding voice.

For a second, I drew back to my childhood, visualizing Mom hitting a wall and landing on the floor in a lifeless heap.

Come here! Brad sounded in my head.

"No," I said softly. I pushed closer to Dillon. "No, let him die."

Dillon looked up and frowned.

"Let him die, Dillon," I said louder.

Sheriff Harvey Jones took my arm, pulling me back.

I shook him off. "Let him die!"

Dillon seemed puzzled by my reaction. He turned his attention back to his patient.

By now, everyone heard my demand, while being forced to back away. I struggled against Sheriff Jones screaming, "No, let the sick bastard die."

Harvey pushed me further away. "Jake, what the hell is wrong with you?"

Memories flooded me. My heart pounded wildly. I placed hands over my ears trying to quiet the crying and shouting in my head.

Where the hell you going, Bridgette? Get your ass back here. Brad please. Hide, Jake.

I began hyperventilating. I had to get out of there.

I jerked my arm from the sheriff's hold, and ran to my car.

Sweat washed over my face. My heart was beating so

fast, I expected it to burst through my chest at any minute. I mentally continued repeating, *Get to the gym and make it go away.*

I raced toward town while scenes of my childhood flickered each horrifying moment. Tires slid to a stop in front of the gym. I didn't take the time to lock the car but ran across the street pushing against the door. It remained shut, only to find the key had not completely turned in the lock.

Near panic, I twisted the key and flung the door open, reaching for the switch to turn on the dim light hanging above the bag in the back. I tore at my shirt, leaving only a spandex sports bra covering my chest. I stormed across the floor, letting bare knuckles pound the bag, and never let up.

Shut up, Brad screamed at my Mom.

Smack. The sound of his hands connecting with her face always followed with the thud of her body hitting a wall or floor. Every time it was the same. He degraded her, beat her, and kicked her to unconsciousness or until he tired, whichever came first.

Stay in your room, she instructed me.

I hid in the closet with hands or headphones over my ears trying to block the terrifying noises of someone thrown over furniture.

One time I left my room to help her. I put all a ten year old could into punching his stomach only to have him laugh throwing me over an end table hitting the wall dislocating my shoulder.

Stupid little bitch, he had laughed. *Get her the hell out of here before I slit both of your throats.*

I crawled on my knees, dragging my arm in agony, seeking refuge under the bed waiting for my mother. I lay there for hours.

When Mom found me, I cried moving from

underneath the bed with the pain throbbing in my shoulder. At the hospital, I lied as my mother had instructed, using the excuse of falling from my bicycle onto the pavement. They knew it was a lie. They saw the swelling on her face indicating something more had happened. Once my shoulder was set, we snuck out of the hospital climbing into the station wagon disappearing into the night.

I punched the bag feeling nothing not even the pain from the raw cuts collecting on my bare knuckles.

"Jake," Dillon called from the doorway

I kept hitting the bag.

"Jake!"

"Go away, Dillon. Go back to your patient."

He moved in long strides coming toward me. "What's going on?"

I wanted him to leave me alone. I wanted the memories to leave me alone. I wanted my mother back. I wanted Brad dead. I punched harder refusing to answer.

The usually composed doctor was angry. "What the hell was that back at the scene? You were screaming like a crazy person to let the poor guy die."

I said nothing but continued concentrating on the bag.

He latched onto my arm. "Answer me," he demanded.

I jerked from his grasp. I wanted to hit someone. I wanted to hit the psychotic pig he worked on. The doctor wanted to get in my face? Fine. I swung at his head in hopes of delivering a right to his clenched jaw.

He stepped aside letting me stumble forward, missing my target. Taking full advantage, two strong arms gathered around my chest, trapping my arms to the side.

"Let go of me, damn it." I bucked against him with my feet off the floor.

"Stop it, Jake."

An agonizing groan mixed with profanity escaped my

throat. I fought to get free. "Let me go," I demanded. I threw back elbows to his midsection to break the hold. He didn't budge.

His voice softened. "Stop, Jake. Stop it."

After several minutes of cursing, I gave one final kick releasing a shout of emotional pain. Everything in my life had been about fighting. The man I hated, the mother I loved. A vow to keep a secret to protect a sister…all sharing in the creation of an apathetic boxer struggling to understand what it was, I had done so wrong, for God to burden me with a life full of such misery.

I grew still letting tears flow freely. Dillon relaxed his grip. I sank wearily to the floor. I bent forward placing my head in my bloody hands allowing myself to cry the tears denied for so long.

Dillon knelt down behind me rubbing my shoulders. "Talk to me, Jake. Please let me help you. Talk to me. What happened back there?"

It was time to tell the truth. The secret was killing me. I couldn't take it anymore. I strained to form the words that desperately needed said.

Dillon remained behind my jerking body, pleading, "Jake, tell me what's wrong?"

Between sobs, I whispered. "He killed my mother."

Twelve years of rage and pain released with those four words. Crying even harder, I rocked back and forth. "He killed my mother."

I felt Dillon's arms go around me, pressing my back against his chest. "My God, Jake. Bill told me your mom died in a car accident. I didn't think about how seeing that wreck might bring back bad memories. I'm sorry," Dillon said.

He held me tight, letting me weep uncontrollably. We sat on the floor, holding each other for what seemed an eternity. The doctor never spoke only waited patiently until I was ready to talk.

"You don't understand," I said softly.

"Jake, I understand hurting."

I crawled forward away from Dillon taking a position facing him. I wiped my wet cheeks with the back of my hands, feeling the salt burning the cuts. I viewed the good doctor. He had no idea the man he gave medical attention to was an abusive psychopath.

Tears ran down to my chin. "You don't understand. My mother didn't die in a car accident. It's what we told everyone around here so Katie wouldn't find out the truth."

"Then tell me the truth," Dillon begged.

The corners of my mouth turned down trembling with sorrowful agony. "The guy on the bike, the one you helped, he's my *father*. He murdered my mother."

16

My earliest memory occurred while living in Dallas, Texas. I was about five years old at the time, sitting in my mother's lap moving back and forth in a rocking chair with my head resting against her chest. Brad came into the room. I was very much afraid of him and closed my eyes. He mentioned a party and asked my mother if she planned to change her clothes. She replied she wasn't going.

His voice was cold and angry, shouting, "The damn kid. Always the damn kid. Why don't you send her to your mother's?"

Momma was upset with him. "I'm not leaving Jake with a sitter, and I'm not sending her to live with my mother, either. She's your daughter. My God, Brad, she's running a hundred and three temperature. Aren't you the least bit concerned?"

His feet shuffled across the floor walking toward us. I squeezed my eyes shut tighter.

"What have I told you about that mouth? Huh?"

A dull popping sound rang out. The rocker moved backward. I opened my eyes in time to witness his wide hand snake out and strike Momma across the face for what must have been the second time.

He jerked her from the chair and hit her again. The force sent her staggering to the side. She dropped me. My body slid across the floor. The shirt rode up my back. My skin burned rubbing against the cold linoleum before coming to a stop near the kitchen doorway.

I looked up seeing his hand connect with her face

again and again. She crumpled to the floor beside me. A single perfect crimson drop of blood ran from her nose, staining the linoleum. Of all the things witnessed in my life, that one moment haunted me the most. It marked the beginning of the end.

My bottom lip trembled, observing the woman who nurtured me lying on the floor in pain.

"Mommy," I whispered.

Her blue eyes glistened with moisture growing larger in fear. "Hide, Jake. Hurry."

I crawled on hands and knees seeking refuge under the kitchen table, staying beneath it for protection.

No other sound was more distinct than flesh meeting flesh. My mother cried loudly each time the echo filled the house. She begged him to stop. After the sixth time, I lay my head against the floor pressing one ear to the tile and covering the other. I placed a thumb in my mouth squeezing eyes shut leaving the horror behind.

A while later, the front door slammed. I let my hand drop from my ear hearing nothing but gentle sobs singing an eerie melody ripping a hole in my young soul. I peeked through a veil of lashes waiting for reassurance the violence had ended.

Once confident that it was over, I crawled to the doorway staying against the wall peering around the corner into the living room. My mother lay helplessly in front of the rocking chair. Blood oozed from her nose and mouth with one eye prominently swelling.

"Mommy?" I called.

She motioned for me to come to her. I lay down next to her, burying my head in her chest trying to understand what had happened. What had I done to make him so angry that he hurt my mother?

"I'm sorry, Mommy," I said, between sobs.

She ran a hand over my hair. "Shhh, stop crying. This

isn't your fault. It's his. It won't always be like this. I promise," she said.

My body continued shaking. My mother captured my chin and raised it. "Stop crying, Jake. It doesn't do any good to cry. We never feel sorry for ourselves. You hear me? We never feel sorry for ourselves."

We didn't leave that night or the next time it happened. My mother took repeated beatings for over a year. There was no rhyme or reason, only because things did not go Brad's way.

It was after one beating in particular we finally left him. He came home. Mom and I sat at the kitchen table doing my homework. She hadn't started supper, and he was furious. He jerked me from the chair, shoving me away. I landed against the refrigerator.

"Get the hell out of here, and do your own damn homework. Then maybe your momma might have time to cook."

My mother pushed past him coming to my aid. "Don't you ever touch my daughter again," she warned.

He grabbed a hand full of her long blonde hair, slinging her over the table with the effort of throwing nothing more than a rag doll. I crawled away afraid I would be next.

My mother rose to her knees. He punched her in the jaw, sending her back to the floor. "We wouldn't have any problems if you would just send that pain in my ass to your mother's," he shouted. He came toward me.

My mother grasped the edge of the table holding on while reaching out, grabbing the tail of Brad's shirt.

"Hide, Jake," she ordered.

The last thing I saw before leaving the room was my father straddling my mother's body with his arm drawn back.

Hours later, I woke in the closet. My mother tugged

my arm.

"Jake? Come on, we've got to go," she said.

Crawling out, I noticing one of her eyes swollen shut, nearly the size of a baseball. She picked me up and carried me to our old station wagon, filled with piles of clothes and toys. I asked her where we were going.

"Away," was all she said.

I looked out the car window while Dallas faded into the dark. I was only six-and-a-half years old with the mindset of an adult and decided that night the man we left behind was no longer my father and glad for it. From that point on, I called him Brad seeing him only as the person who abused my mother.

The next morning, my eyes fluttered opened in Brownsville, Texas. Within three months, Brad found us. This became a routine, we ran, he found us. He kept his hands off my mother and I for a while but inevitably, the beatings began and we ran once again. Sulfur Springs, Texas; Shreveport, Louisiana; Bright Star, Arkansas; Oklahoma City, Oklahoma; Paris, Texas, and other places I've forgotten with St. Louis, Missouri, as our last home.

I considered the revolving way of life normal behavior. Mom trained me well. Whenever Brad found us, I went directly to my room or somewhere out of sight staying put until she came for me. No matter where we lived, we had an exit plan most of the time. I always kept a suitcase under my bed with the things I treasured most and another full of clothes in the back of the station wagon. I understood. We had to leave with very little time for gathering things.

With every new town, making friends was out of the question. I knew it was a matter of time before we would have to leave. I kept my head down at school and was labeled the weird kid. I didn't venture beyond our yard. My greatest fear was getting too far from the house and

Brad showing up, forcing Mom to flee without me.

My mother created a normal life when it was just the two of us. She was smart, and witty, and read constantly, mostly poetry with a particular admiration for D. H. Lawrence. The passion with which she read, somehow erased everything bad occurring in our lives.

She radiated intelligence expecting the same of her daughter. I went to school during the day and Mom taught me at night trying to keep me ahead of the class so I wouldn't fall behind during the times we were forced to move. Once a teacher gave me a placement test during my fifth grade year. I scored at the level of an eighth grader.

We lived in Paris, Texas, when I was twelve. The kind biker, Z lived across the street. He helped my mother so many times yet in the end, he couldn't save us from Brad. It was shortly after fleeing Paris and finding a new home in St. Louis, Missouri, my mother told me she was pregnant. I was excited by the thought of having a little brother or sister but at the same time, very much worried about Brad showing up hurting Mom because of another child he didn't want.

Katherine Glenn Conner came into the world on a late August afternoon. I was there in the birthing room with Momma. Being tall, the hospital staff thought me older and let me stay with her. I often joked with my mother about how I saw Katie before she did.

I fell in love with my sister upon first sight becoming overly protective immediately. My mother failed many times where Brad was concerned. I was the only person who could protect Katie from him and vowed to keep her safe no matter what came our way.

We lived in St. Louis for three years. Each passing day brought hope. It had been the longest we went without Brad discovering our whereabouts. My mother promised that if he did show, she would call the police. She never broke a promise and I was naïve enough to believe the police would save us.

It was heavenly watching Katie grow, seeing the world through her innocent eyes. I began to relax somewhat making friends with a few kids on our block.

An elderly woman named Mrs. Walters lived across the street. We tortured the woman by playing stickball in front of her house, letting a few balls land in her landscaped flowerbeds. She loved scolding the juveniles on the block to stay out of her yard. She called each one of us hooligans.

"You hooligans stay out of my yard or I'm gonna call the cops."

On August first, the day started like any other. It was summer with no school. Mom left for her waitress job that morning. At fifteen, I cared for Katie to save on daycare, and I wouldn't have had it any other way. I trusted no one to care for the soon to be three-year-old. Katie was my responsibility, or so I felt.

Around six, Mom usually arrived home from the job she referred to as, "slinging hash." Whether she ate with us or not, she always sat down to discuss our day.

I cooked in an effort to help my mother. Mac and cheese was the only thing I knew how to make without destroying the kitchen. It happened to be Katie's favorite. I noted the clock on the stove read five-thirty. Mom would be home soon.

I was helping my sister with her spoon when Momma crashed through the front door screaming for me to take Katie and hide. I didn't hear his motorcycle. I didn't have to. *Hide* was one word that confirmed our life of bliss was over. Through the large double windows in the living room, I saw a truck pulling into the drive with Brad getting out.

I panicked thinking of what he might do if discovered

he had fathered another child. With Katie in one arm, the bowl of Mac and cheese in the free hand, we went out the back door to the storage shed located a few yards from the house. It was the safest place to prevent him from hearing Katie jabbering and making noise. I walked down the steps staring at Katie apologetically. I never wanted her to live in the same traumatic world where I grew up. I vowed, pushing the worn door to the side, Brad Conner was not ever touching my sister.

Flipping the switch, the dim light came on. I searched for a weapon and found an old broom handle. I carried it along with Katie to the far corner of the shed. The two of us crouched together. I continued feeding my sister the Mac and cheese while keeping surveillance on the door.

My mother shouting from the kitchen demanded he leave.

Brad yelled, "Call the cops. Here let me help you dial the number, and you'll be dead before they get here."

I didn't consider myself a child. I was fifteen going on fifty. I wanted so bad to leave the shed to help her, but I couldn't abandon Katie.

The sounds coming from the house clearly indicated the fight had begun with furniture being overturned and a person hitting the wall. My mother let out a bone-chilling scream.

Katie stopped eating hearing the shrill. Her frightened eyes collected tears with a lip quivering. "I want Mommy."

"Shhh, it's okay, Katie," I consoled, kissing her hair. "Someday when I'm older and stronger we'll never have to hide again, I promise."

Footsteps running across the living room floor brought me erect. I sat Katie down and walked to the shed door to peek out. The sound of the front door hitting the wall with the screen door slamming soon after. I could hear the fight escalate outside.

Good for you Mom, I thought, *let the neighbors see and call the cops.*

I ventured further out the door looking back to Katie. "Stay here. I'll be back."

I stepped out of the building securing the door behind me making my way to the corner of the house. Muffled cries started inside the shed followed by light pounding. "Jake. Let me out. I don't like it in here, please, come get me."

I ignored Katie's loud wails placing my face against the side of the house easing around the corner. Mom took off, running down the road. Brad's truck started almost immediately.

Katie continued to pound on the door wanting out. I was torn between going back for Katie and following my mother.

I couldn't stop myself. I ran around the front of the house scanning the street in the direction where Mom ran. She was two houses away. The truck pulled from the driveway spinning gravel. Brad produced a smug grin on his face staring directly at me.

The neighbors along the block came out of their houses watching the event unfold. I later discovered Mrs. Walters had called the police.

Running down the street four houses away with the truck on her heels, Mom turned to go into the ditch. She never made it. The truck sped up connecting with her hip. I froze unable to process what I just witnessed. Every woman, man, and child on the block watched her body roll under the front and rear tires run over her mid-section. I forgot about Katie and ran to my mother's mangled body.

I passed the truck hearing, "Run now, bitch," with a sarcastic laugh coming from Brad before he pulled away.

When I reached my mother, I sat down with blinding tears and held her hand. She turned her head toward me. I couldn't believe she was still alive. There was no hint of the pain she must have felt, only worry in her eyes.

"Don't cry, Jake. We never feel sorry for ourselves. Remember?" she whispered. The last words she uttered were those from the D.H. Lawrence's poem of Self Pity. 'I never saw a wild thing sorry for itself, a small bird will drop frozen from its bough never having felt sorry for itself.'

She smiled and then her lips relaxed.

By now, the whole neighborhood gathered around with sirens in the distant. I knew she was gone and nothing was going to bring her back. Remembering Katie, I ran back to the shed, picked her up, and walked to the spot where we sat hiding from Brad. I fed her the cold Mac and cheese and felt nothing. A part of me always knew it would end like that. The only hope I carried was that if it happened, Brad would die, too.

It wasn't long before the door creaked open revealing Mrs. Walters and a police officer on the other side.

"Jake, let me take Katie," the elderly woman offered.

I was surprised she knew our names. I never spoke to the woman for the three years we lived across the street. I refused to release Katie. "No, I'm all she has and she's all I have."

I walked to the door with Katie attached to my hip. Mrs. Walters put an arm around me, leading my sister and me into the house with the officer close behind.

It was at the kitchen table, he questioned what happened. I left no details to mystery. "The man who hit her is Brad Conner, my father," I said with no emotions in my voice. "We've run from him for over ten years."

"Do you have any relatives?" he asked.

I recalled the metal security box Mom kept under her

bed. With Katie clinging to my body, I went into Momma's bedroom locating the box bringing it back to the kitchen.

I removed an address book flipping to the P's showing the officer the name MOM beside the entry of Chelsea Parker with a phone number.

"This is your grandmother," he inquired.

I nodded.

He explained he would call her from the station but for now, Katie and I had to go with another woman standing in the kitchen.

"She's from Social Services. We can't leave the two of you alone. You have to stay with the family she places you with until your grandmother arrives," he said.

I panicked. The thought of a grandmother, whom I never met, who might not even be alive, meant Katie and I would became wards of the state, foster children, and possibly separated.

"No, I can take care of Katie," I pleaded.

Mrs. Walters, the last person I expected to come to our defense, interjected, "I'll stay with them until their grandmother arrives."

The woman from Social Services said, "Ma'am, we don't know how long it may take to get in touch with her or if we can."

Mrs. Walters shook her head firm in her decision. "It doesn't matter. I'm not leaving the girls."

I never imagined the woman who yelled every day for the kids to get off her lawn was the same person standing before me vowing to step in and help my sister and me. The elderly woman never left our side that night. The next day, Gran arrived, packing our things, and moved us to Arkansas.

17

❡ never allowed myself to go completely back to the beginning of the nightmare called my life. I told Dillon more about my childhood than even Gran knew. I raised my head searching the face across from me filled with sympathy and shock.

"Regardless of the number of witnesses who saw my father chase my mother down and run over her, Brad managed to plea bargain a twenty-five year sentence. I guess that's what happens when you're poor. Get it over quick with the least amount of cost to the state," I said in disgust.

The look on Dillon's face was one that matched my own the day I watched my mother die, unable to comprehend the heinousness that happened.

Dillon's eyebrows raised in question. "How did you survive all this?"

"Boxing," I said.

I shifted positions looking at my bloody hands. "First time I met Gran was the morning after Mom died. I was hurting from losing Momma, pissed off Brad took her, and scared. I didn't know how Gran would treat us or even if she wanted us. I started using drugs and drinking, stole Tom's truck, and that's how I met Bill. He was part of my community punishment. If it wasn't for him, I don't think I'd have made it."

Dillon took my arm, pulling me to his chest. I squeezed my eyes shut, letting him comfort me in the way

I should have let Gran so many years ago.

"My God, Jake, I'm so sorry. I understand now," he said.

It was unnerving having someone feel sorry for me. I never felt sorry for myself.

"What do you understand?" I asked pulling away.

He brushed loose strands of hair from my face. "The toughness, why you're so skeptical."

"And stubborn. You forgot that one," I added.

I hugged my knees resting my head. "He came here earlier waiting on me to come out of the dressing room."

Dillon took one hand examining the abrasions. "What did he want?"

I felt tears building in my eyes once again. "Money. If I don't give him what he wants, he's going after Katie.

Dillon raised my chin. "Katie? What do you mean he'll go after Katie?"

"He knows she lives with Gran and me, and that I call her my sister. We left Paris before Mom knew she was pregnant. He didn't see Katie in St. Louis. He doesn't know she's his, but he knows she's important to me so he'll use her."

I searched the dark brown eyes realizing he did not comprehend the weight of pure evil carried inside Brad Conner. "He will do whatever it takes to get what he wants, no matter who he hurts or kills. Do you understand? He is a sick murdering bastard who doesn't give a damn if you're his wife or kid. He gets what he wants and will destroy anyone in his way."

"Then we've got to go to the police," Dillon said.

I gave a derisive snicker, and moved my face out of his grasp. "Do you think he's scared of the cops? My God, Dillon, he's been in prison for over a decade, and the first thing he does when he gets out is come after me. No. All I can hope for is that he's dead. Is he? Did he die?"

Dillon stood his full height pulling me to my feet. "He was alive when the chopper left. Come on, we need to clean these up before infection sets in. Do you have a first aid kit around here?"

We went into the office. I opened the metal cabinet getting a bottle of antiseptic. The courier package of pictures fell out. I shook my head, picking it up I tossed it back into the cabinet.

Dillon took a seat in Bill's chair. I perched on the corner of the desk, watching him clean my battered hands.

"How much does Katie know about your parents?" Dillon asked.

I shook my head watching the gentle hands examining my knuckles. "Nothing. Gran and I agreed to tell everyone around here Momma died in a car accident, and that's what we told Katie when she started asking about her. She asked me about her father when she was around nine. I told her he left us before Momma found out she was pregnant, and we never saw him again. Heck, after a while I tried to convince myself that's what happened."

He poured peroxide on the cuts several times allowing the chemical to bubble the abrasions. "Why didn't you tell her the truth?"

"Katie was never a part of it. I've lived my whole life with what happened. Katie deserves better."

"You're going to have to tell her, Jake."

I pursed my lips. "Not if he dies. If he lives, I hope he goes back to prison. There's no reason to tell her anything."

He dabbed the cuts with four by four cotton pads. "You need to tell her. She should hear this from you, not someone else."

I pulled my hands away. "Who's going to tell her? You?"

He took my hands and continued working on them.

"I'd never repeat something told to me in confidence. But, Jake, he's out and he knows about her. Don't you think she might get curious someday and run a search on the internet about him?"

I replied, "I don't know, maybe, I just… I just want to protect her for as long as I can."

He stopped working on the abrasions. "Is it the fact she's going to know he beat and killed your mother that worries you or are you afraid she'll ask questions about what you went through?"

I swallowed the emotions rising in my chest. "What I went through? I hid. My mother took the brunt of Brad's wrath. I don't want to tell Katie about the things I saw or heard. Why would I ever put those images in her head? I survived. That's all that matters."

When finished, Dillon applied antibiotic cream on the abrasions wrapping my now swollen hands. "I'll make a call. See if I can find out about his status. If he'll make it, you need to tell Katie the truth. From what you've said, if he came after you once, he'll do it again."

I didn't respond. He reached out touching my face. "I am so sorry this happened to you."

I pulled away not wanting to talk about it, nor did I want the pity shining from his eyes.

He placed a call to the Hope hospital asking one of his co-workers to inquire about the status of Brad with instructions to call him back.

"We need to get you home," he said.

I let him know my car was outside, and was able to drive myself.

"I don't think so. With your hands swollen and everything that's happened tonight, you're not driving," he ordered.

"You're on your bike, right? I wouldn't leave it on the street if I were you," I argued, trying to convince him to let me drive myself.

He took the keys to the gym ushering me out and locked the door. "We're riding it. Your car locked?"

I shook my head. He jogged across the street.

Standing with only the shorts and spandex bra covering my body, I shouted for Dillon to grab the extra tee shirt off the back seat. He locked the car, coming back, he placed the shirt over my head, and pulled it down.

He climbed on the Harley waiting for me to sit behind him. Trying to postpone getting on the bike, I said, "No helmets? I mean, you're a health driven man, right?"

"Get on," he said, jokingly, annoyed at my hesitancy while lowering the foot pegs behind him.

With a defeated grunt, I climbed onto the back holding on with my throbbing hands.

It took some time, but I finally understood. The man riding in front of me was a genuinely caring person. The proof was on his face in the boxing area listening to the gruesome details of the childhood from hell. No one can fake the sorrow he displayed.

The feel of the wind felt good blowing the hot humid air away from my body. Since I told Dillon the truth, the stress and pressures carried over a decade eased. New worries developed wondering if I were indeed rid of Brad or faced telling my sister the truth about our parents.

Dillon pulled the bike to a stop near the front steps of the farmhouse, into the welcome glow of the porch light. I climbed off the motorcycle making my way up the steps hearing Dillon's cell phone ring. The conversation was short. He provided his thanks placing the phone in his pocket.

My swollen hands were unable to turn the key in the lock. Dillon took the keys and unlocked the door.

"What did they say?" I asked.

"He's in a hospital in Texarkana and will make it. He has a serious concussion, bruised everything in his chest but nothing that he can't recover from."

I turned on the living room light.

Dillon moved forward, gently touching my cheek. "What happen to your face?"

I felt the tender spot created by my father's fist. "Brad and I had a father-daughter moment in the gym."

Fury shrouded Dillon, "He hit you?"

I nodded lifting a brow. "Haven't you been listening? He doesn't care. All he wants is money. I'm not giving the man who killed my mother one red cent, and he wasn't happy about it."

"This won't happen again, I promise you that," he vowed tracing the bruise.

I pulled away wagging a finger in his direction. "Now, now don't go all boy friend on me, and besides I hit him first," I admitted, trying to lighten the mood.

He narrowed his gaze. "It's not funny, Jake. It doesn't matter who hit who first. He's your father. I can't understand what thrill he gets from hitting a woman, especially his own daughter."

I spoke in a serious soft tone touched by his words. "You're right. it's *not* funny, and it's not supposed to be like this but it is what it is Dillon."

I left him in the living room making my way into the kitchen. I opened the fridge with my wrapped hands. "We were supposed to have dinner. You hungry?"

"No, but I'll take one of those beers," he said, looking over my shoulder.

"I think tonight calls for one." I handed two bottles for Dillon to open.

Seated at the table, I mused, "He's like a roach. Everything else around him can die or fall apart, but Brad

Conner survives."

"You have to tell her," Dillon said.

I leaned back running the bandages over my sweaty, matted hair. Good lord, I bet I looked a sight. "I know. I'll call Harvey in the morning, See what he can do to help. Then I'll tell Katie when they get in from the tournament."

Dillon took a sip from the beer. "What about Bill?"

"He knows everything."

Finishing the first beer, I retrieved two more rounds. "Gran's going to wonder what happened to her beer." I returned to the table handing the fresh brews to the doctor.

Reaching out, Dillon lightly stroked my swollen cheek. "Does it hurt and tell me the truth please?"

"Yeah, it's tender but I've had worse."

A deep sigh escaped. He leaned back in the chair. "Never give an inch do you?"

"I'm a boxer, or I was a boxer. You get use to being battered and bruised."

He said nothing in return. I placed elbows on the table resting my head in a swabbed hand. "I know you don't like hearing about my boxing days, but it was the only thing I found that felt right when my mother died."

He set the beer down. "Can I ask you something, and don't get all ticked off?"

I nodded.

"When you're fighting, do you see yourself hitting your father? It that why you love it?"

It was a fair question.

"In the beginning, but then after a while I came to love it because it was a challenge, never the same, always different opponents and learning to anticipate their moves. It's actually a rush when you're in the ring."

He bobbed his head gesturing he understood.

I smiled at his attempt to swallow his dislike for the sport. "I don't expect you to understand, Dillon. I was hurting so bad I had to get rid of the rage," I said.

He took a drink from the bottle. "I understand hurt and anger, wanting to know why. Really I do. I went through something similar when my wife, Anna, died. I came close to dropping out of med school because I thought, what the hell. Just because you're a doctor doesn't mean you can stop people from dying so why bother."

I searched the dark eyes across the table. "What made you go on?"

He smiled. "Something Sam said to me."

He placed a hand on his chin giving a rub and recalling the words."You should know better than anyone, when God closes a door he opens a window. Then he laid Josh in my arms."

Both of us lost someone we loved and were left with kids to raise. Bill said we had a lot in common. He was right.

According to the clock hanging near the back door, it was ten-thirty. Bill's plane landed at eight. I decided to wait and call him in the morning to bring him up to speed. Brad was subdued in the hospital, and my cuts were clean. There was nothing for Bill to do.

After finishing the second beer, Dillon stood. "It's late. You need to get some rest. I don't want to leave you here by yourself. I'll stay if you want."

I thought about the conversation and the fight in the gym. Did Brad act alone or was someone helping him? The pictures and the flowers made it to Hope while he was in Missouri or so I thought. "Do you mind staying?"

"Not at all. I'll camp out on the couch." He took the phone from his pocket. He spoke to Josh saying an emergency came up, and he planned to stay at the hospital all night. When he ended the call, I thanked him for staying and for the discretion. The last thing I needed was rumors of the doctor spending the night at the house circulating throughout the county.

I went upstairs with Dillon following. We located sheets and bedding in the upper hall closet to make up the sofa. Dillon insisted on doing it himself.

"I'm so sweaty. I need to take a shower," I said.

"Go ahead. I'll take this stuff down."

I went off to the bathroom. Once inside, it was impossible to untangle the hair from the banded braid. My hands were too bulky. I couldn't get the shirt over my head either, plus the bandages were going to get wet. Hesitantly, I opened the door calling downstairs. "Hey, um, I need a little help. Can we take off the bandages?"

Dillon jogged up the stairs and stepped inside the bathroom unwinding the yards of gauze.

"Thanks," I said.

Dillon went back downstairs.

I grasped the hem of my tee shirt feeling the full weight of pain in my side where Brad planted the toe of his boot. I couldn't raise the shirt. I pondered on calling Dillon upstairs again. The last time I ignored an injury it nearly cost my life.

"Dillon?"

He bounded up the steps. "Yeah?"

I hated asking anyone for help. "I can't get the shirt off and my side's hurting pretty bad."

"What happened to your side?"

"Reunion injury."

A warm rush swept over me when his hands slid the shirt upward. I winced when his fingers pressed the rib cage.

Dillon knelt down getting a better look at my side.

"He hit you in the side?"

"Kicked," I corrected.

Dillon scowled. "Jeez, what a creep. Nothing feels

out of place. Probably just a bad bruise," he surmised, rising from the floor.

I clawed at my braided hair. My puffy fingers were unable to grasp the band.

"Let me," he offered, pushing my hands away.

I kept my gaze on the floor while he removed the band from my braid, running his finger through the matted mess and untangled the strands. I raised my head capturing his stare. He was kind, gentle, understanding, everything a woman wanted. Any other man would have run after the way I treated him so rudely, not to mention listening to my screwed up life. Not him. He related to the pain.

I reached out tracing the high cheekbones. "Thank you for everything," I said. I rose on toes and softly pressed his lips.

Dillon grasped my chin with his thumb and forefinger brushing his lips against mine.

He smiled. "You're welcome. Are you able to take off the rest of your clothes?"

My swollen hands didn't want to work right. Pulling off the spandex would prove difficult and painful. Blushing, I lowered my head, "I…"

Without saying a word, his fingers stroked my rib cage lifting the spandex sports bra over my head. His thumbs hooked on each side of the tight shorts peeling them away leaving me practically nude with only the thin material of panties covering the lower part of my body.

My face grew hot from the nakedness exposed in front of him. He never acknowledged my nudity. I preferred to think it was his professionalism kicking in.

I raised my gaze, and could feel my face turning red. We stared at each other for what seemed an eternity. I've experienced a lot of emotions in my life, mostly negative and angry. For the first time, a positive yearning pulsation rushed through me. Many questions went through my mind, each answered by a simple response of take a chance.

I reached out laying a hand on the chiseled jaw caressingly cupping my palm under his chin, running a thumb over the smooth lips. I spread a hand over the hard muscled shoulders, drawing his lips to mine.

His arms went around my waist embracing and deepening the kiss. Fingers traced my spine and tangled in my hair. We both breathed rapidly. He pulled me closer then stopped with the soft lips leaving mine.

"I'm sorry," he said, turning his back to me.

I know he wanted me with the same intensity that I wanted him. I took his hand. "Don't go."

A turn showed his silent contemplation to stay or go. "I can't, not this way, not tonight," he said softly.

Lowering my head, I whispered in disappointment. "I understand. A little too much baggage."

I started the shower. Two strong arms captured my waist bringing me around with his lips crushing mine, lifting me from the floor. I met his force with an urgent need, wanting to be closer to him with each passing second.

He pulled his head back. "You misunderstood. I want you. I really want you, but not if it's a means to get over everything happening tonight."

My feet once again touched the floor. His arms let go, starting to turn and leave. I stopped him. "If I wanted a distraction, I'd be at the gym punching the bag. I gave up reckless behavior a long time ago, Dillon. I've never felt like this. Never wanted someone as much as I want you."

Dillon waited by the door with his head lowered. He looked over his shoulder trying to read my thoughts and feelings.

"Don't go, please. I want this to happen," I

whispered.

He released the black hair held behind his head letting the ends hang loose, flowing over his shoulders. He lifted the shirt revealing a smooth chest trailing to narrow hips. He was perfect in every way.

My attention returned to the handsome face losing myself in the dark eyes filled with a promise of passion. Removing the remainder of his clothes and mine, he gathered me in one arm, cradled my face with his free hand while pressing lips to mine, lifting my body against his and stepping into the shower.

In the early morning hours, we lay in my old metal framed bed with only a sheet covering our bodies. The light between the barn and house showed through the window, illuminating the room. I lay my head on his chest feeling everything that occurred between us was natural.

Twining his fingers in my hair, he tilted my head upward and placed a tender kiss on my forehead. "Go to sleep, Jake. Let me worry and watch over you tonight."

I lay my head onto his chest and fell into a deep sleep dreaming for the first time of what could be instead of what had been.

18

The morning sun filtered through the window rousing me to consciousness. I woke in the same position where I fell asleep. My fingers traced the smooth chest lying beneath me reminiscing about the wonderful hours spent in the arms of the man.

Many times throughout my adult life, I wondered at the possibility of intimacy but did not allow myself to open the door in fear of the monsters lurking and pulling me into the same living hell where my mother lived for many years. I never imagined the gentleness he possessed invoking such euphoric feelings. For one brief moment, I saw myself in his eyes. Not Jake Conner, the fighter, or the woman haunted by a past, but the person I desired to be, one capable of giving and receiving love.

Raising my head, I lingered on his face memorizing every line and curve, afraid it was just another dream waiting to disappear. The dark eyes peeked through slits delivering high cheekbones rising into a sly smile.

"Good morning."

I felt a smile of my own creasing the corners of my mouth. "Mornin'."

He stroked my bruised cheek. I moved higher onto his chest delivering a light kiss. I started pulling away when I felt a hand on the back of my head pulling me downward joining our lips together once again and rolling me to my back.

I stretched my arms around his shoulders spreading finger on the flawless skin wanting to melt into his body.

Before the surging passion deepened, a vibration rattling on a surface interrupted the moment breaking the seal between our mouths. We reached for our respective phones lying on the night tables beside the bed.

"It's mine," I announced, noting the number belonging to Bill.

Dillon rolled to his back.

"Hey, Bill."

"Where are you, kid?" the trainer asked with a note of worry.

Moving to a sitting position with modesty to my appearance, I gathered some of the sheet and replied, "Home."

He asked why my car was still at the gym.

"Long story. I'll be there in a few hours and fill you in," was the only explanation I provided.

"Everything okay? You sound funny?" he asked somewhat badgering.

"I'm fine," I reassured him. "How did it go in Chicago?"

He confirmed the gym exchanged hands with no issues. After promising to see him soon, I closed the phone.

I raised a brow to the man across the bed. "You know he's going to give me a hard time when we pull up on the bike."

A hearty laugh escaped the doctor. He moved over to my side, urging me back to the place where we left off.

It was sometime later standing in front of the mirror that I caught a reflection of the prominently bruised cheek.

How bad is it?" I asked turning to Dillon.

"Not bad," he said.

Shirtless, he came closer examining the bone. "Nothing feels broken," he concluded, brushing my forehead with lips and embracing.

I lay my head against his chest wishing the moment never ended. Nothing in my life had ever felt this right. I didn't want it to stop upon rejoining the world.

We made our way downstairs entering the kitchen. "I can try to make eggs if you're hungry," I offered.

He gave a cautious decline. "The bakery's open. We can go next door when we get to the gym."

I took the slam against my culinary abilities in humor before closing the refrigerator and moving to the phone in the living room. I rang Harvey Jones asking him to meet me at the gym.

"Something wrong, Jake?" The sheriff asked.

I answered, "Yeah, Harvey, there is and it has to do with the guy on the wrecked motorcycle last night."

He agreed to meet me within the hour.

I followed Dillon to the waiting motorcycle to carry us into town. I climbed behind him leaning forward to insure he heard me. "Thank you for everything. It's all a little strange for me."

I thought about how it sounded and knew it deserved further explanation. "I don't mean last night or what happened between us was weird. It was great. I just can't believe I told you about Brad and...."

Dillon turned craning his neck pecking my lips. "I know what you meant. I'm glad you trusted me enough to share something so painful. And last night was special for me, too."

We rode into Hope with my arms wrapped around his waist. Dillon eased the motorcycle to a stop directly in front of the gym door. Everyone in town out and about that time of the morning saw the two of us. It would certainly start the tongues wagging in the small town.

I entered the office, locating Bill behind the desk reading the paper. He did a double take seeing the bruise on my cheek. "What the hell happened to you?"

Dillon came in behind me. "Doc? Can you take a look at Jake?" the concerned trainer asked, rising from his chair.

I waved Bill off. "He's all ready seen it."

Bill gave a curious lift of the brow.

"Brad was here last night in the gym," I said.

Bill flopped back onto the chair with a reddening face. "What?"

"Calm down, Bill," I ordered. "I came out of the dressing room, and he was here."

"And he decided to beat your ass?"

"He wanted money," I said. I went on explaining the details of what happened including the wreck. "Harvey's on his way. Maybe he can lock him up and send him back for breaking parole, and I'm telling Katie the truth."

"So you told the Doc everything?" he said.

"Yeah, Dillon knows everything."

Bill smiled hearing me use the doctor's given name. "He wanted money, huh? What a low-life bastard. I'm sorry, kid, I should have been here."

"It's okay, Bill. I think it was planned, and I think someone helped him. He picked the right time to approach me when you, Gran, and Katie were gone."

I told Dillon everything that happened from the time I left the hospital until last night. Walking to the cabinet, I removed the box holding the photos and handed it to the doctor.

"No return address?" he asked, mystified.

"No, and we know when it arrived Brad was still in Missouri," I said.

Dillon sat the box to the side, pulling a ringing phone from his pocket. The portion of the call I heard identified the caller as Josh. I wasn't sure where he wanted to go, but Dillon gave his permission and advised the seventeen-year-old to be home by eight that evening.

Before closing the phone he added in a louder tone, "Because I want you close to home tonight, Josh."

This was my fault. I should have kept my mouth shut. "I got you mixed up in this insanity. Call Josh back and let him know you're not angry with him."

Reaching out he stroked my bruised cheek with the back of his hand. He said, "I'm here, and I'm not going anywhere."

Following my direction, Dillon walked from the office to place the call leaving me alone with my trainer.

I caught the smug grin on Bill's face. Pointing toward the door my friend chuckled. "So, you and the doctor?"

Great, here we go. "Yes, Bill, me and the doctor, you and Shirley, everything just rosy and sweet."

Bill gave up another chuckle.

"What happened with Carter?" I asked.

Bill took a drink from the coffee cup on his desk. "He signed the papers. The little wanna-be hired Angela to run the office. He made it a huge affair with the press like he was a long lost son helping his momma."

I was skeptical Bill let it go at that. "So is he still able to box?"

Bill placed his hands behind his head. "Last time I saw him he was smiling for the camera showing a kid how to use a jump rope. We're clear with each other. We have no other business. He stays away from me, and I stay away from him."

The door opened. Harvey Jones stepped inside. The first time I met him he was gray with a few hints of dark hair sticking out from under his hat. He was older now, completely gray, a little thicker in the midsection.

"Hey, Bill, Jake," he said, taking a spot on the corner of the desk.

Dillon joined us listening while I relayed the identity and history of the man involved in the motorcycle accident leaving out most of the sordid details, revealing only the parts relevant.

"You can arrest him, right, Harvey. I mean he left Missouri. Surely that's a violation," I said with hope.

Soaking everything in, the sheriff replied. "Yeah, if he left the state without permission that should be reason enough to revoke his parole. I need to check everything out though."

Bill offered the phone. Harvey called his office. "Run a search on the guy in the motorcycle wreck last night a Brad Conner. Do you know his middle name, Jake?"

"Bradley James Conner. He should be about fifty," I said in disgust.

The sheriff continued on the phone. "Bradley James Conner, age fifty, parolee from St. Louis, Missouri." The sheriff paused then added, "He's in a Texarkana, Texas, hospital. I need to know if he's got permission from his parole officer to leave Missouri. Call me back at the gym when you hear something."

Replacing the receiver, the sheriff brought his attention back to me with sympathy appearing on the aging face. "Even if he has permission, you can still press charges for assault," he said.

I clucked a near laugh. "No, I actually hit him first, Harvey. So he'll plead self-defense."

Harvey moved his head disapprovingly. "I told you when you hit the Simpson boy three years ago, keep your hands to yourself. You're a professional boxer and hitting folks will get you in a heap of trouble."

Dillon cut a questioning look in my direction. I shrugged, "He made Katie cry. He was eighteen picking on a twelve-year-old girl. I didn't punch him. I kind of slapped him."

The four of us sat in the office waiting. Finally, the phone rang. Bill handed it to the Sheriff.

After a brief conversation, he announced, "He's out on parole, but it'll be Monday before I know if he has permission to leave the state. Do you know if it's possible for him to get out of the hospital today or tomorrow?"

Dillon advised him of the injuries, and doubted Brad would be released any time soon.

The sheriff rose from his perch on the desk. "You need to tell your grandma. Go to the prosecutor's office and get a restraining order on Monday. I'll have one of my guys patrol the house until he's back in Missouri."

A restraining order was not stopping Brad. I humored the sheriff anyway, thanking him for his help.

After Harvey left, I walked to the door.

Bill leaned forward. "Whatever you're thinking, Jake, drop it."

"I'm taking care of this once and for all."

Dillon took my arm, stopping my advance. "Where are you headed?"

According to the expression on his face, I must have sent cold chills down the doctor's back when I replied, "Texarkana to finish this."

Dillon shifted his gaze trying to read my mind. "Not by yourself."

It was probably a good idea for him to accompany me in case I ran into trouble gaining access to the patient.

"Suit yourself but stay out of my way. This is between him and me."

Dillon left for home to change and wait on me to pick him up. I walked to the office door stopping before I turned the knob. I let my hand slide off the handle seeing my best friend making a call.

"Who're you calling?"

Bill's eyes were icy staring back. "I'm calling in a favor."

I took the phone from his hand placing it on its cradle.

"No, this is my fight. I'm not scared of him anymore."

Bill narrowed his eyes. "Yeah, I know you're not, and I think that's what make you more of a danger to yourself."

I searched the trainer's face. "I've run and hid from him all my life. I've had enough. I'm not running, and I will not hide. I'll make sure he understands I'm not Mom, and I'll see him in hell before he hurts anyone else I love."

Bill moved around the desk taking my arms. "Kid, let me take care of this."

I tilted my head to the side smiling upward at the man who meant so much to me. "I know you'd move heaven and earth for me. I'd do the same for you. This is something I have to do on my own. This is my fight. It's always been my fight. I've just been afraid to accept the challenge until now."

He drew me into his arms. "Don't do this, Jake."

I let him go. "I have to."

I drove to Texarkana with Dillon in the passenger seat. There were very few words exchanged between us. Once inside the hospital, with Dillon's help, we discovered Brad was in intensive care on the fifth floor. We made our way to the waiting room where I pressed the call button for assistance.

"Can I help you?" came the voice on the other end.

"My name is Jake Conner. I believe you have my father, Brad Conner, in a room."

It wasn't long before the door opened.

"Ms. Conner?" asked the woman waiting on the other side.

I nodded.

"We've been trying to locate a family member since last night. Well, hi, Dr. Lawrence," she said.

Dillon addressed the nurse, "Marie, good to see you."

The three of us walked down the hall toward the Intensive Care Unit. Dillon explained he had met the nurse while working at Hope hospital.

"What's Mr. Conner's status?" Dillon inquired.

She handed the chart to Dillon. "He's got a head injury. Nothing serious, but he seems disoriented at times."

"Which room?" I asked.

The nurse pointed to a door across from the nurse's station. I asked Dillon to wait. He was hesitant but obliged.

Upon entering the grayish room, I saw Brad lying in the hospital bed with his eyes closed. He appeared to be asleep.

"Wake up, Brad," I said, loudly after shutting the door.

His eyes fluttered open. A slow smile crept across his lips. "Who are you?" he asked.

I shook my head, thinking, *What a terrible actor*.

He gave himself away with the hatred in his eyes. "I'm your daughter," I said, oozing with the sweetness of pure sugar.

He continued the charade. "I have a daughter?"

I snorted a laugh in disgust. "Don't you remember me?"

He shook his head. Leaning in, I stroked his face with my hand placing a thumb on his chin changing it to a firm grip.

"There's no one around, Brad. Just you and me," I said. "You may have the doctors and nurses buying your line of bullshit, but we both know different."

He kept up the façade narrowing his eyes. "What are you talking about? Leave now."

I gently patted his face before moving a hand to each side of his head and leaning over close. "Oh, that's right.

You have a head injury."

No matter how much he tried to hide it, the hatred pooled in the green eyes. "You don't remember me?" I asked innocently. "What about your wife? Do you remember her? Remember the one you ran over and killed?"

His face darkened with the mention of my mother. I went on. "I'm surprised you can't remember beating the hell out of her every chance you got."

For one second, I considered placing a pillow over the evil man and ending his miserable existence.

"You can't remember chasing her down the street in your truck? The front and rear tires running over her?"

I swallowed hard fighting the building tears. I clenched my teeth so tightly, I thought they might crack. "I do, every day of my life!"

From the corner of my eye, I saw his hand lift. Knocking it back to the bed, I grasped his wrist."You don't remember coming to the gym last night, knocking me to the floor, then kicking me like the cowardly dog you are?"

Lowering my mouth within inches of his ear, I whispered, "You hit like a little bitch."

I raised my head staring hard into the face of the man who murdered my mother. "I am not scared of you. Understand? I'm not Mom. I'm not running. This is between you and me. Any time you want me, come get me. One of us won't walk away. You get me, Daddy?"

Standing upright, releasing his arm, I continued, "Carry your ass back to Missouri or I swear the next time I see you, the conversation we had last night will end a whole lot different. I promise."

He pressed the call button. The all too familiar evil grin appeared on his face. "Don't bet the farm on it, Jake."

A nurse's voice came over the speaker located on the

wall above him. "Can I help you, Mr. Conner?"

He yelled pathetically. "I don't know this person. Get her out. Please, get her out."

Within seconds, the nurse and Dillon rushed into the room. He took my arm leading me into the hall. Glancing over my shoulder at the despicable man, smiling, I acknowledged the first round goes to Brad Conner, but the second round I'm ending the fight.

Once in the car, Dillon asked, "What did you do?"

I stretched my neck. "Oh, just shared some memories I thought might help the poor guy."

Dillon furrowed with skepticism.

I rolled my eyes. "He's faking."

"He has a small fracture. The neurological test are normal."

Tilting my head in his direction, I restated, "Like I said, he's faking."

Lifting a brow, he asked again, "What did you do?"

I leveled to a cool tone. "I did nothing to jeopardize his healing if that's what you're worried about."

Dillon touched my arm.

I shifted my eyes in his direction.

"I'm not the enemy, Jake. Don't shut me out," he said.

I sucked my upper lip between my teeth, biting and fighting tears. "I hate him."

"You have every right to hate him, but don't let that hate drive you to his level," Dillon warned.

While turning onto the freeway heading east toward Hope, Gran called. I swallowed hard, producing a facetious happy tone. "Hi, Gran, how's it going?"

My grandmother sounded tired letting me know the Heat played in the finals later."We should be home around eight. So everything okay, farm still standing?" she inquired.

"Yes, ma'am." I replied. "Be careful, Gran. Tell Katie I love her and go Heat."

After the call, I slumped into a slightly depressive state thinking this time tomorrow the truth would came out with Katie knowing everything. How she reacted remained a mystery I did not want to solve.

At least their getting home late helped delay the impending conversation. Too many people already knew what happened last night. I had to tell Gran and Katie, but it would wait until tomorrow morning.

The worried emotions were showing on my face. Dillon reached out, taking my hand bringing it to his lips. "It's going to be okay, Jake."

I shook my head. "I have to tell Katie the truth. How do I make her understand? No matter what I say or how I try to justify it, the only thing she'll hear is that I lied to her."

He leaned in looking at the speedometer. "First thing you do is slow down before you get a ticket or kill us."

The speedometer registered ninety. I release the pressure on the accelerator.

"You need to clear your head and be straight with her. Katie'll be mad at first, and it may take some time for her to understand but she will. She loves you, Jake," he said.

The rest of the ride went by in silence. I pulled into the doctor's driveway killing the engine resting my head against the steering wheel, tired and starving.

Rubbing the back of my neck, he said, "Come on, get out. We haven't eaten all day. Let's see what I can throw together."

I declined. "I'm tired. I just want to get home, take a shower and go to bed."

He did not push the issue. "Do you want me to be there when you talk to Katie?"

"It's best if you're not. If she finds out other people

knew before I told her, it'll only make it worse."

Leaning across the seat cupping my chin, he brushed my lips with his. "Let me know if you need me. I'm not on call until Tuesday." He opened the door.

"Dillon?" I called out. "Thank you."

"You're welcome." He gave wink and walked away.

On the way home, Bill called, offering to be at the farm in the morning to help with Gran and Katie. I told him no.

Later in the evening, I went into the kitchen searching for sustenance. The only thing that did not require cooking was a sandwich. I began smearing the bread with mayonnaise, stopping the knife mid-spread when my mind flashed to the house in Dallas.

I hid inside a kitchen cabinet under the sink with the door cracked watching my mother huddled in the corner. Her hand covered her bleeding mouth.

"You wanna rethink that sandwich thing, Bridgette? I told you I want chicken. Get your ass up, and it better be ready when I get back," Brad yelled, slapping her one last time before he left the house.

Droplets of water coursed my cheek and fell from my chin, hitting the bread below. I slid to the floor, still holding the knife and rested my forehead against the cabinet. I hated him. God help me, I hated him for everything he did to my Mother, and to me. But most of all, I hated him because I had to tell my sister we were fathered by a sadistic abuser who killed our mother. How would I ever protect her when I lived the truth and failed myself?

I'm not sure how long I sat there. When I brought my head upward, darkness filled the sky. I rose to my feet. My appetite was gone so I tossed the bread into the trash, and put things away. I wandered onto the porch, trying to think of Dillon in an effort to take my mind off the past while waiting for the sound of the Cadillac to come up the drive.

At eight-thirty, headlights came into view. My family was home. The car crept down the drive with Katie hanging out the window, shouting, "We did it. Yeah, baby, the champs."

She's so happy, I thought. How can I cause her so much misery tomorrow?

Once the car came to a stop, Katie jumped out rushing up the steps presenting a trophy for Most Valuable Player.

"Way to go, Sultress. I hate I missed it," I said.

Katie noticed the bruise on my cheek. She reached out touching the area. "What happened?"

"Hit it on the corner of the car door," I lied.

Sitting around the kitchen table, Katie filled me in on winning the tournament. Gran surveyed the kitchen before commenting on the depressive state shining from my eyes. "Something wrong, Jake?"

I replied, "No, I'm just tired."

With the good nights said, we each entered our rooms. It would be the last night living life as we knew it. In the morning, everything would change.

19

❡ woke with Dillon on my mind, thinking of our night together. I felt alive in his arms with a blissful exhilaration that was borderline sinful. A twinge of sadness pierced my happiness wondering if my mother ever experienced those feelings. Did she ever feel real passion?

I turned my head glancing over to the photo on the dresser of Katie. The disheartening time of telling her the truth edged closer. I rolled over onto my side, resting my arm beneath my head, pondering about what was to come. There was no way around saving my sister from knowing the hellish nightmare I lived for so long. I never wanted her to know the truth behind our parents marriage nor the end that came so violently.

I released a deeply-drawn breath, rose reluctantly from the bed, and dressed slowly. I prepared to walk out the bedroom door, stopping and holding the knob. A walk through to the other side and there was no turning back.

I stepped into the hall. The house was quiet. Poking my head into Katie's room, a sense of relief washed over me seeing her asleep. It allowed an opportunity to speak with my grandmother alone before facing the teen.

I went downstairs. Although she was nowhere around, the lingering dread hung inside contemplating the correct method of explaining Brad's freedom to Gran. I poured a cup of coffee, relaxing against the counter, taking a sip of the hot liquid. Through the window, the woman who raised my sister and me sat on the patio enjoying the morning solace engrossed in a gardening magazine. I leaned my head back, looking upward, closing my eyes, gathering courage.

Just go out there and tell her, I coaxed myself

A long sigh escaped. I pushed away from the cabinet and left the house.

A morning breeze blew loose strands of hair away from my grandmother's bowed head. If anyone deserved to loath the world and the cruelties it held, it was Gran. She lost her daughter twice. She raised a troubled teen with such love and understanding. It broke my heart knowing old wounds must open.

"Mornin', Jake," she said.

I glanced downward fearing they might lock on hers.

"Mornin', Gran." I replied, taking a seat.

There was no easy way to tell her about Brad. I took a sip of my coffee setting the cup down. Straightening up, I stared at her across the patio table.

"Katie's still asleep. We need to talk."

She met my stare directly. "All right, Jake. I know something's going on with you, has been for months so spill it."

I opened my mouth slightly chewing a bit of the corner. "Brad's out on parole."

Gran's a hard person to read. Very little gave way to her reaction. "He can't be out. He got twenty-five years," she said in a low voice, returning to her magazine.

"He's out," I repeated.

"When?" she asked, turning a page.

I shifted in the seat regretting keeping the events of the last months from her. "Maybe seven months."

She massaged her temples. "Are you sure?"

"Yes. I found out a month ago he was out, and I've seen him."

Gran's head jerked up. Her eyes grew large. "You

what?"

"He came here while you and Katie were in Little Rock."

I went on to explain everything that had transpired, including the altercation at the gym. When finished, I waited, wondering what she was thinking.

She let her gaze trail toward the pasture and wrinkled her forehead. "Take Katie and leave."

I reached out taking her trembling hand. "Gran, I'm not running. I'm telling Katie everything."

A well of tears brewed with a few sliding down her cheek. "Please, Jake. Take Katie and go. I lost my Bridgette to him. I *won't* lose ya'll."

I pushed the chair back, rounding the table. My arms gathered the weeping woman."He broke his parole coming here, I'm sure of it. He's going back to prison. I promise he won't hurt us. I won't let him, Gran."

Lifting a worn hand, she caressed my face, forcing a smile. "I know and that's what scares me. You've been fighting since the day you were born. I worry you'll die fighting him just like my Bridgette."

She lay against my shoulder with both of us crying for a past we couldn't forget. Once we gained control of our emotions, I sat back in the lawn chair, wiping my face. "I just don't understand. Mom was so smart. How did she ever get tangled up with him?"

Gran dabbed tears on the hem of her apron. "She met him right after graduating high school on her senior trip. The class went to Dallas for a weekend. She came back head over heels. Your grandpa knew he was a good-for-nothing, but Bridgette wouldn't listen. We tried everything in the world to talk her into breaking up with him. Herman even threatened to call the cops 'cause he was so much older than her."

She raised her cup of coffee, taking a drink, frowning

from the strong flavor. "One afternoon they came in and said they got married, even showed us the license. Your grandpa and I knew it wouldn't end good and thought for sure she'd be back in a month. She called every once in a while. Then, the calls came fewer and farther in between."

"She never came back?"

Gran took a cleansing breath. "She came here, once, right after you were born."

Bewilderment flashed across my face. I never knew she came home to Gran, ever. "She came here?"

Gran nodded bringing her cup to her trembling lips but sat it back down, recalling. "One night after we went to bed someone knocked. I guess it was around midnight. Herman opened the door, and there the two of you were. I reckon you about three months old. I didn't even know she was pregnant."

She gave a halfhearted smile. "You were the prettiest little thing. So tiny."

Gran let out a breath, wringing the hem of her apron in one hand. "Bridgette looked bad, eye swollen shut, lips all busted up."

She stopped and closed her eyes. "I took you. Herman helped Bridgette upstairs and cleaned her up. Before our heads hit the pillow, Brad showed up pounding on the door, begging Bridgette to come back."

I sat, listening to what I feared. The beatings occurred long before my first memories.

My grandmother rubbed her forehead reliving the rest of that night. She wasn't going. She said, I'm not raising my baby around you. He told her, she could leave you here, but she was coming back with him. And if she didn't, he would kill us all."

Resting her arm on the table, the older woman's dark eyes appeared drained. "She took you from my arms, and said she wasn't leaving her baby. She cried and cried when telling us how sorry she was for all the trouble. Last thing I said to her was never be sorry for something that's not your fault. I watched her get in an old station wagon and follow Brad's motorcycle. That was it. Never saw her again until…until I saw her in the morgue in St. Louis."

My heart ached for Gran. Her pain matched mine. My mother knew Brad was capable of carrying through with his threat. All the years spent running. Never meeting my grandparents had been to protect them. My mother seemed to want to defend everyone but herself. I asked my grandmother for wisdom. "How do I explain this to Katie?"

The weary sixty-nine year old eyes met mine. "There's no easy way. The truth is the truth no matter how much it hurts. I'll tell her, and she can be mad at me for lying to her. You've suffered enough."

"We've both suffered. I just never wanted Katie to suffer. When she comes out, I want you to go in the house. I'll tell her. I can take what ever she dishes out," I said.

We both sat in silence waiting for the teen while reliving our own personal sorrows. An hour later, a cabinet opened and closed. Katie was awake, searching for breakfast. My grandmother and I looked at each other. The screen opened. Katie said good morning and planted herself in the chair next to me.

"Mornin'," we returned.

"Jake, I found something," she said, peeling an orange and sounding serious.

She shifted her gaze toward my grandmother then continued, "In the, uh, living room. You may want to return it."

I asked what she was talking about and saw a plastic card pulled from her pocket. It was Dillon's hospital badge. Gran said nothing. She rose from the table and left the room. I reached for the ID card. Katie jerked it out of reach.

"Oh, no, no, no, sis, we need to talk," she chided.

I ran my stare over the pretty features struggling with the job ahead of crushing her innocent world.

Not getting the reaction she hoped, she drew back, narrowing her eyes, reading my stress.

"What?" she asked.

Sitting back in the chair, I met her squarely. "Katie, there's some things I need to tell you. Things I should have told you a long time ago."

She shook the plastic in the air laughing, "Ah? Yeah."

I took the distraction away from her. She frowned. "You're no fun."

She went back to peeling the orange. "So tell me. When did Dr. Lawrence come to the house?"

"This isn't about Dillon," I said.

"Dillon? You say the name like you're real familiar with the man. Exactly what went on while Gran and I were in Little Rock?"

I moved closer clasping my hand over the orange. "I'm serious, and I need you to be serious. We need to talk about Momma."

Our mother was one subject I never discussed. I had her full attention. "What about momma?"

"There's some things I should have told you a long time ago. Things that are bad. Things I didn't want you to know. Heck, I wish I didn't know."

Katie squinted skeptically. "What're you talkin' about Jake?"

I let out a deep breath rubbing fingers over my forehead. "I told you Mom died in a car accident. That's a lie."

Katie released a chuckle. "Stop messing with me," she said, continuing to peel the orange.

I ran my fingers through my hair gripping the sides of my head. I rested my elbows on the table feeling a pounding headache building in my temples. "A man ran over her with a truck. That's how she died."

The crease in her forehead deepened with frustration. "This ain't funny, Jake, what's the punch line?"

"It's the truth. He hit her with his truck and killed her."

She stopped working on the orange. "Why would you lie about that?"

"Because the man who hit her is our *father*. Brad Conner."

Katie looked at me in disbelief, frowning. "What? You said he ran off. What are you saying? She died in an accident. You said it was an accident."

It was going to hurt her deeply. I agonized over how to tell her what happened. "No, Katie, he meant to do it."

I rolled my neck prepared to come clean. "Brad didn't run off. We left him. He found us in St. Louis. They got into a fight, she took off running—"

Katie interrupted. "What are you talking about, Jake? This makes no sense. Wait a minute, back up. Why did we run from him?"

I swallowed hard. "Because he was mean. He beat her a lot."

Katie grew still.

"He beat her, we ran from him, he found us, the beating started again and we ran until—"

Katie's head popped up. "Until what?"

I held her gaze answering, "Until the day he found us in St. Louis. They got into a fight, she took off running, and he chased her in his truck and ran over her."

A mouse-like sob slipped from her. "You're lying. Why would he do that?"

The one question I knew the answer to better than

any. "Because he's a sick, evil bastard."

Moisture collected in her blue eyes. "You told me he left. You said Momma died in a car accident. Why did you lie to me?"

I took a deep breath. "To protect you."

Tears fell down my sister's face. I reached out taking her hand. She jerked away. Katie shook her head pursing her lips. "I don't understand. Protect me from what? Knowing the truth?"

I leaned back in the patio chair rubbing my throbbing head. "You were so little when she died. Brad didn't know about you, and I wanted to keep it that way so I decided it was best to tell you she died in an accident and that Brad ran off before you were born."

Katie shut her eyes for a moment, drawing in a deep breath and letting it rush out. "He didn't know about me? How could he not know about me?"

I looked away, not sure I could keep it together with the image of the truck crushing my mother's body playing in my mind. "Because we hid in a shed, and he never saw you."

Katie kept her blonde head down. "Why did we hide? What happened, Jake? Tell me."

I chewed on my bottom lip, fighting tears. "We lived in Paris, Texas, before St. Louis. Brad found us there. Momma got pregnant, and we left before he found out. When he showed up in St. Louis, you were three years old. She told me to take you and hide, and I did." I stopped and swallowed hard, fighting the sobs gathering in my chest. "We were in the shed out back, and I could hear them fighting and...," I squeezed my eyes shut. "I heard the screen slam. I left you in the shed and went to see what was going on. He got in the truck an...and he ran over her."

"You saw it," she choked out between sobs.

I nodded brushing tears from my face.

Silence filled the air for several minutes.

"What did they do to him?" Katie murmured.

"Charged him with manslaughter and gave him twenty-five years."

Tears ran down her cheeks, hearing the truth kept hidden all her life. "Why didn't you tell me?"

I was openly crying in front of my sister. "You were so little when Mom died. I prayed you didn't remember that day."

Katie kept picking at the orange peel, not looking at me. "Did he ever hurt you?" she asked, softly.

I wiped my cheeks with the back of my hand, nodding.

Katie's body jerked in spasms.

Gran appeared on the patio, handing tissues to both of us keeping one for herself.

Katie dabbed her eyes and blew her nose. "Why didn't you tell me the truth? Why did you keep this from me?" she insisted, looking between Gran and me, sobbing loudly.

I fixated on my grandmother. "I thought it best if you didn't know. I couldn't see any point in hurting you," I said.

Katie looked between my grandmother and me once again. "What made you decide to tell me now?"

I hesitated.

"What?" Katie demanded.

"He got out on parole," I said. "He came to Hope a few days ago wanting money, and I refused give him one dime."

I didn't tell her about the things occurring over the past few months or the entire story of the altercation in the gym. "After I told him I wasn't giving him any money, he took off on his motorcycle and got hit by a car. He's in

Texarkana, in the hospital, and I'm going do everything I can to make sure he goes back to prison for leaving Missouri."

My sister rose and paced the patio. Finally, she stopped and turned toward me. "You lied to me. My entire life, you've lied," she said.

My sister's grieving turned to anger. I expected it. I stood quickly, hoping to quell her ire. "I never wanted you to get hurt. I didn't say anything because I wanted to protect you."

She brought her tall frame into direct eye contact with mine standing within inches."From what, Jake? The truth? Why are you telling me now? Why not continue to lie?"

I broke away from her glare, stepping away.

She came after me grabbing my arm. "Why, Jake? After all the years of lying, why are you telling me now, or should I ask what are you still lying about?"

"Somehow he found out about you. He threatened to contact you if I don't give him money," I said.

Katie tilted her head jutting her chin. "Tell me something dear sister…if he didn't find out about me, would you have ever told me the truth?"

I replied honestly. "No, I would have never told you."

The angry teen took several steps back, her eyes shown in a venomous rage. She threw the uneaten orange across the yard. "I had a right to know. She's my mother, too!"

I reached out to capture her shoulder trying to calm the irate girl. Katie jerked away.

"I did the right thing. Do you think it's been a bed of roses for me? I wish someone had lied to me. Not one day goes by that I don't see him hitting her or…" I stopped before spouting the horrid detailed images haunting my memories.

Katie stiffened with rage."At least you knew her.

Everything I built in my mind came from you and Gran. It's a lie. Maybe all of it is a lie. Did he really kill her or do you just hate him so much you want to keep me away?"

Her last words plunged a dagger into my heart. Tears flowed freely down my face. "It's not a lie. She was a beautiful, smart woman, and he took her from us. You can be mad all you want, but I don't regret keeping you from knowing about Brad. If I had it to do all over, I would do it *exactly* the same way."

"It wasn't your choice to make, Jake. I can't believe this. How could you keep this from me? You're my sister. You're the one person I trusted to always be honest with me. Now I find out you've been lying to me all my life," she shouted.

I couldn't defend myself. She was right. I was supposed to be the one person she could trust, but here I was the biggest liar she had in her life. "I did what I thought was best. I never wanted you to feel..." Katie cut me off dashing into the house refusing to listen.

"Katie?" I called after her. My heart sank. Gran and I followed her into the house. "Katie?"

By the time we made it to the kitchen, the front screen door slammed. I picked up the pace making my way onto the porch in time to see my sister speeding down the driveway in my truck.

"Katie? Katie," I yelled to no avail.

I rushed to the buffet to grab my car keys discovering they were gone. "She took the truck and car keys. Gran give me your keys."

My grandmother shook her head. "Leave her be."

I threw up my arms. "Gran she's upset and driving around with no license."

Gran refused to hand over the keys to the Cadillac. "Give her time, Jake. You go after her, and she'll only get madder. Trust me, I know. That's exactly what you did."

She was right. I was the last person Katie wanted to talk to, but someone had to go after her. I went to the phone and called Bill.

"Stay there, kid, in case she comes back. I'll go look for her," he said.

The next two hours were the longest of my entire life. I sat on the porch watching for my truck to pull into the drive, thinking of the years I spent protecting my sister. I didn't regret keeping the truth from her. At least fifteen years of her life was untouched by the ugliness I'd witnessed firsthand.

Hearing the phone ringing, I dashed inside with Gran saying, "Thanks Bill." Hanging up, she turned to me. "He found her. They'll be home later."

I let out a breath, relieved. "How is she?"

Gran rolled her head slightly. "Upset. Confused. Bill wants some time to talk to her."

I hoped with all my heart that my best friend helped my sister the way he had me years ago. I went upstairs to wash my face and change to boots. I had to get out of the house away from Gran to think.

I went to the barn. Sluggo followed on the other side of the fence. My hands were still sore from punching the bag without gloves. I didn't care. I winced lifting the hay bale tossing it through the door to Sluggo.

The animal seemed to sense the depression I carried inside me. She moved closer nudging my arm to gain attention. I moved my hands over the black mane.

"What do you think, girl? Will she ever forgive me?" I lay my face against her nose, smoothing the soft hide of the animal's head.

I went back inside the barn, wandering in circles, trying to think of a way to fix the situation when I noticed the bridle on the ground. The nail holding it was gone. I grabbed a hammer on the nearby workbench and began pounding a nail into the post. I tapped lightly then escalated to wild slams against the post. The more I thought of Brad, the angrier I became. It was his fault. He ruined my life. He ruined my mother's life and he was the reason I hurt the one person I spent years protecting.

"Why didn't you die? I hate you." A cry of anguish thrust from my body. "I hate you." I kept beating the post.

From behind, a strong hand grabbed my wrist stopping the hammer in mid air. "Stop, Jake," the calm, low voice of Dillon Lawrence ordered.

I willingly let go of the tool. I raised my hands to my face sinking my head. A loud thud of the hammer rang out hitting the workbench. Dillon wrapped his arms around me turning me toward him. I burrowed in his chest.

"It's going to be fine. Give Katie time," he whispered, brushing his lips on my temple.

I hoped he was right. "I never wanted to hurt her." I choked through a sob.

He held me tight. "She knows you love her. Just give her time."

I moved out of his embrace taking a seat on the workbench. Dillon approached kneeling on one knee. His fingers lifted my chin. "Don't be mad, I know you told me you didn't need my help. Bill called and asked me to check on you. What can I do?"

I met his sympathetic eyes. I stroked the smooth shaven face, thankful he came. Everything I thought in the beginning about the doctor was wrong. He was a good man with a kind heart. I lay my head on his massive shoulder. "Nothing. There's nothing anyone can do."

His arms went around me stroking the length of my back. We continued in the position until the barn door opened.

"Katie," I cried, jumping to my feet.

With a sobering face, she requested, "Dr. Lawrence, I need to talk to my sister if you don't mind."

Walking past, Katie reached out touching Dillon's arm stopping him. He smiled down at the teen's sad yet mischievous eyes.

"We'll discuss this later," she said, pointing between the doctor and me. With a chuck under her chin, Dillon left us alone.

No words passed between the two of us for a few minutes. I broke the silence. "The day you were born, I promised never to let anyone hurt you." I choked back a sob. "I didn't know it would be me that would hurt you the most. I swear to you I lied because I love you so much and never wanted what happened between Mom and Brad to touch your life."

She raised her hand, waving me to stop. Rushing to me, she threw her arms around my neck holding me tight. "I love you, Jake. I'm sorry for what I said and running out like that," she said, quietly.

We held each other until the summer heat inside the barn sweltered encouraging the two of us to move outside to the nearby oak tree. Taking a seat on the grass, Katie propped her chin on her knees.

"Bill told me a lot that you probably wouldn't have. He said you saw things no kid should see, and to try to imagine growing up hiding and moving around all the time never having friends, and living in fear. He said I should be thankful you lied and gave me a childhood."

I didn't reply. My sister stared off toward the pasture with a glisten in her eyes. "You never had a childhood. He's the reason you push people away," she stated.

I lay back against the tree trunk, listening to my younger sibling. "I know you don't want to talk about the details of what happened, but I'm here, Jake, if you ever do."

I picked up a twig off the ground beside me, toying with it between my fingers. I never really talked to anyone other than Bill and Dillon about the years spent running with my mother. I wasn't sure why but I said, "Mom made me hide when he was around. I usually sat in the closet with my hands over my ears to block out the noise."

Breaking the twig in half I went on. "I think he hated me from the moment I was born. I don't know why, but I think he did."

Katie reached out grasping my hand "It doesn't matter, Jake. I love you, Gran loves you, and Bill loves you in his own mean ass way."

I smiled, patting the slender hand on mine. "It wasn't all bad. When he wasn't around things were great. She was the best Mom anyone could ask for," I said.

I pushed a wisp of hair from Katie's face. She resembled our mother so much. It was a comfort yet painful at the same time. "When you were two, she made a bunny cake for your birthday. She set the cake on the table. I stood you in the chair and all three of us blew out the candles. You dug your hands in the cake trying to feed mom and me. I worried because you had icing all over you. Momma said, 'Leave her alone, she's a free spirit.' Don't ever break her spirit. I kept the truth a secret because I wanted you to always have that wild spirit."

Katie shifted her head in my direction. "I know, and I love you for it."

She shifted positions laying her head in my lap. "Do I look like him?"

I smiled. "No, you look just like Momma."

"What's gonna happen now, Jake? Will he go back to prison?"

I stroked the blonde strands to comfort my baby sister in the same way Mom had done for me so many times. "We hope he violated his parole and goes back to prison, or he'll go back to St. Louis and forget about us.

She straightened holding herself up on one hand. "He knows about me," she said, with a worried voice.

I nodded. "Yeah somehow he found out. I won't let him near you."

She jutted her chin defiantly. "I'll be sixteen in a few weeks. Stop treating me like a baby. I don't need you to protect me. Be honest with me. This ain't just your fight anymore. We're sisters grieving the same mother. It's our fight."

I reached out touching the soft face, seeing my sister not as a toddler clinging to my hip, but the young woman she had become. "You're right. It's *our* fight."

It felt good having everything out in the open. I gave a laugh changing the mood. "How many dents are in my truck?"

She chuckled whole-heartedly. "None. I guess all I needed was to get pissed off to keep it between the ditches."

I pushed her and stood.

"Oh, yeah," she said, striking a cord of curiosity in her voice. She rose to her feet, brushing the grass from her knees. "Since we're being honest, I said I found the badge in the living room floor which was a lie. So tell me sis, how did Dr. Lawrence's hospital badge end up on our bathroom floor?"

I could feel my cheeks turning pink.

Katie doubled over giving a howl of laughter, "In our bathroom?"

"For the love of God, Katie, don't say anything in front of Gran," I begged.

She regained her composure, trying to fight back giggles. "I won't tell her, but I get to drive your car the first day of school, or I'm *tellin'*." She took off across the back yard with me chasing her.

I caught her at the front steps reluctantly granting her ransom for keeping silent. "Fine, but I'm riding shotgun. Deal?"

She agreed.

We walked into the house where Bill, Dillon, and Gran gathered in the living room. Katie went immediately to our grandmother, hugging her.

Bill held out his arms, "What about me, my little demolition princess?"

I waited for a cutting remark to come from the teen but was surprised when she approached the trainer hugged him, and planted a kiss on his cheek. "I love you, too, you old buzzard." The afternoon grew late. I was starving from the lack of food all day and worrying about Katie.

"Well I don't know about everyone else, but I am hungry," I proclaimed.

Gran rose moving toward the kitchen, "Yeah, me, too. Let me see what I can fix."

"I can cook if your tired, Gran," I offered.

A resounding, "No!" came from everyone in the room then laughter with Gran's being the loudest leaving the living room.

Bill moved toward the door. "I got to go."

Disappointment crossed my face."What? No. Stay and eat supper with us."

He smiled. "Shirley's cookin' supper tonight."

It filled my heart knowing my best friend and I both took down the fences that once stood pushing the world away. I hugged him and thanked him for all his help.

Katie grabbed the hospital badge from the buffet and sashayed over to the chair where Dillon sat. She perched on the arm. "So, Dr. Lawrence, or are we all on a first name basis now?" she teased, dangling the hospital badge.

"I suppose we are," he replied, in discomfort taking the badge from her slim fingers.

Feeding off his uneasiness, she remained on the arm of the chair. "Now that we are all so close, tell me Dillon, boxer or briefs?"

Dillon removed himself from the chair, red-faced from the inquisition. Thank God, Josh pulled into the driveway at the precise moment ending the examination.

"I called Josh earlier before Bill found me. I didn't know who else to talk to," she said.

I hugged her. "It's okay. Talk to whoever you need to."

Katie met Josh on the porch. The pair stayed outside. Once alone, I apologized for Katie's behavior.

Dillon gave a chuckle. "Actually, I'm glad she found it. I looked everywhere for that badge."

I walked toward him. "Thank you for coming. I owe you so much," I said with sincerity.

"I'm here whenever you need me, Jake."

We stood in the living room studying each other's face trying to decide what should come next. We didn't have to wait long. Gran interrupted the moment by clearing her throat. "I could use some help setting the table."

Gran insisted upon using the formal dining room. I set the table calling Katie and Josh to eat. It seemed natural the five of us sitting down together for an early supper.

After the meal, Katie and Josh left going to Ali's house to meet Clint. Dillon ushered Gran from the kitchen insisting he and I would do the dishes. She claimed the garden needing her attention and left the two of us alone to manage the clean up.

Dillon hooked Gran's apron over his neck. I burst into laughter. Raising an eyebrow he asked, "What's so funny?"

I tried to stifle the laughter, "You seem a little too comfortable in aprons, Dr. Lawrence."

He raised a brow moving toward me. I backed away until I felt the counter pressing into my back. Dillon stretched a hand to each side of the counter trapping me between his arms. "Really? Are you questioning my masculinity?"

Lashes fanned my cheeks. I could not bring my eyes to meet his. A mixture of shyness and desire clouded my thoughts.

I heard a light chuckle escape Dillon, and he leered. "Not so brave, now, are you champ?"

My head jerked upward with his words. "And if I am questioning your masculinity?"

With no words or warning, he bent, placing his lips against mine with no mistaking the desire they held. His mouth moved away trailing kisses down my neck. My breathing quickened from the yearning building inside.

I felt myself lifted from the floor with my rear coming to rest on the counter top as Dillon's lips returned to mine, pressing the kiss and knotting his fingers in my hair. I pulled him closer. His lips pressed against mine, spread into a smile and withdrew.

"Nope, I don't think my masculinity is in question," he said, moving away to begin washing plates, leaving me sitting on the counter with mouth agape. I gave a low growl of irritation for falling into the trap.

After all was finished, he glanced at his watch. "I really need to get back," he stated with a note of disappointment.

We walked out the back door.

Dillon waved to Gran, "Thanks for supper, Mrs. Parker."

She waved back. "Come back any time, Doc."

Standing beside his car, he asked, "What are you doing Tuesday night?"

I teased, "Washing my hair."

Pulling me to him, he whispered in my ear, "Good. When your finished, I'll see you at seven for dinner."

He planted a searing kiss, strategically located behind my ear. He quickly retreated inside the car and pulled away before I had a chance to answer.

20

On Monday, I dressed for the ride into Hope asking Katie and Gran to stay home. How much of the encounter with Brad leaked from the sheriff's office remained an unknown. Distancing the two from the possibility of wagging tongues in the small town was important to me.

The Hempstead County Police Station parking lot held only a few patrol cars. Pulling the truck to a stop, I sat inside gathering my thoughts before opening the door. I prayed in all earnestness for the first time in what had been a while for God to grant one thing: Let them revoke Brad's parole.

Inside, glass separated visitors from the female officer on duty. Harvey walked through a door behind her. He noticed me at the window and waved. A loud buzzing from the electric door lock filled the air with the aging sheriff sauntering through.

"Morning, Jake. Let's go to my office," he said. We crossed the hall with the same noise clearing entry into another secured area.

Harvey took a seat at his desk motioning me to join him. I eased into an old cloth chair holding my breath anticipating the news.

"Conner's parole officer's contacted Miller County. When he's released from the hospital, Texarkana Police will take him into custody," the sheriff said.

A bit of relief washed over me. "Tell me he's going back and serve the rest of his sentence?"

The sheriff gave me a disheartened look. "I wish I could say yes, but, Jake, it's up to his Parole Officer. I talked to him this morning, and explained what happened. He didn't indicate which way he was thinking."

Harvey picked up the cup in front of him taking a long drink before setting it back on the coaster. "I've seen some parole officers send a violator back quickly and I have seen 'em give a second chance."

I sat back in the chair disappointed. I sought the sheriff's guidance. "What do I do now?"

The explanation of an order of protection he provided sounded good in theory but not enough to guarantee safety for my family.

"What good will it do? How's a piece of paper going to stop him?"

Harvey held empathy for the situation. "I'm sorry, Jake, all I can offer is patrolling the house and to call me if he comes near you, Katie or Chelsea."

I rose, preparing to leave. "Could you give me a call when they transfer him?"

Harvey nodded. "Sure, I'll let you know when he's in custody."

I thanked him and left.

From the sheriff's office, I went to the gym. Bill was in the back lying under a sink wrenching a pipe in the men's room.

"Hey, kid," he said.

I took a seat on the worn floor. "Harvey talked to Brad's Parole Officer. When the hospital releases him, they'll take him into custody, but he doesn't know what will happen after that."

Bill slid from the cabinet. "So that's good news."

I said nothing. It might have been even better if I knew for sure Brad was going back to prison.

After a few minutes of silence, Bill asked, "What's eating you, Jake?"

I lay back against the white paneled wall. "My gut

says this isn't over."

Bill wiped his hand on a towel. Resting arms on his knees, he spoke softly, sympathetically, "The offer still stands. It'll only take one phone call, and you won't have to worry about Brad Conner again."

I shook my head. "No. You and I, we'd be no better than him."

Rising to his feet, the trainer turned on the water. He shut off the faucet. Satisfied with the work he picked up the toolbox. We left the dressing room.

Stopping in front of the ring, Bill paused, scanning the area where the two of us spent so much time over the past twelve years.

"Do you remember the first time Sven punched you?"

Did I ever. The Swedish monster hit me in the abdomen doubling me over. I puked in middle of the ring.

"I thought I was dying, couldn't breathe," I chuckled.

My friend faced me. "What did I tell you that day?"

I thought for a moment. "You said suck it up, Jake. Don't let your opponent see you hurting. They'll feed off your pain."

He gave a wink and walked away toward his office.

I left the gym a few hours later and headed toward Washington. I passed the cemetery making a quick turn and came back to the entrance. I walked across the freshly cut grass deep in thought. Bill was right. The more I fought against Brad Conner, the harder he'd come at me. The more I let the past haunt me, the weaker I became.

I bent down tracing my mother's name feeling the grooves of each letter cut in the granite wishing for her words of wisdom to come to me.

"You put up with Brad for years. I wish you were here to tell me what to do. I can't keep doing this. I want a life of my own. I want to be happy," I whispered.

Resting my head against the cold stone, I uttered a

plea. "Momma, help me find the strength to put it all behind me so I can move on."

My mother's voice eased into my thoughts. "It can't be sunny every day. You need to have some rain if you expect to grow."

I placed lips to the ends of my fingers, laid them on the stone before I rose from the burial site and went home.

Gran was in the laundry room.

"Katie still at Ali's?" I asked.

Pouring the detergent into the loaded washer, she replied, "Yeah. What did Harvey say?"

"The Parole Officer's having Texarkana Police take him into custody when he's released from the hospital. He doesn't know what will happen after that."

Gran closed the lid of the washer, pushing a button to begin the cycle. She grabbed a pair of jeans from the floor and straightened. "Harvey give you the number to the Parole Officer?"

"No, why?"

She removed clothes hanging on a hook near the folding table, and handed them off to me. "I'm calling Missouri."

Chelsea Parker was a headstrong woman. Once she got something in her head, she didn't let it go.

I went upstairs to put away the freshly ironed apparel. The last few items consisted of Katie's jeans. Passing the teen's cluttered desk, a paper caught my eye lying on her laptop. I saw the headline, MAN SENTENCED TO TWENTY-FIVE YEARS FOR VEHICULAR MAN-SLAUGHTER OF ESTRANGED WIFE. I fingered the sheet, scanning the old article from one of the local paper in St. Louis printed from a web site.

Who could blame her for researching Mom's death? If I had been the one lied to for twelve years, I would have wanted to verify the facts for myself, as well.

The article described several neighbors accounts of the tragedy leading to my mother's murder. The only reference to Katie or me was, "Minor children were present at the time of the incident."

I finished reading the article, placing the paper back on the laptop. Katie was so little when we sat huddled in the shed. I had been a scared teenager clinging to a toddler feeding her cold macaroni and cheese, her innocent blue eyes staring up, so trusting, and counting on me to take care of her. I was still there, maybe not in a shed, but still clinging to my sister to protect her from Brad Conner.

I went downstairs.

Gran's voice rose. "Mr. Bryant, he killed my daughter and now he's after my grandchildren. Please, I need assurance he's going back to prison."

Then there was a long pause with Gran thanking the person on the other end.

"Who was that?" I asked.

"Mr. Bryant, Brad's Parole Officer. I called Harvey and got the number," She said. "He's revoking Brad's parole and recommending he serve the rest of his sentence behind bars."

I pulled Gran into my arms. A wave of relief washed over me. "Thank God it's over," I said.

Gran kissed my cheek giving the other a pat.

The rest of the afternoon, we moved around the farm cleaning and mowing with a peace that neither of us had experienced in the last twenty-seven years. We carried our own painful memories yet there seemed to be more closure with no secrets holding us hostage. We knew exactly where Brad was and where he would be for the following years. Eventually his time would end, but it meant thirteen years of peace. Maybe the years might deal harsh aging leaving him an older, weaker man. Maybe it would be enough time to strengthen Katie.

21

ℑ drove to Dillon's that Tuesday with a newfound happiness feeling free to move forward with a future filled with possibilities. I was almost to the point of giddiness.

I pulled my Camaro into the driveway meeting Josh who was leaving. I stopped and rolled down my windows. "Hey, where you going?"

"Following Dad's orders and disappearing. Wanna switch cars for the night?"

I grinned. "Can't. I didn't bring the two-hundred page contract you'd have to sign swearing your first born if you bring it back damaged."

He laughed loudly.

"You don't have to go," I said.

He smiled. "I don't want to hang out with the old folks."

I found the statement rather amusing considering I only had ten years on Josh.

"Clint and I are takin' the girls to a movie then getting up early and going fishing," he said.

"Good luck." I waved, moving on toward the house.

I walked up the steps and rapped on the screen door. No one came. I entered without invitation, making my way through the house. Dillon was on the patio. His back was to me, he wore no shirt. Well-toned shoulders moved while he cleaned the grill.

I sighed taking in the scene. Fate sure had a way of bringing a person to the one place she thought she never wanted to be. It was funny when I thought about it. In the beginning, Dillon Lawrence was the biggest, irritating pain the rear. The man before me was more than I ever imagined. He was handsome on the outside but more importantly, he was beautiful on the inside.

"What's cooking Doc?" I asked with enthusiasm, stepping onto the flagstone.

"You're early," he said before turning around, flashing a grin. The smile broadened while trailing his eyes over my body clad in jeans, blue tank top and sneakers.

"You seem to be in a very good mood," he said.

"Why, yes, I am."

He washed his hands in the nearby sink. "Want to share?"

"Brad's going back to jail."

"That's good news indeed," he agreed, drying his hands and maneuvering around the bar to stand in front of me.

The bare chest sent a surge of butterflies to my stomach. He placed fingers under my chin raising my eyes to meet his. I drew in a breath, anticipating a kiss. Surprisingly and somewhat disappointingly none came.

"Now," he said, giving a wink, "stop worrying and have fun."

He walked to the patio door, stopping short. "I'm going to shower. When I get back, I'll teach you how to cook shrimp."

I grinned. "I'm domestically challenged. You really need to talk to Gran first before trying to turn me into a chef."

He gave a chuckle. "Katie told me you have issues in the kitchen. Something about obliterating a food processor and tomato sauce on the walls. Anyway, maybe grilling's your niche."

I was thankful she didn't tell him about the fire.

Dillon disappeared from the patio returning with a large bowl containing jumbo shrimp and two lemons. Taking a knife from a nearby drawer, he asked, "You ever peel shrimp?"

I raised a brow taking the knife. "No, but it can't be that hard. I think I can handle peeling shrimp without destroying anything."

"Good. Peel the shrimp, and squeeze the lemon juice over them. I'll shower." At the door, he paused. "Um, I'm fully insured for fires, and the band-aids are under the counter."

I shot him a agitated look. "Go take a shower." With this, he left me alone to tackle removing the shells.

Dillon returned twenty minutes later dressed in jeans and tee shirt with his wet hair hanging loosely. I cleaned the counter top with him standing behind me, inspecting my work.

After retrieving several spices and skewers, he looked me up and down. "Very good, and no wounds."

I presented a mischievous grin. "None yet."

I sat at the bar skewering shrimp watching the good doctor preparing chicken. The menu seemed in line with the first meal we shared. Remembering the delicious food, I hoped my involvement with the preparation did not spoil the flavor. The cooking lesson actually went very well, a complete success, although the doctor completed the majority of the culinary tasks.

I started the dinner conversation, telling him about the in-service meeting coming up at school.

"This isn't the first one is it?" he asked.

"No, we had one on the twenty-fifth. It was more of a meet and greet. The next one is going over class schedules and lesson plans. I have a meeting with Mr. Morton tomorrow, too."

"So you think you're ready for school to start?"

My mouth was full. I gave a nod and swallowed. "I'm kind of scared about the in-service meeting after the way the last one ended."

"What happened?"

"Mr. Morton talked me into taking over the cheerleading squad. He was rather insistent so I couldn't say no. We're having our first practice in the morning."

Dillon choked on a piece of shrimp. "Whoa, whoa, back up. Hope High School wants you to take over the cheerleading squad?"

He gave a snicker, sitting back in the chair. "I have to get a visual on this. You and a bunch of teenage girls throwing pom-pom's at each other give new meaning to school fighting spirit." He closed his eyes, building a grin that widened with each passing second.

I threw a wadded napkin at him.

"They want you to coach the cheerleaders, and you agreed?"

"Against my better judgment, I said yes," I admitted, without a hint of enthusiasm. "At least, it might keep me in shape."

The smile faded, replaced with a serious expression. "Is this what you want, Jake, to teach and deal with cheer-leaders?"

I thought for a minute, wondering if I should just reply yes and be done with it, or say exactly how I felt. "Honestly?"

"Yeah, honestly. Is this what you want?"

I stared at my plate. "No. If I could do what I want, I'd be boxing or at least involved in some way. Maybe training a female fighter. Hope doesn't have a lot of women interested in boxing, and I'm not leaving my family to move somewhere to find one."

I forked a piece of chicken. "Changing professions was the right thing to do. I mean who knows? There could be a kid out there I might inspire."

"Not if it means you're unhappy," he said. "Have you thought about going back to school for sports therapy?"

Sports therapy was a thought. "It's a possibility. I'll try my hand at teaching and Cheer Coach first, and, hey, if I make it through the first year without clocking a student or strangling one of the little drama queens, then maybe it's my calling."

He reached across the table taking my hand. "I've seen you with Katie. You're actually patient, kind, and whether you admit it or not, you have a big heart. I think you'll be great."

I smiled at the observation. He returned attention to the food on his plate. I continued staring.

What have I've done to deserve such kindness from this man? I wondered. *Since the first time I laid eyes on him in the green scrub with the half glasses, he's received the brunt of my rudeness and has been drawn into a hell no one person deserves to experience. He should have run in the opposite direction yet remained beside me with the compassion of a true friend.*

I bit the inside of my lip, realizing what I felt for Dillon Lawrence was more than friendship.

We finished the meal rising from the table to clean up the aftermath. Once again, Dillon looped an apron over his neck taking the helm washing the dishes while I dried.

He caught the corner of my mouth turning upward. "Are you laughing at my apron again?" he asked cupping a handful of water.

I grabbed his hand. "No, not at all."

After the clean up, Dillon tossed the dishtowel to the counter. "How about going for a ride?"

"Yeah sounds like fun." I enjoyed riding the bike the night he took me home.

I wrapped arms around Dillon's waist, relaxing, and

enjoying the ride. Turning east, we rode several miles then took the back paved roads toward Hope once again. Halfway back, he brought the cycle to a halt turning off the engine. He retrieved the cell phone from his pocket that must have vibrated. Checking the number, he flipped the cell open. "Dr. Lawrence."

There was a pause. "I'll come by and sign the order. No, no problem. I'm out riding so I'll just stop by on my way home."

He stuck the phone back into his pocket, turned to me and said, "Quick stop by the hospital."

We parked on the sidewalk between the main entrance and the emergency area. I climbed off the back running fingers through a tangled ponytail, smoothing my windblown hair. I didn't want to go inside and face the gawking co-workers. "I'll hang out here until you're finished," I said.

He smiled, took my hand, and pulled me along. We made our way through the hospital passing patients rooms and stopping at the nurses' station.

A small, young nurse with short, strawberry-blonde hair sat behind the desk. "Hi, Dr. Lawrence, sorry I disturbed your evening."

I looked down avoiding her smile knowing it was public knowledge the doctor and I were officially an item. "No problem Natalie," he replied, signing a paper on a chart.

"Have you met Jake?" he said.

The petite nurse extended a small hand. "Hi, Jake." Taking her hand, I returned a greeting.

"Anything else going on?" he asked handing the chart back to the nurse.

"No. Rather quiet tonight."

The two exchanged goodbyes. "Nice to meet you, Jake," she said.

Dillon's large hand holding mine, tugged me along the hall. We did not leave the same way we came in but detoured through the emergency room. The first person we met was Nurse Mary, the woman who took care of me the night of the boxing injury.

"Jake Conner, how ya doin', girl?" she inquired, stopping for a moment.

"I'm fine Mary, and yourself?"

"Slow night," she responded, adding, "And look at you Doctor Lawrence dressed up in your jeans, I don't think I've ever seen you in anything but scrubs, you clean up pretty good." She gave a toothy grin with a wink in my direction before disappearing into a room.

We went toward the exit. The only person at the desk was the same rude, skinny nurse I encountered on my previous visit.

"Evening, Dr. Lawrence," she said in a flirtatious manner.

"Evening," he responded, not bothering to stop and socialize.

It was apparent she did not see or recognize me at first until we passed by. I gave her a twist of a wave. The same icy stare seared with recognition reflecting on the slim face.

We arrived at Dillon's house a few minutes later. "Well, Mr. Entertainment Director, what's next on the fun list?"

The high cheekbones rose into a grin. My face flushed knowing the thought crossing the doctor's mind. The memory of the night alone at the farm seared mine as well.

"I thought maybe just relax and enjoy each other's company," he responded taking my hand leading the two of us through the kitchen toward the patio.

He flipped a few light switches along the route

illuminating the patio with lights and music filled the air. We made our way beyond the crepe myrtles to a double chase lounge chair angled toward a wooded area behind the house.

We stretched out beside each other on the comfortable recliner. "This is the best view," he stated, assuredly.

"Best view for what?"

"Josh and I put a feeder under a tree. The deer come around this time. It's a full moon. We should be able to see them pretty good."

We watched for a few minutes. It was quiet except for the rustling of leaves in the nearby woods. On cue, a doe and her baby appeared at the edge of the woods. The doe inspected the area checking for danger before moving closer to the food on the ground. The yearling followed.

After eating every grain under the tree, the mother eased her way back into the woods with her baby following, watching, and listening to ensure it was safe. Mothers protect, I thought. They look out for their babies, give up everything for their babies.

"Amazing, isn't it?" Dillon said.

I remained quiet.

"You okay?"

"That deer, she watches, listens, she can sense danger. All creatures sense danger," I said, turning to Dillon. "Why aren't you running in the other direction? Why do you want to spend time with me?"

A soft hand captured my face. "The first time I saw you on the gurney with a punctured lung all feisty and stubborn, my God you were stubborn, I thought now here's a woman who's either tough or just a pain in the ass. Then, I looked in your eyes and saw it. Something I recognized all too well, hurt. My life was not as bad as yours, but I know how it feels to have something chasing you inside every day. I have no idea why fate threw us together, but I'm glad it did."

The moon light was bright shadowing his features. I reached out to stroke the smoothly shaven cheek, tracing the bones. "A wise man once told me life's about taking chances. I'm glad I took a chance on you."

With my last words, his lips joined mine. Wrapping an arm around my waist, he rolled me onto his chest. His fingers laced into my hair, pulling me closer.

I maneuvered my body to a sitting position, straddling his hips. Lowering my head, I brushed his lips with mine, growing hungrier. Swinging legs to the side of the lawn chair, he stood with mine wrapped around the trim waist carrying me with ease into the house and lowering our bodies onto a soft bed with our lips never leaving one another.

That night, lying in Dillon's arms, my way of thinking started changing. Part of the old philosophy held true. What was in front of me was real. Nothing else mattered as long as I embraced reality and kept the things that had passed far behind me. It gave me a new lease on life, exhilarating yet frightening, strange but comfortable, a beautiful spring after a life of bitter winter. It was something I lost long ago but found, hope and belief.

22

I fell asleep beside Dillon waking hours later to his warm breath brushing the curve of my neck.

"What time is it?" I purred.

"Four-thirty," came the soft reply.

An arm crossed my waist. Pads of soft fingers brushed hair away from my cheek. Lips lingered on mine. I knew I should dress and leave for home before Gran woke finding my room empty. At twenty-seven, I was old enough to spend the night with a man but felt the necessity to respect my grandmother by applying discretion to behavior. Desire triumphed.

In time, I reluctantly rose from the bed and showered. I followed the aroma of coffee into the kitchen. Dillon leaned against a counter handing me a travel mug filled with needed caffeine.

We walked to my car unable to speak due to the smiles paralyzing our mouths.

We stood, looking at each other, when Dillon laughed easily.

"I'm thirty eight years old standing here with my heart beating like a boy kissing a girl for the first time."

"I know it's crazy," I said, wrapping arms around his waist resting my head on his shoulder.

Dillon tilted my head upward with an amused glint in his dark eyes. "We're going on a real date this weekend."

I agreed.

A long kiss goodnight and I left, hoping to get home before Gran woke.

It was six when I turned into our driveway noticing the light shining from the kitchen. With no way to sneak in undetected, I prayed Katie still slept. The little cutup would never let me hear the end of it if she knew I spent the night with Dillon.

I paused at the back door eyeing Gran frying bacon. I walked inside passing through to the dining room quickly setting my bag on the buffet and returning to face the music.

"Morning, Jake," she said.

"Morning, Gran," I murmured taking a seat at the table waiting for her to unleash the riot act.

She laid a fork on a spoon rest and took a seat at the table. Gran craned her neck checking the doorway.

"Next time, call and let me know if you're not coming home. I was worried sick something happened to you," she said.

I did not expect this type of reaction from the woman raised with the fiftyish-style values on premarital sex. "I'm sorry. I meant to come home before you got up."

She cut me off. "You're a grown woman. All I ask is be a little mindful. You have a teenage sister."

I agreed and promised to call the next time.

She pushed the chair back, leaning forward, opening the oven expelling the scent of homemade biscuits beginning to brown. "Is he a distraction, or are you in love with him?"

The question caught me off guard. "I am not promiscuous," I said, more quickly than I intended.

She returned to the previous position resting an elbow on the table edge. "I didn't say a thing about you being a floozy." A smirk crept to the corners of her mouth. "I asked, if he was a distraction, or are you in love with him?"

I frowned not wanting to admit anything I felt for

Dillon Lawrence aloud. "I enjoy spending time with him. I never thought…"

"You never thought what?"

I averted my eyes. "I never imagined I could feel something other than contempt for a man. Okay?" I rolled my head to relieve the stress in my neck growling, "Good lord, what's happening to me. I'm getting too soft."

She snorted and rose from the chair removing the biscuits from the oven. "Nothing's wrong with you, Jake, except you're falling in love. Stop fighting it and let it happen."

"What if I don't want it to happen?"

Gran moved about placing food on a plate and handing it to me. "Then you're lying to yourself."

After breakfast, I went up stairs readying for practice with the cheer squad. I peeked in on Katie still asleep before going down stairs. A hug to Gran, a "Wish me luck," and I was out the door.

I hoped God gave me strength to deal with the ten drama queens waiting on me. When I arrived at the school, some of the girls waited, watching the football team practice drills. I decided to linger back until the others arrived.

After fifteen minutes, they were all present. I shook my head surveying the group of giggling teenagers seated on the bleachers. Letting out a sigh, I wondered how I went from a champion boxer to this.

"Good morning ladies, my name is Ms. Conner and I'll be your coach for this school year," I said giving no hint of a smile.

I started the speech prepared over the past week. "I was a professional boxer for ten years. In order to do some of stunts and moves to shock and awe the crowd, you'll have to be in the best shape of your lives and with total concentration."

Pausing to draw a breath and reading the faces in front of me, I continued. "I'll require each of you to find your way to the gym at least twice a week. Mr. Monroe is offering his facility free of charge. We will practice three times a week starting Monday then twice during the week and some Saturdays when school starts. We will run, we will exercise, we *will* get strong, ladies. Any questions?"

I paced a few feet away with my hands on my hips in frustration. I sounded like a drill sergeant. It wasn't how I wanted it to come out. I turned around to see ten frightened faces staring back. I couldn't tell if it were me or the exercise that scared them.

One tiny girl who introduced herself as Lana spoke low. "Ms. Conner can, I ask you a question?"

I nodded.

"Didn't it hurt, getting hit?"

This brought a smile to my lips. "Yeah, it hurt, but you learn to condition the body and mind to endure the pain," I said.

I asked the others to tell me their names which they did in turn.

Taking the opportunity to bond somewhat, I added, "I never was a cheerleader. Not sure what kind of coach I'll be, but I can show you how to make your bodies stronger and focus. In turn I will learn the routines and do them. I will never ask you to do anything I am not willing to do myself. We work together and maybe we come out the strongest, most athletic cheer squad in the state."

It sounded corny but heartfelt.

The same tiny elf raised her hand again. "Will I be the egg again this year?"

They could see the confused look on my face.

A girl named Amy, spoke up. "The smallest person on the squad is the one we toss in the air. Egg toss."

"Um, Lana isn't it?" I asked.

She nodded. "I would say since you're the smallest then you'll be the egg. Let's just hope the rest of the squad works out like they are supposed to so you don't become the scrambled egg."

Laughter erupted easing my nerves. We warmed up running a couple of laps around the ball field. No complaints came from the girls. They demonstrated some of their past routines. I managed to complete some of the drills and added a few things along the way showing the girls how to move on toes to quicken movement and balance. I was amazed realizing they were in great shape. They jumped, bounced and pyramided little Lana to the top, tossing her to two girls below. The girl called Catlynn proved her flexibility with back flips across the field. I was impressed realizing how wrong I had been about their capabilities.

After a two-hour practice, the heat was unbearable. We broke for the day. I made my way to the truck.

The cheer captain, Tisha, called after me, "Ms. Conner?"

I stopped and waited for her to catch up. "Ms. Conner, you're pretty cool."

I smiled. "So are you guys."

"Do you think you can show us some boxing moves? Maybe work them into a routine like mixing fighting with fighting spirit?" she asked.

I smiled thinking of Dillon's description of school fighting spirit. "I think that would be a good idea."

"See ya," she said, while running to catch up with the group of girls walking away from the field.

I drove to the front of the school and walked inside anticipating the redheaded secretary. No one was within sight. I waited for a moment then cleared my throat to gain attention.

Mr. Morton appeared from a door into the school hall.

"Hey, Jake, come on in."

I followed him into his office.

"Sorry about the wait. Miss Martin called in yesterday and quit. No notice just quits," He said. "How did practice go?"

"It went well," I said.

He gave a nod. "I knew you were the right person for the job. And trust me. I know you don't want to coach a bunch of cheerleaders. I appreciate you taking on the position at the last minute."

I took a seat. "Actually I'm impressed. I thought they would be a bunch of whining teenage girls, but they're in great shape."

"Good. So let's talk about teaching history."

After a long discussion of the expectations of a high school history teacher, I was free to leave. My thoughts found their way back to the night before and the morning spent in bed with Dillon. Flipping open the cell, I pressed the numbers connecting me to the doctor.

"Dr. Lawrence," came the professional sounding voice.

"Do you make house calls?" I asked.

I heard a deep laugh. "Depends. When you say house do you mean your home or the big house? You're not in jail, are you, or did you make it through practice?"

"I made it. Actually it was not that bad," I admitted. I went on detailing my morning session.

"Good, glad it went well," he said. After a few minutes of banter, and a promise to talk later in the evening, we said our goodbyes.

I stopped by the gym to check in with Bill and grabbed some lunch next door. Bill took a drink of soda with a glint of humor in his eyes. "So how'er things with you and the doc? Rumor has it you two were seen yesterday riding around town on a motorcycle."

I rolled my eyes. "People in this town need to get a life. If it's any comfort, yes, we rode the bike, and, yes, we are officially an item."

He nodded. "Good. I told you he was a good guy and exactly what you needed."

I huffed hearing the remark. "All right, I admit it. He is a good guy, and, yes, I like him. Are your happy?"

He leaned back, folding hands behind his head. "Ecstatic."

I hung out at the gym until three. I had to pick up Katie for the softball game.

"Tell her to hit one out of the park for me," Bill said.

I left the gym heading home. Near the tractor dealership, my phone rang.

"Jake, where are you?" Bill asked with an unusually frantic tone in his voice.

"Just left town. What's wrong?"

There was a long pause before he spoke. "Harvey called right after you left. Brad's missing from the hospital."

My heart leaped into my throat. Please let Bill be wrong.

"You there, Jake?" Bill said.

"They don't have any idea where he is?" I asked.

"No. A nurse said a woman came to visit him last night, and when the cops came to pick him up this morning, he was gone. She remembered hearing Brad call the woman Teyla and her description matches the new secretary at the school."

I squeezed my eyes shut feeling the bile rising in my throat. Teyla Martin was the one helping Brad. It all made sense. The weird looks, the pictures during the Fourth of July celebration, her asking Dillon questions. It all added up.

"No wonder he knew about Katie. She saw us and

had access to all my information at school."

"It gets worse, Jake. Miller County found Teyla Martin's car on a back road west of Texarkana. She's dead. They told Harvey a motorcycle was missing from a neighbor's house and they think he's making a run for Laredo, trying to cross the border."

"I need to call Gran," I said frantically.

"Bring Chelsea and Katie to the gym. Harvey's going to keep me up to date," Bill said before hanging up.

I called the house phone. It was busy. I pressed the numbers to Gran's cell phone. No one answered. I didn't want to call Katie and send her into a panic, but I had no choice.

The phone rang three times. My sister came on the line with a shaky voice.

"Jake?" she choked.

"Katie, what's wrong?" I asked, stepping on the brakes and easing to the side of the road.

"Jake," Katie screamed. "Jake!" Her cries faded.

"Katie? Katie?"

"You invited me to come get you. Well, I'm here waiting for you. Don't be stupid and call the cops, or I might get a little nervous. We wouldn't want anything to happen to your sweet little Katie now, would we?" Brad released a cruel laugh.

I steadied my voice. "How much do you want?"

"Oh Jake, it's not about money. We're beyond that. Just get your ass here. We're having a family reunion."

"Don't touch her. I'll do whatever you want," I pleaded.

"Brad? Brad," I rushed.

The line was dead.

For years, I kept secrets from my sister to protect her. I kept hidden Brad's release for months from my grandmother. Bill told me not to play Brad's game.

I called Bill.

"He's at the farm, and he's got Katie."

Bill breathed hard through the line. "I'm calling Harvey. Come back to the gym or wait where you're at, and I'll be there in a minute."

I closed my eyes and saw my mother's bruised and battered body crumbled onto a floor, bleeding from her nose and mouth. Then I pictured Katie in the same state. I felt a calmness come over me. I knew what had to be done.

"I want you to call Harvey, and let him know Brad's at the farm. Call Dillon, tell him I appreciate everything he's done for me and my family. I've got to go. I can't let him hurt Katie."

"Kid, wait. I'm on my way," Bill shouted.

"Bill, I wish you were my father."

I pressed the END button and turned off the phone.

23

 $\mathcal{W}$ e spend our lives waiting for one monumental moment that defines our sense of purpose. For many years, I believed my moment came when Mom died leaving me with a three-year-old and a soul full of heartache headed toward the boxing ring. I was wrong. Every step in my life was for preparation. My moment had arrived. My moment waited in a two-story farmhouse. Whether I triumphed or became the sacrificial lamb, I finally understood my purpose. Save Katie no matter the consequences.

I raced home paying no attention to the oncoming traffic or any sense of the familiarity to the landmarks in passing. Securing freedom for Gran and Katie eclipsed all other thoughts. Different scenarios played out in my mind, each ending with the possibility of one or both of my loved ones caught in the chaos between Brad Conner and me. I did not want my sister exposed to the same violence I grew up with. There was no way of avoiding it, either. Running and hiding were options no longer valid. I knew first-hand they didn't work.

I rewound the last remarks made by Brad.

"It's not about money. We're beyond that," I muttered. The game had changed. He found something else he wanted more.

I passed the cemetery glancing to the spot where my mother lay. With a sudden clarity I had not experienced, I understood the sacrifice she made for her family. She spent her days swallowing her own pain to protect the people she loved eventually giving up her own life. The day she ran from the house in St. Louis, it wasn't about getting away from Brad. She lured him from her children allowing outsiders to bear witness to the violence hidden behind closed doors for so many years. The way she chose to deal with her abusive husband was the choice she thought best.

It was my turn to choose between two options. The first: Storm the place attacking the man head on, chancing my grandmother and sister's safety. The second: Enter the lion's den, offering myself in hopes of bargaining my love ones from him. I chose the latter.

I turned the truck onto the drive idling the engine for a minute while scanning the area. Gran's Cadillac parked in front of the garage was the only vehicles in sight. I searched the front porch for a sign indicating Brad's whereabouts within the house. Was it possible he took Katie somewhere else leaving me to think they were at the farm?

Stepping from the truck, I walked to the porch cautiously making my way up the front steps. No sounds came from inside. I opened the front door pushing it wide with my foot. Looking straight ahead, Brad stood at the bottom of the stairs behind my sister with a hand around her throat. He lowered his head close to her neck encompassing her waist drawing her into a cuddling embrace.

His lips grew to a twisted grin. "Come on in, Jake."

I stepped inside the screen keeping eyes forward on the man holding my sister prisoner. A figure on the sofa across the room caught my peripheral vision. Gran lay on her side with eyes closed.

"Gran?" No answer.

"I knocked her out. Crazy old bitch tried to cut me with a butcher knife." Brad laughed.

I kept eyes on him while moving toward my grandmother. "Gran," I called again. My fingers pressed on her wrist checking for a pulse. A purplish bruise formed on her cheek.

"Gran?" I shook her lightly trying to rouse her awake.

"Hell, Jake, I may be a lot of things but a liar's not one of 'em. She's fine. Just taking a nap," he said.

I saw her chest rise and fall. She was alive. I peered at the man I never considered my father. Hate-filled green eyes flashed in my direction. He tightened his grip on Katie's neck, reading the same sentiments from me. Katie shook in fear. I needed her calm and controlled. One wrong move,and Brad might snap her neck.

I threw myself at his mercy. "Let them go. I'll do what ever you want, just let them go."

Brad gave a demented howl. "You know your mother said about the same thing the last time I was in this house. Leave them alone, Brad, and I'll do what ever you want." He sighed with the laughter fading to contempt. "Lying whore. How did she repay me? By running away, over and over."

Tears ran down Katie's cheeks. He let go of her neck and wrapped both arms around her waist. Laying a cheek against her blonde hair he closed his eyes, "Shhh, Don't cry, baby, it'll be over soon."

The way he held her, speaking lovingly, reeked with a hint of perversion.

"Brad," I shouted in an effort to bring him out of the trance.

His eyes snapped open with a hideous smile. "She looks just like her, doesn't she?"

"Yes, she does," I said, calmly.

I took a step forward hoping to take advantage of the soft moment. Biting back words of nausea, I said, "I know you loved Momma but she's gone. Katie's never been a part of this. Let her go, Brad, and I'll do whatever you want."

He took a deep breath releasing the hold on my sister. At first, I thought he was actually letting her go. Katie struggled to move from his reach unsuccessfully. Grasping her arm, his demeanor changed to a tone of hatred. "She's the proof of what a lying unfaithful bitch of a wife I married."

He was crazy. My mother never gave any other men the time of day. Katie struggled fighting to free herself from his squeezing hold. He returned his hand around her throat to still her movements pulling her tight against him.

"Please, let us go," she sobbed.

"Stop moving before I have to hurt you, sweetheart," he said in a lover's whisper.

I tried to make sense of everything. "Momma was never unfaithful to you. She got pregnant in Paris when you found us. Katie's *your* daughter," I said in a steady voice.

His eyes narrowed. "Nothing like a family reunion to get the truth out in the open." He leaned in close to Katie's ear. "Jake, ever tell you the reason Bridgette died? Hmm? That's right, honey, your momma died because Jake made her run away. It was all about Jake. She ever tell you about that?"

Katie closed her eyes, crying, uncontrollably.

"Every time I turned around, Jake was in the way. I couldn't have a minute alone with my wife because Jake needed her. If she had stayed with me and let the old bat have your sister," he said, nodding toward my unconscious grandmother, "she would have never left me and never been a cheatin' whore. So now, you know. Jake is the reason your momma's dead. She killed her."

I could no longer control my temper. "I'm not the one who chased her down the street and ran over her!"

He laughed loudly, enjoying the rise in me. I was

playing into his hands. Losing my temper made me careless. The incident in the gym proved it.

I shook the anger away changing my tone. "I was just a little girl. She was supposed to take care of me. You were supposed to take care of me."

I should have felt no shock by the next words coming from his mouth, but they still delivered a stinging slap. "I never wanted you," he said, tightening the grip around Katie's throat.

Clenching my fist, I fought to gain control of my emotions. I had to think and think quickly to get my sister away from him. "What do you want, Brad? Money? I can get you money. Just let Katie go. We can take my truck and go to the ATM. I'll drive you wherever you want to go."

His arm tightened around the teenager's waist, molding her body against his. "All I want is what I have right here. You took Bridgette. I'm taking Katie. Fair trade. Don't worry, Jake. I'll take care of her."

His next action shocked me so much I lost focus. He spun my sister to face him planting his lips on hers. She pushed against him grappling, to free herself.

Brad was quickly avalanching into a pit of insanity. I rushed forward, hearing my sister screaming and fighting for release. He saw me coming and slung Katie toward the stair railing with one of her arms still in his grasp. The other curled into a fist finding its mark on my chin.

My head spun back.

"Jake? Jake! Let me go you freak," Katie cried fighting against the hand on her arm that prevented her from escaping.

I took a few staggered steps backward shaking the blow from my head. Recovering quickly, I prepared to return the favor. He planted my sister in front of his body using her as a shield. I shifted my eyes over him hoping for clearance to land a fist on his smug face. There was no way to attack without injuring Katie.

"She's your daughter, you perverted bastard," I screamed in blind rage.

He displayed a white flashing grin. "No."

He was completely over the edge.

"Momma got pregnant when you came to Paris. Katie was born nine months later. She's your daughter. What part of this do you not get?" I shouted.

"There's no way I can be her father," he said defensively, through tightly held lips. "I didn't sleep with Bridgette in Paris. That's what started the fight. She fought me, and wouldn't let me touch her."

It made no sense. There was nobody else. Mom was always with me except when she worked. She had no male friends that I knew about. The only man she ever spoke to was Z.

I reeled for a minute letting it sink in. If Brad spoke the truth, then it was reason to believe my mother shared more than meals with the kind biker who lived across the street from us in Paris, Texas. I shook the thought from my head, returning attention to Brad and my sister searching desperately for a way to save her.

He read my thoughts. "Jake, I am taking her. What you have to decide is if you and the old woman want to live?"

Katie ceased struggling. Tears streamed down her face. Her eyes searched mine not with hope of rescue, but with one of a made decision.

A small trembling voice erupted from the teen. "Promise me you won't hurt Jake or Gran, and I'll go with you. I won't fight. I'll go willingly."

"No," I panicked, taking a step forward.

"Stop, Jake," she begged. "Please, let me go."

I loved my sister, and she loved me. The sacrifices we

prepared to make were obvious with each giving a life for the other. I raced for options, discarding one after the other. Nothing seemed to offer a solution. I wasn't going to lose Katie.

Katie. Suddenly it came to me, hearing Katie's voice in my head from the afternoon when I told her the truth about our mother.

I locked eyes on my sister. "It's our fight," I said.

"I don't give a damn who wants to fight. We're leaving," Brad said, preparing to walk away, dragging Katie with him.

I raised my arms in surrender. "You win, Brad. At least, let her get some of her stuff to take with her. She loves softball, and she's really good."

"Fine. Get some of your stuff but you won't have time to play ball." He put his mouth to her ear, slapping her rear-end with a sickening grin. "If you're not back down here in five minutes I'll make sure you watch while I beat Jake to death then slit the old bat's throat. You hear me, Bridgette?"

Brad let go of Katie. She took the first step with a hint of sadness. The same despair I saw many times on my mother's face. I gave a stern narrowing of my eyes, reminding her, "Don't forget your gear."

She wrinkled her forehead in confusion. I raised a brow repeating, "Don't forget your gear. It's our fight." She nodded, understanding my meaning, and moved up the stairs with haste.

Once she was out of sight, I glared at the man standing before me. "You know I will never let you walk out of this house with her."

He replied, "And you know I'll never leave here with you still breathing."

I watched his every gesture calculating the best point of attack with the same method I used to size up my boxing opponents."Teyla Martin helped you. Did you plan on killing her all along?" I put myself between Brad and my grandmother edging him closer to the bottom step of the staircase.

"We had our run. She took care of things while I was a guest of the state of Missouri. Then you turned her against me just like you did your momma."

"What are you talking about? I didn't know her. I spoke to her a couple of times."

Brad shook his head. "It doesn't matter really. She was so stupid. She felt sorry for me being a father whose wife kidnapped his daughter. She helped me find you and Bridgette in St. Louis."

"She knew you killed my mother?"

He gave a wicked laugh. "I didn't kill my wife. You did. You see when I found you in Missouri, Bridgette tried to stop me from reclaiming my daughter by jumping in front of my truck. It was an accident."

I nearly vomited. "She believed that sick lie?"

"Jake, she spent the last twelve years coming to see me in prison ever Saturday. Now that's devotion. And she would still be if she hadn't heard you in the hospital."

"She was there," I said.

He nodded. "In the bathroom. All it took was hearing your version of what happened and bam, she grew a conscious. She actually thought I was gonna go to Mexico with her, forget about the money, and leave you alone."

"So you killed her," I surmised.

"She was a means to an end," he said, admitting to murdering the redhead.

"Story of your life, isn't it, Brad? Using, then killing."

He raised a brow."Actually you can blame yourself for Teyla dying along with your mother. This all started because of you."

I took a small step toward him. "Because I was born? Is that how I caused all this?"

He laughed. "Exactly. You were a mistake that cost me everything. Bridgette knew I never wanted kids. When she told me she was pregnant, I told her to get rid of it. But I loved her and gave in. So you can thank me for your existence."

Katie appeared at the top of the stairs with the softball bat in hand. He caught the shift in my eyes and looked up the staircase. My opportune moment arrived.

I crossed the short distance delivering a right hook. His blonde head swung around, losing his balance. He reached out, grabbing the banister to brace his fall. Katie raced down the stairs swinging the bat, connecting with Brad's back. He fell to his knees.

I threw an upper cut under his chin sending him to the floor. Katie swung again missing him. He quickly rolled away. Cat-like movements righted his frame. He grabbed one end of the bat trying to jerk the weapon from Katie. I took another swing at his chin. He ducked from the punch, causing him to release the bat.

I pushed my sister out of the way ordering her up the stairs. Iron knuckles connected with my upper lip. The taste of blood entered my mouth with it trickling down my chin. I kept my mind sharp, immediately throwing a right jab to his stomach followed by a left to his cheek. His head reeled forcing him to take a step away from me. I'd waited for this moment my entire life to make him feel the same pain my mother felt. I closed the distance, throwing another jab.

"Come on, you son of a bitch," I snarled.

I continued to pound alternating between fists moving him closer to the screen door with each hit. Brad staggered backwards falling through the screen. He tried to stay on his feet. His foot slid off the porch step sending him sprawling down to the sidewalk.

I stalked after him, moving quickly. He tangled his leg with mine tripping me to the ground face first. My ribs crunched hitting the brick border lining the flowerbed. It knocked the breath from my body. I attempted to force myself upward. Brad flipped me onto my back. My head connected with the bricks shooting white pain.

He straddled my waist drawing back and hit my cheek. My head snapped to the side. He swung a second time on the opposite side then repeated the series. Blood oozed from my nose and lips.

"I want you dead." He wrapped both hands around my neck pushing his thumbs into my windpipe. Blood dripped from his nose onto my shirt mingling with my own. He completely cut off my air. I fought the clamped hold on my throat trying to tear it away. My eyes grew heavy, and I found myself wanting to drift to unconsciousness, feeling the strength leave my body. I slid half-closed lids to the side seeing a figure lying beside me.

My mother was there. She looked exactly the way she did the day she died. "Remember?" she said.

I shifted my eyes forward fixating on the figure hovering over my chest. I pushed against him.

Brad loomed above clamping his jaws and increasing the pressure to my throat. "Give it up, Jake. That's right, lay there feeling sorry for yourself just like your momma used to. Not so tough now, are you?"

"Remember," my mother's voice said again.

I scratched the ground searching for something to help get the monster off me. I felt a brick above my head. I grasped the hard masonry, slamming it against the face a few inches from my own, unbalancing Brad's body. I bucked myself upward, throwing him off my torso curling to the side holding my throat. Several coughs escaped me as oxygen filled my lungs.

Gasping for breath, I pushed myself to shaky legs and staggered over to the man who tried to kill me. He was on his knees holding the side of his head. Dragging all the air I could into my chest, I shouted, "I never saw a wild thing sorry for itself."

I hit the already bloody face. Brad's head snapped right.

"A small bird," I gasped delivering a right punch.

"Will drop frozen."

A left.

"From it's bough."

Right hook.

"Never."

A left.

"Having."

A right.

"Felt sorry for itself."

A right upper cut sent the man to the side and face down onto the grass.

I bent over resting my hands on my upper legs.

"Jake?"

I raised my head. Katie was on the porch with the bat in her hand.

I was afraid for her. Brad was unconscious but could wake any moment. I shouted the same words to my sister that my mother said so many times in my life. "Hide," I said. "Hide!"

She obeyed. I took a step and went down onto my knees bracing my hands on the ground fighting to draw a breath and gather strength in case Brad came to.

The sound of sirens filled the air with vehicles speeding up the drive.

"Jake? Jake?"

I drew my head around. Dillon was a good distance

away running across the large lawn toward me with Bill close behind. I pushed myself to stand, stumbling in Dillon's direction.

He was worried. I lifted an arm to show him I was fine. I didn't understand why he was so worried. I won. I beat Brad Conner.

Dillon ran faster toward me. "No!"

He was looking beyond me. I followed to see what had his attention. Brad struggled to stand pulling something from the band of his jeans. He held a gun pointed at me.

It's a game, I realized. He could have killed me anytime he wanted. Just another sick twisted game. I turned back to Dillon.

"No," Bill belted.

A shot rang out. Sheer burning seared into my back a few inches below my shoulder blade. The impact sent me slightly forward. I caught my balance and remained on my feet. A second shot rang out. I waited for the thud of the bullet but it never came.

I rolled my stinging shoulder, turning my head back to the porch in time to see Brad slipping to the ground. Beyond him, my grandmother stood on the porch with a shotgun in her hands. The barrel lowered to her side and dropped to the porch.

Gran's mouth moved. I couldn't hear what she was saying. She took the steps quickly. I came around to Dillon. I smiled taking a step stumbling into his arms. He held me for a moment before pulling his hand from my back covered with blood.

I held onto his arms trying to maintain my footing. I was exhausted, so tired. I felt a smile stretch across my lips, laid my head against Dillon's chest, and relaxed.

"Jake, stay with me, stay with me," he said while easing my body to the ground. "Don't do this, Jake."

I didn't understand anything else he said. I recalled every wonderful second that we spent together over the past months. There was so much to tell him. So much, he should know. Most of all I wanted to tell him I loved him. My mouth struggled to form the words but they never came. I drifted into an abyss of darkness.

24

I opened my eyes, unable to see anything in the dark-ness. A light, humming noise vibrated in my ears. I stretched my jaw, hoping to pop my ears to rid myself of the noise. It took several tries to visualize my surroundings. A television stationed on the wall played with the volume turned low.

Pain radiated throughout my body. I narrowed eyes recalling the last memories clouding my mind. Brad was at the farm trying to take Katie. We were fighting in the front yard, and he shot me. I panicked wondering if my sister and grandmother were okay. I moved my shoulder trying to position myself on the edge of the bed. I dropped my shoulder back, it was too painful to move.

I turned my head, looking for a call button. The blinds concealed the windows but allowed enough light into the room to see a figure lying in a chair beside the bed. It was the most wonderful sight. Katie lay with her head resting on a pillow propped up on the arm of the chair. Her long blonde hair streamed over the sides. I drifted back to the mattress with relief washing over me. She was here.

I managed a rough whisper from my raw throat. "Katie?"

She stirred a little.

"Katie," I said louder.

The teen's head came up quickly. "Jake?"

"You okay?" I asked.

She leaped from the chair coming to my side and laying her head on my chest. I felt the tears falling from her cheeks landing on the exposed skin above my hospital gown. I brushed the crown of her head with my hand. "It's okay. Everything'll be fine.

She gave a convulsive cry. "Thank you, God, thank you."

I stroked her hair saying a prayer of my own, thankful my sister was with me. I kissed her hair. "Tell me you're all right?"

She rose and gave a sniffle. "I'm fine now that you're awake. I was so scared."

I pushed the blonde strands over her shoulder. "I know, but you were brave. If you hadn't hit him with the bat…"

She shook her head. "No, Jake, I wasn't talking about him. I was scared you were gonna leave me. Please, don't ever leave me."

I smiled. "I'm not going anywhere."

She returned her head to my chest. For the past fifteen years, I've always thought my sister and I complete opposites. It's sad that it took something of this magnitude for me to see how much we are alike. We both carry the same fear of losing each other.

We stayed attached for a while. Finally, Katie brought her face upward, smiling. "Dillon was right. I'm so glad he was right."

"About what?" I quizzed stroking the blonde strands.

Katie choked a sob mixing it with a laugh. "He said you were too stubborn to give up. He was right."

I returned a grin pulling her closer. "I love you, sis."

"I love you, too, Jake."

After the reunion, Katie righted herself, blowing her nose. I wanted to know about Brad. It might have been wrong for a daughter to wish her father dead, but I wasn't ashamed. "Is he dead?"

Katie gave a nod. "He's gone for good. I was standing

there when they pronounced him dead and loaded him into the coroner's van. He can't hurt us anymore."

I blinked hard. "I never wanted any of this for you," I said.

Katie took a seat on the bed beside me holding my hand. She appeared older. Gone was the once innocent look in her blue eyes."Mom didn't want this for either of us. It happened. All we can do is pick up the pieces and be better for it," she said. She sounded wise beyond her years and mine as well.

"Is Gran okay?" I asked.

"She's still shaky. Dillon had a doctor in the ER check her out. Said she's fine. Bill made her stay at his house and get some rest. I'll call her in a bit."

Katie's chin quivered. "I can't believe you made it. There was so much blood."

I reached out rubbing her arm. "Hey, stop crying. It's over. I'm here, you're okay. Gran'll be all right," I said.

Katie shook her head going on."I don't know how Dillon did it, but he was so calm."

She gave a shiver. "He did it, though. He didn't wait for the ambulance. He made 'em take you in Harvey's car. They told him at the hospital he couldn't operate on you. He said if we wait for another surgeon, she'll die. And you would've."

I began to worry he was in serious trouble. "Did they fire him?"

Katie shook her head. "No, his boss said he would have done the same thing."

A twinge of pain sent a frown across my face.

"You hurtin'? I'll call the nurse or go get Dillon. He's asleep in a room across the hall," Katie said, moving away.

I caught her hand. "No, stay with me."

She sat back down and rubbed my hand. The corners

of her mouth rose with a hint of sweet honesty. "He's in love with you."

I gave no indication the words affected me. She lowered her head then brought her eyes to mine. "He didn't know I was standing in the doorway. He sat here holding your hand begging you to come back to him and then said, 'I love you, Jake'."

I turned my head away fighting my own building emotions remembering, wanting desperately to tell Dillon Lawrence how I felt about him while laying on the grass at the farm.

"Don't make Dillon pay for what Brad did to you, to Mom, heck, to all of us. He's a good guy and deserves a chance," Katie said.

I drew my face around to my sister feeling the tears brewing in my eyes. "Why?"

Katie frowned. "Why? He's a good guy, Jake."

"No, I mean why does he love me?"

Katie gave a perplexed glare as if offended by the question. "Don't you think you're entitled to be loved? My God, Jake, why wouldn't he fall in love with you? You're beautiful and smart. You're the most unselfish person I've ever known. You put everyone ahead of yourself. You're perfect. Any man would be lucky to have you."

I shook my head. "You're wrong. I'm damaged here," I said, pointing to my head. I moved my hand to my heart. "And here."

I covered my mouth hushing the sob about to erupt. "He's a good man," I said. "Probably the best. I want him so badly it hurts but…"

"But what, Jake?

"He deserves someone better. Why would he want to love someone like me?" I asked, choking back the lump building in my throat.

A deep voice came from the doorway, "Because I can't imagine my life without Jake Conner."

Dillon came closer. Katie moved away giving him access. "I'll go call Gran," she said and left.

Dillon took a spot on the bed and ran a smooth thumb over my cheek. "I love you, Jake. Just give me the chance to prove it. I have no hidden agendas. I won't take anything your not willing to give. Just give me a chance, and I promise you won't regret it. I love you, Jake. I love all of you, the good, the bad, everything."

I gasped trying to fight a full-blown cry. "When I was lying on the ground, I wanted to tell you something, but I couldn't get it out."

"Tell me now," he said.

I choked back a sob. "I wanted to say how thankful I am you came into my life, and how sorry I am for treating you so badly."

"You don't need to be sorry for anything."

I covered his lips with my fingers to quiet him. "I was afraid of leaving before I told you how I felt."

He kissed my fingers, drawing them down. "Tell me."

I placed my hand against his cheek letting tears flow freely. "I am so in love with you that it feel like my heart's going to bust right through my chest."

I saw a hint of a tear escape from the dark eyes with a smile playing on his lips. "That's exactly how I feel every time I look at you."

Dillon held my face in his hands. "Amazing."

"What's amazing?" I asked.

He shook his head giving me one of his famous grins. "We've never been on a real date yet somehow fell in love. It's kismet."

I remembered Katie using the same word to describe Dillon and me. He was everything I never wanted but everything I always needed. Maybe we were predestined.

I smiled. "Pure divine, heavenly, written in the stars, kismet." Then I kissed the smooth lips I once denied noticing.

EPILOG

On a warm summer day, I lay on the grass of our farm fighting for my life. The nightmarish hell that engulfed my mother and me started with Brad Conner and ended with him. I was the fortunate one. Folks around Washington said it was by the grace of God I survived. I do thank God for sparing me and believe with all my heart he sent the vision of my mother to provide the strength for fighting back.

I worried about Katie, wondering how everything affected her. At first, she was quiet clinging to my every movement. Over the following weeks, she seemed to be her old self with questions about her biological father.

I believed Brad about his relationship with our mother in Paris, Texas. My gut feeling leaned toward the kind biker known only as Z as the father of my sister. I told Katie everything I knew about him and promised to help her find Z and the truth if that was what she wanted.

My grandmother, Chelsea Parker, took the word of God to heart and was the sweetest woman a person would ever meet. It took a lot for her to make the decision to pull the trigger on Brad. She was justified in shooting him and received no repercussions. Like my mother and me, she did what she had to in order to protect her family. No matter how many people told her she did the right thing, Gran carried guilt for taking the life of the man who killed her daughter and attempted to murder her granddaughter.

It did not have to be like that. It shouldn't have been like that. Fathers were supposed to love and protect their children, not hurt them. All my life, I never understood why Brad hated me. In the end, I realized it wasn't about me but his inability to let go of a woman who chose her child over her husband.

In death, I refused to allow Brad Conner near my mother's grave. He was a disturbed man with no living family except for me, his daughter. I sent his body to Dallas to have him buried in a small cemetery near the home where the insanity started.

Teyla Martin was a victim of a twisted man's revenge. Like my mother, she fell in love with Brad only seeing his true colors when things did not go his way, and, she paid for the mistake with her life. My grandmother said Harvey managed to find a brother in Oklahoma who wanted nothing to do with Teyla in life or death. At my request, we buried her in the cemetery a few yards away from Momma.

It had been two months since the shooting. I made a full recovery and prepared for another life-changing event. My best friend stood beside me nervously picking at the nonexistent lint on his jacket. I loved him so much and never imagined life without him. He took an angry emotional train wreck of a girl and turned her into a fighter that exceeded the boxing ring. He taught me life's about taking chances. You can be the most physically strong person in the world but if you're afraid of living then you've lost already.

Bill tugged on the tails of his jacket.

"You okay?" I asked.

"Fine. Ready, kid," He said.

I nodded. "Been waiting a long time for this."

Music played on the other side of the door cueing our entrance. I hooked my arm in his and walked through the door to face the friends and family, waiting inside the old church in Washington decorated with fall flowers and leaves.

As we neared the altar, I focused on the dark eyes lingering on me. My heart swelled so full of love. Twice Dillon Lawrence saved my life after a fight. The first time came ending my career, the second, ending the reign of terror brought on by a deranged father. He was the one chance fate brought into my life making me a better person.

The music ended. I released Bill's arm taking my place, listening to the pastor recite, "Do you William Monroe take Shirley Dobbs to be your lawfully wedded wife?"

Bill remained silent. I've never seen my friend as rattled as he was at that moment. I lowered my head hiding a smile on my lips placing an elbow in the trainer's ribs.

"I do," he said loudly.

I glanced over my shoulder hearing the giggles coming from my sister seated between Gran and Dillon. I drew my brows together sending the message for her to stop laughing. She covered her mouth attempting to cease the mirth.

Bill and Shirley exchanged their vows. Just about the time he bent down to seal the moment with a kiss, Katie yelled, "Go, Bill. Get your game on."

I closed my eyes and let a sigh escape, knowing we should have expected Katie to have the last jab. Bill shook his head and moved in kissing his bride.

At the reception, Katie positioned herself close to Gran and Cora Mae Jackson with Clint by her side. Over the past few months, Clint and I came to know each other. He was a sweet boy and a saint to put up with the most audacious girl in Hempstead County.

Dillon and I took a spot on the old courthouse steps watching Bill and Shirley cutting their cake. From behind,

Dillon leaned in whispering, "You are the most beautiful best man or should I say best woman I have ever seen."

I tilted my head to him. "Why, thank you, Dr. Lawrence."

He kissed the crown of my head wrapping his arms around my waist.

When they finished exchanging bites of cake, Bill took Shirley's hand walking to the front of the crowd. "Folks, can I have your attention for a minute?" he said.

A hush fell over the guest.

"This day would not be complete if I didn't thank the one person who made me take my own advice. Jake, come up here."

I took slow steps making my way through the crowd reaching Bill. He held both my hands in his. At first, he said nothing and then raised his head. "You know I love you, Jake. You are my daughter in all the ways that count."

I always felt Bill's love, but it was something else to hear it. Tears stung my eyes.

"I love you too."

"Good. Remember I'm doing this for your own good. Doc? She's all yours." Bill dropped my hands, ushering Shirley a good distance away.

Dillon appeared in front of me. I looked up to the familiar grin I loved so much. "Bill once told me if I want to spend time with you to just do it. I figure that philosophy holds for anything."

I gave him a long look.

"You are the most stubborn person I've ever met. The words give up don't exist in your vocabulary. You fight for the people you love."

I looked down at the ground with my cheeks growing warm. Dillon raised my chin. "I love you, Jake. I want to spend the rest of my life fighting for you, if you'll let me."

I blinked several times, taken aback by what I knew was coming. Dillon pulled a ring from his pocket and knelt down on one knee. A gasp went out among the wedding guests followed by silence. His soft finger massaged my hand followed with lips brushing the backside. "Jake, will you marry me?"

I felt the tears sliding down my cheeks. I expected to wake any minute and discover the past months had been a dream, Brad was still alive, and my life as empty as it had been the day my mother died.

I brought my head up, struggling to find my voice. "I never thought…" I choked back a sob. I released a rush of air over my lips before continuing. "My mother used to read me fairy tales about a prince who rescued a princess from an evil wizard. The last time she wanted to read the story, I told her no. I hated that story and didn't want to hear it anymore."

I drew in a long breath looking into Dillon's eyes. "All my life I thought it was a lie. There are no princes and the princess gets tortured by the wizard the rest of her life. Then I met you. I love you. I want to marry you more than anything."

Dillon slid the ring on my finger and gathered me in his arms. We held each other with the crowd shouting its approval. He lifted me from the ground and whirled me around. Josh stood behind Katie and Gran smiling the same grin he inherited from his father.

When Dillon sat me back on the ground, Bill approached taking me in his arms.

"You did it, kid. You really are the champ."

It was later after moving through the gauntlet of congratulatory friends, that we made our way onto the dance floor to finish celebrating Bill's marriage and my engagement. Dillon and I moved across the floor happier than I thought possible. I felt a tap on my shoulder.

Looking to my right, Katie swayed to the music in Clint's arms.

She presented a grin with a raised brow. "So, Dillon, since it's official, we're going to be family, I think I deserve an answer to my question."

My sister grinned with a hint of mischief in her blue eyes. "Boxers or briefs?"

Dillon bented his face to mine lightly caressing my lips. Raising his head, he gave a wide grin. "Neither."

We waltzed away leaving Katie speechless.

I laid my head on Dillon's shoulder looking up to the sky that Fall day thinking of my mother, sure, somewhere beyond the clouds she was there smiling. She said it can't be sunny every day. You got to have some rain if you expect to grow. I've grown a lot. But, I know I wouldn't have survived without a wise poem etched in my heart. I forever thank my mother for the love of D. H. Lawrence.

B. R. Almond resides in Southwest Arkansas on a slice of acreage referred to as heaven on earth.

The self proclaimed product of the middle child syndrome discovered a passion for story telling through the teaching and encouragement of two creative parents. She soon learned limitations of a story were endless as long as she could imagine it. She maintained her love for writing poetry and short stories throughout her life placing the desire of authoring a full length novel aside while rearing two children. When the nest emptied, she wrote her debut novel, For the Love of D. H. Lawrence. She is currently hard at work on her next series of books.

VISIT THE AUTHOR AT
www.bralmond.com

For additional copies of :
        For The Love of D. H. Lawrence

Name:________________________________

Address:________________________________

City:________________ ST:____ ZIP:______

E-Mail:________________________________

No of Books ______ @ $15.95 ea.……$______

       Postage and handling……. $__3.00

       Total Enclosed $______

Please enclose check or money order made to:
GTWG
(Golden Triangle Writers Guild)

Mail to:

Golden Triangle Writers Guild
PO B0X 541
Hillister, Texas 77624